true blue forever

Book Three of the True Blue Trilogy

A novel by
Joyce Scarbrough

Blue Attitude
BOOKS

For Tony
Who will always be my Mickey

From the Author

This book exists because of something my dear friend David Hodges said to me in August of 2000 at our twentieth reunion for the Vigor High School class of 1980. When we were seniors, David wrote in my yearbook that if I didn't someday write the Great American Novel, he was going to kick my butt, so when he asked me at the reunion if I was still writing, it just about killed me to tell him I hadn't written anything in a long, long time.

I turned 39 that year, so I figured I had one more good year at the most. On my birthday in November, armed with the shiny new thesaurus my husband and kids had given me, I began writing this book. It took me six months to write it, only because I occasionally had to stop for sleep, work, and feeding my kids something besides frozen pizza. Other than my husband Tony, I have never been as obsessed with anything as I was about writing this book. When I wasn't writing, I was thinking about writing, and I missed more than one day of work and a few family gatherings because I faked an illness to stay home and write.

That was 16 years ago, and in addition to finding out that I actually did have a few more good years left, I've learned a lot about the publishing business, had my aspirations trampled on and been disillusioned more times than I can count. But I've also met some of my dearest friends because of writing, including my best friend and literary sister Lee Ann Ward, the only person in the world who loves these characters as much as I do. The rest of the world may not consider this the Great American Novel, but at least two people do. So I'm grateful for this journey, potholes and all.

Last year, I discovered that I wasn't done with this story and these characters, so I wrote a prequel to the original book and turned it into this trilogy. I think this is its last incarnation, but I won't swear to it. There may be another chapter to their story somewhere down the line.

We'll see.

true blue forever

Prologue

Vigor High School, 1979

Coach Carter shoved Mickey and Wade into the football equipment room and flipped on the light.

"You two badasses want to kill each other so much then go right ahead, but you're not taking up my practice time with it anymore! Stay in here and beat each other's brains out while the rest of the team practices. If one of you is still alive when I come back, maybe I'll let you stay on the team!"

He slammed the door, and they heard the deadbolt slide into place. Mickey and Wade glared at each other in the dim light of the bare bulb suspended from the ceiling.

"See what you did, Strickland!" Mickey said. "Why do you always have to start something with me out there?"

Wade pushed him in the chest with both hands. "Shut the hell up! Why don't you go play your sissy-ass baseball and stay off my football field?"

Mickey pushed him back and Wade lunged at him. They fell onto a pile of old shoulder pads, both of them landing a few random punches until a blow intended for Mickey's jaw missed and hit the concrete floor with a sickening crack of bone.

"Shit, I broke my frigging hand!" Wade held up his decimated left fist in disbelief. "Sonofabitch!"

Mickey rolled away from him and sat up, wiping his mouth with the back of his hand. "Brilliant move, Strickland. That's gonna be hurting like hell by the time Coach comes back to let us out."

1

Wade picked up a stray arm pad and threw it at Mickey's head. "You better be glad this happened or you'd be the one hurting like hell!"

Mickey shook his head and sighed. "Fine. You sit over there and enjoy your busted hand. I'll shut up and wait for Coach to come back."

"Stupid Yankee asshole." Wade leaned back and closed his eyes, holding his left wrist against his chest.

Mickey resisted the urge to respond in kind and closed his own eyes in the hopes that he might be able to doze until they were liberated. But the stifling heat and rank smell of the room, coupled with the aftereffects of Wade's punches that hadn't missed, made him too uncomfortable to sleep. He glanced at Wade and could tell from the grimace on his face and his gray color that his hand was killing him.

Mickey looked around the room with a sigh and finally spied a white box in the corner under a weight bench loaded down with old practice jerseys. When he got up to retrieve the first aid kit, Wade didn't even open his eyes, so Mickey wasn't sure if he was still conscious. He opened the box and found one of the instant cold packs they used for injuries on the field, then he nudged Wade with his foot.

"Here, put this on your hand before you pass out."

Wade's eyelids didn't quite make it all the way open. "Go to hell, Yankee-boy. I don't need shit from you."

"What you need is your stupid head examined, but this'll have to do for now."

"Kiss my ass!" Wade tried to kick the cold pack out of Mickey's hand and ended up banging his busted hand on a pair of shoulder pads when he missed. His next words were a string of unintelligible curses mixed with groans.

"God, why do you always have to be so bullheaded, Strickland?" Mickey tossed the cold pack onto Wade's lap then went to sit on the other side of the room.

Wade glared at him, but he picked up the cold pack and wrapped it around his left hand. "Don't worry about why I do anything, asshole. Just stay outta my way."

"Kinda hard to do with you in my face every time I turn around at practice," Mickey said. "You could at least give it a rest until football season is over."

"Why? You afraid I'll kick your ass and keep you from playing the big football hero in front of Jeana?"

Mickey scoffed. "If you knew anything about Jeana at all, you'd know she wouldn't care if I never played any kind of sports."

Wade's face flushed a deep crimson. "I do know that about her! And I've known it a helluva lot longer than *you*."

"Yeah? Then you should also know that she's the only thing keeping me from putting you on the disabled list for good, so why don't you lay off for her sake?"

Some of the anger disappeared from Wade's face. "What does Jeana have to do with anything between us?"

Mickey hesitated a second, then he said, "She asked me to try and get along with you. I told her it was pointless, but she made me promise."

Wade seemed to think about that a moment. "Yeah, she always hated it when me and DuBose would fight when we were kids. She'd get so mad and call us stuff like Neanderthals and barbarians."

It was the most civil thing Wade had ever said to him, but Mickey hated being reminded of those years when Jeana hadn't known him and had been so close to Wade. And he also didn't like the unmistakable tenderness that was always in Wade's eyes and voice when he talked about her. It was bad enough that Mickey knew Billy Joe had loved Jeana since they were kids. He was starting to feel sure that Wade was in love with her too.

"You're right, Strickland. She hates violence of any kind, and since she asked me not to fight with you anymore, how about we call a truce? At least until football's over."

3

Wade's customary smirk appeared. "Sure, Yankee-boy. I'll let you live for her sake. I'll always have a soft spot in my heart for Redhot."

"I told you not to call her that," Mickey said.

"And I told you to kiss my ass." Wade's smirk widened. "She likes me to call her that, and she always has. You just can't stand it 'cause you know she's got her own soft spot for the Wademan."

"You're even crazier than I thought you were," Mickey said, disgusted. "Jeana loves me and nobody else."

"You trying to convince me or yourself?"

"Shut up, Strickland! Just stay outta my face on the football field so Jeana will be happy!"

Wade looked amused that he'd gotten under Mickey's skin. "Tell the truth, Yankee-boy. I know you wish you'd finished me off when you had the chance. Why'd you tell Jeana yes when she asked you not to mess up my pretty face?"

Mickey leaned against the wall and folded his arms. "If you ever stayed with a girl longer than one date, maybe you'd understand what it's like to have a real girlfriend."

Wade snickered. "Yeah, well you better make sure you keep Jeana happy, 'cause I know she's just waiting for me to make it back around to her again."

Mickey knew he was just trying to provoke him, but his words hit a little too close to home, so he did a little provoking of his own.

"That reminds me, Strickland. You're always talking about how Jeana used to like you so much when you were kids. What exactly did you do to make her stop? And how hard is it to live with knowing that you had a girl like her and were stupid enough to lose her?"

He knew he'd struck a nerve when Wade's smirk disappeared and his eyes darkened with fury.

"I'm not telling you shit about me and Jeana!"

"Why not? I'd love to know how a big shot like you

screwed up bad enough to lose the most amazing girl in the world. Especially since you think you know so much about her."

"I'm warning you, asshole! If you're serious about not fighting with me anymore, you better shut up right now."

Mickey looked surprised. "You're agreeing to a truce?"

"Sure, what the hell." Wade closed his eyes again. "If that's what Jeana wants, then fine. Besides, my old man's got a ton of money riding on us against Murphy. He'll kill me if I get in trouble and don't get to play."

"You think you'll be able to play with that busted hand?"

Wade scowled without opening his eyes. "What the hell do you care? I thought you were such a superstar linebacker that it wouldn't matter if I played or not."

"Yeah, but with both of us playing, that cocky little running back Murphy's got will be lucky to gain twenty yards total. Don't you want to shut him down?"

Wade opened his eyes slowly. "You mean that mouthy little Jackson punk?"

Mickey nodded. "He's been telling the newspaper that he's gonna run over you *and* me."

Wade sneered. "He couldn't run over DuBose. I'll put him out for the season." After a pause, his smirk returned. "Broken bones might stop a wuss like you, but it won't bother me none."

"Great," Mickey said. "Because you know nobody's scored more than twelve points against us since Coach started playing both of us at linebacker, right?"

"Yeah. What's your point?"

Mickey sighed. "Look, you might be batshit crazy and a major pain in the butt, but you tackle better than anybody else in the county—except me. And I also know you hate losing as much as I do. If we can forget about how much we hate each other long enough to work together on the football field, we should have a real shot at taking state our senior year."

"Not only can I tackle better than you," Wade said, "I put your Yankee ass on the grass plenty of times when you were playing fullback."

Mickey scoffed. "And since we both know you're way too slow to ever play fullback yourself, I guess I won't get the chance to return the favor."

"Slow my ass," Wade said. "You only beat me by a quarter second in the forty. And I sure as hell don't need *you* to tell me we got a good chance at state next year. Why do you think I said I'd let you go on breathing, Yankee-boy?"

"I thought you said it was for Jeana."

"No, I said I'd let you live the rest of this year because of Jeana. Next year's for my state championship ring."

Mickey laughed. "I'm sure that's the closest thing to a compliment I'm ever gonna get from you, so thanks."

"Don't thank me, asshole. It wouldn't break my heart to see you leave the last game on a stretcher."

A few minutes later, they heard the deadbolt turning. When the door swung open, they both got up and faced Coach Carter sheepishly.

"What happened to your hand, Strickland?" Coach asked.

"It's nothing, Coach. We were doing a few tackling drills to kill time and I missed the dummy." Wade glanced at Mickey and snickered.

"Yeah, right," Coach said. "Well, at least I don't see any blood or detached limbs lying around. Does that mean you two boneheads are ready to play some football?"

"Yes, sir," they said in unison.

"Praise Jesus, Mary and Joseph!" Coach held his hands to the sky. "I'm thrilled to see you in agreement about something finally, and that better be the way it stays if either of you wants to remain on this team. You can hate each other's guts all you want in private, but you'd better work together and have each other's back when you're on the field. Now get your ass out there and run wind sprints until I get tired!"

He grabbed them both by the shirt and shoved them behind him out of the room. When they reached the door leading to the practice field, Wade shouldered Mickey aside and turned to sneer at him.

"I hope you like the sight of my ass, Yankee-boy, 'cause that's what you'll be looking at when I leave you in the dust. We'll see who's slow."

"Keep dreaming, Strickland," Mickey said as he sprinted past him to the field.

Chapter One

By the time they were seniors, Jeana Russell and Mickey Royal had a love based on a mutual trust and respect that shielded them from the petty arguments and jealousies most young couples have to endure. In fact, the only source of conflict between them was the subject of Jeana's college plans. She was sure to be the valedictorian of their class and therefore be awarded the George C. Wallace full academic scholarship to Troy State University in central Alabama. Based on Mickey's stellar performance his junior year as a pitcher and center fielder for Vigor's baseball team, he would likely be offered a scholarship to the University of South Alabama where his dad had played.

Jeana refused to even consider leaving Mickey for four years. She told him that if she couldn't get her own scholarship to USA, she'd get a job to pay her tuition so she could go there with Mickey. He insisted he would change her mind before they graduated.

Mickey and Wade had finally come to coexist on Vigor's football team without any serious conflict. They would never be friends, but they recognized in each other the drive to play hard and win, and they both grudgingly respected it. Wade surprised everyone by getting even bigger, and he began his last year in high school at six feet four inches and close to two hundred fifty pounds. But even with the size advantage over Mickey, Wade still wasn't guaranteed the middle linebacker position. Mickey started as a fullback when they were juniors, but the coaches had quickly learned how well he played linebacker and began alternating him with Wade in the middle.

Wade's constant parade of girlfriends continued. They

all eventually tired of his unpredictable temper, lack of respect for them, and his erratic behavior when he was drinking—which was every weekend. Remarkably, no one but Jimbo had ever made any sense of the references Wade frequently made in his alcohol-fueled tirades to someone he called Redhot.

Jeana's attitude toward him had softened a little once he'd stopped his blatant efforts to cause problems with Mickey. She still wondered what had changed him so much from the boy she'd grown up with, and she hated the thought of his father abusing him, but he had a talent for irritating her. And she still couldn't forgive him for what he'd said about her in middle school, nor had she ever spoken about it to anyone, including Wade.

Billy Joe remained close to Jeana and became best friends with Mickey as well. Always the one to be different, he'd chosen a 1970 El Camino when he was able to get a car the summer before he turned seventeen. He spent most of his spare time—and most of his paychecks from working as a stock boy at Delchamps supermarket—customizing the car to fit his personality. The first thing he did was paint it metallic purple.

Jeana also got a car for her seventeenth birthday: a red Volkswagen Beetle with a tag on the front that read JEANA LOVES MICKEY.

They all expected big things to happen for them as seniors in the fall of 1980.

They weren't disappointed.

~ * ~

Mickey and Jeana pulled into Vigor's parking lot on the first day of school and parked next to Billy Joe's El Camino.

"Hey, buddy," Mickey said when they got out of the Mustang. "I see you got the steering wheel cover you wanted."

"Put it on last night." Billy Joe ran his hand over the

faux leopard fur. "Devastatingly cool. Huh, Jeana?"

"That has to be the ugliest car on the face of the Earth," Jeana said. "No girl in her right mind is ever going anywhere with you in that, Billy Joe."

"Who said I wanted a girl in her right mind? I hear crazy girls are easy."

Mickey laughed and Jeana rolled her eyes. "Did you ever get your schedule, Billy Joe?"

"Nope," he replied. "Gotta go to the counselors' office this morning. They still don't have me registered for some reason."

"They probably did it so you'd have to get counseling," Jeana said.

When she got to her first period Psychology class, she took a seat in the front of the last row by the windows, her favorite spot. She'd always been fascinated by what motivated people in their actions and behavior, so she was really looking forward to this class.

She was leafing through her textbook, engrossed in some of the odd pictures, when a large hand covered the page, and she recognized Wade's diamond-studded class ring. He kept his hand on her book and left his arm draped over her shoulder as he took the seat behind her.

"Look into my ring and tell me my future, Redhot."

She picked up his hand and tossed it aside. "This is Psychology, not fortune telling. Don't tell me you're actually in this class."

"Okay, I won't tell you."

She turned around and arched her eyebrow. "What on Earth made you take Psychology?"

He shrugged. "Maybe I thought it would help me figure out what you see in Yankee-boy. Why isn't he here glued to your side?"

"He took Mechanical Drawing for his elective."

"Getting awful brave, ain't he? Leaving you unguarded and all."

Jeana frowned. "What's your point, Wade? I know you're not really interested in what Mickey does."

"You got that right," he said with a scoff. "I just wondered why he's not following you around like he usually does." He fingered one of her auburn curls absently, his gaze darting up to her face and back down again. "You didn't break up, did you?"

"Did Hell freeze over?" Jeana said. "Did the world stop spinning? Is it the Twelfth of Never? Do pigs fly? Is the sun—"

"Okay, I get it!" He looked ill and leaned back in his seat. "Jeez."

Jeana smiled and went back to her book while Wade stared out the window. When the bell rang, Ms. Majors greeted everyone and called roll, then she talked about the basic concepts of Psychology and the different schools of thought they would examine during the course. She also outlined the papers and projects that would be required.

"You'll be assigned a partner for a project in which you'll conduct your own experiment in behaviorism," Ms. Majors said. "This will constitute a major portion of your first semester grade."

Jeana hoped the partners wouldn't be assigned alphabetically. She glanced behind her and got a wink from Wade that made her wonder if he was hoping for the opposite.

When she got to second period, Mickey was waiting for her outside Mr. Brownlee's Biology II class, and they sat together at one of the two-person tables in the room. Jeana had been in Mr. Brownlee's class for Biology I as a sophomore and knew the class would be enjoyable, but Mickey hated Biology and had made her promise they could be partners before he would agree to take it with her.

Midway through the period, Billy Joe came in and handed Mr. Brownlee a roll addition sheet.

"I don't believe it," Jeana said when she saw him. "This

is the first time we've ever had a class together."

Billy Joe spotted Jeana and Mickey and smiled mischievously while he waited for the teacher to add him to the roll.

Mr. Brownlee looked up from his grade book. "Okay, Billy, have a—"

"Excuse me, sir," Billy Joe said, "but it's Billy *Joe*. My mama's a stickler for that Southern three-name tradition. My sister's name is Peggy Sue, and my brother is Jim Bob."

Scattered laughter from everyone who knew Billy Joe was an only child.

Mr. Brownlee looked suspicious. "Okay then, Billy *Joe*. Find a seat somewhere."

He still didn't move. "Excuse me again, sir, but I have to protest the seating arrangement. Jeana Russell needs to sit with me."

"I'm going to kill him," Jeana said, hiding her face.

"And why is that?" Mr. Brownlee asked Billy Joe.

"I started tutoring her in Biology when we were two years old. We still got a few things to clear up."

More laughter filled the room.

Mr. Brownlee smiled slightly. "Well, I would hope that being in my class will answer any questions she might have. I think you can sit elsewhere."

"Sorry, Jeana," Billy Joe said. "You're stuck with Mick."

She still had her hand covering her eyes, but Mickey laughed. Billy Joe took an empty seat two tables over beside a blonde girl who smiled at him as he sat down.

"Hi," she said. "I'm Allison White."

"Billy Joe DuBose. Mind if I sit with you?"

She shook her head. "Not at all."

"Are you new?" he asked, looking at her thoughtfully. "I don't think I've seen you before, and I know I'd remember you if I had."

"We just moved to Chickasaw," she said. "I went to Murphy last year."

Billy Joe patted her hand. "That's okay. We won't hold it against you." When he got a funny look from her, he said, "Just kidding. Welcome to Vigor."

"Thanks," she said. "I really like your hair. Is it natural?"

"Yep. One hundred percent pure Billy Joe."

He introduced her to Jeana and Mickey after class and Jeana said, "Don't pay any attention to that stuff he said to Mr. Brownlee. He's certifiably insane."

"I think he's funny," Allison said, smiling at Billy Joe. "He kept me laughing all period."

"Who do you have next?" Billy Joe asked her. "Need any help finding your classes?"

Allison looked at her schedule card. "Mr. Harris for Advanced Government and Economics."

"I have that too," Jeana said. "I'll show you how to get there."

She gave Mickey a quick kiss, and Billy Joe puckered up as though he were expecting one too.

"See what I mean?" Jeana said to Allison. "He's hopeless."

As the girls walked to class together, Allison said, "How long have you and Mickey been going together?"

"Two years next month," Jeana replied.

"Wow, that's great. He's a good football player, isn't he? I remember hearing his name a lot when Vigor played Murphy last year."

"He's the best player on the team," Jeana said with a proud smile.

"Have you really known Billy Joe since you were two years old?"

She nodded. "He's lived across the street from me my whole life. He's really my best friend, but he loves to embarrass me."

13

"Does he have a girlfriend?"

"No, most girls don't understand him I guess. Why?"

Allison shrugged. "I figured some lucky girl had already snagged him. I think he's cute, and he's *so* funny."

Jeana's eyebrow went up as she shifted into matchmaking gear. "He's a football player too, you know. He kicks it."

Allison laughed. "You mean he's the kicker?"

Jeana nodded. "That's what I meant. Do you like jocks?"

They sat next to each other in Mr. Harris's room, and Allison said, "Sure, I play basketball and softball myself."

"Oh, really?" Jeana smiled. "Billy Joe plays basketball too."

She checked Allison's schedule after class and saw that she had English with Mickey the next period, so she sent him a note to meet her at her locker before sixth period.

"Hey, baby," Mickey said when he walked up. "Is something wrong, or did you just miss me?"

"I think Allison likes Billy Joe," she said. "Talk to him and see if he likes her too."

"Are you playing matchmaker, Jeana?"

"Somebody has to help him. His car is enough by itself to keep him celibate for life."

Mickey laughed and flicked her ear. "Don't talk about him like that, baby. Besides, we're celibate too."

"But definitely not for life." She poked him in the chest and gave him a cajoling smile. "Talk to him for me, okay? You know he'll never give me a straight answer."

Billy Joe was talking to Allison in the bleachers when Mickey entered the gym. When he came in the locker room to change a few minutes later, Mickey asked him why she'd been there.

"She's got Varsity Athletics for basketball and softball," Billy Joe said. "How 'bout that? Beautiful *and* talented."

Mickey sat on the bench to take off his shoes. "Guess I

don't need to find out if you like her. Jeana told me to grill you."

"She's jealous, huh?" Billy Joe sat down and put his arm across Mickey's shoulders. "You need to be there for her, Mick. She's gonna be crushed when she hears I'm taking Allison out Saturday night."

"That's great, buddy." Mickey started to pull his shirt over his head and then stopped. "Wait a minute, has she seen the El Camino yet?"

He ducked the arm pad that flew across the room toward his head.

Chapter Two

Monday morning, Allison was wearing Billy Joe's class ring. She and Jeana became close friends despite their different interests, and the two couples frequently double-dated or just hung out together. They had fun no matter what they did because it was one of those rare cases where all four of them were friends.

Vigor's football team squashed Satsuma 21-0 for a spirited start to the season, but the offense still struggled for the most part, and the defense was again the team's stronghold. Mickey and Wade were a formidable pair of tacklers, and Mickey's ability to read and predict the other team's plays gave them even more of an edge.

The last regular season game against McGill gave Vigor the chance once again to play for the Region One championship and advance to the state playoffs. Coach Carter had Mickey playing middle linebacker and Wade playing strong-side linebacker for the match-up. They both played a great game and it looked as though the Wolves were going to state until Vigor's quarterback threw an interception with two minutes to go in the game, and McGill ran it in for a touchdown to win 14-10.

To mark the end of their high school football careers, the senior players had big plans for after the game. Jimbo had scored a keg, and since his parents were gone to Jackson for the Alabama-Mississippi State game, he was hosting the party at his house. When the team got back to the school and everybody was leaving after the coaches were gone, Teddy Greer asked Mickey and Billy Joe if they were coming to Jimbo's.

"Sorry," Mickey said, "but I got somebody a lot prettier

16

than you guys waiting for me."

Billy Joe occasionally drank a beer or two, but he had no desire to get falling-down drunk with a bunch of football players. He slung his arm around Teddy's shoulders and said, "Damn, Greer. I told you I was taken the last time you asked me out. You gotta get over me, man."

Teddy laughed. "If you change your mind, we'll be at Jimbo's getting shitfaced."

"You're wasting your breath on those two, Teddy." Wade walked up with a beer already in his hand. "Besides being a couple of Boy Scouts, they're both totally whipped."

"Whipped like you wish you were, Strickland," Billy Joe said. "The only steady date you ever have is a six-pack."

Wade tossed the beer aside and Mickey stepped in front of Billy Joe, but Jimbo and Lamar grabbed Wade and pulled him away in the direction of their cars.

"Uh-uh, not tonight, man," Jimbo said, throwing an arm around Wade's neck. "Those girls we talked to at Colonel Dixie the other day said they'd only come to the kegger if the Wademan was gonna be there."

Wade snatched another beer from the ice chest in the back of Lamar's F-150 and sat on the tailgate to open it, still glaring in Mickey and Billy Joe's direction. Jimbo downed half his own beer then poured the rest over his head with a Rebel Yell, shaking it and slinging the amber droplets onto Wade and Lamar.

"Forget about those losers," Jimbo said. "DuBose don't know shit. How many girls you got waiting in line to get it on with the Wademan?"

Wade kept his gaze on the beer in his hand and didn't say anything.

"Come on, man." Jimbo took a dime bag from his pocket and dangled it in front of Wade's face. "You just need to get mellow with Miss MaryJane and get you some lovin' from a couple of girls at the party. Shit, I bet the most action those two jackoffs see tonight is a kiss on the frigging cheek." He laughed and crushed the beer can against his forehead.

"Naw, Jimbo," Lamar said. "The Yankee's been with Jeana for two years. He's gotta be banging her."

"I'll kill you!"

Wade slammed into Lamar and they crashed against the side of the truck. Jimbo ran over and tried to wedge himself between them and break the hold Wade had on Lamar's throat.

"Let him go, Wademan! You know he's a frigging halfwit. He don't know any better!"

Wade's eyes bored into Lamar's, his grip tightening. "I better not ever hear her name come outta your mouth again! You got that, shit-for-brains?"

Lamar nodded and managed to croak out a *yes*. Wade released him and turned to grab a six-pack from the ice chest before storming off to the Corvette.

Lamar bent over, holding his throat and coughing. "What the hell is *his* problem?"

Jimbo looked at him in amazement. "Come on, dumbass. Let's get outta here."

~ * ~

When Jeana and Mickey came back from the band room to get in the Mustang, she stopped him before he opened the door.

"I know we lost, Mickey, but you still deserve a big kiss for the way you played tonight." She pushed him against the car and put her arms around his neck. "They were announcing your name for making the tackle every time I turned around."

He ran his hands over her back and pulled her hips against him while they kissed. "Mmm... too bad this was our last football game. What do I have to do in basketball to get kissed like this?"

She laughed. "Show up for the game."

"I think I can manage that." He smiled and kissed her again.

Wade watched them from where the Corvette was parked in the shadow of the gym, and he could see them clearly in the glow of the parking lot light they were standing under. He hated the way the Yankee's hands knew their way around her body and the way she laughed up at him. He hated that Yankee even more than he hated himself.

"She's supposed to be *mine*," he said to the empty car. "It's time I did something about it."

Chapter Three

Ms. Majors routinely got to school about forty-five minutes before the first bell so she could get a cup of coffee from the teachers' lounge and take it back to her room with her while she prepared her lesson plan. Only twenty-three and still filled with new-teacher idealism, she had encouraged all her students to come to her if they needed to talk about anything, so she was surprised but pleased when she walked into her classroom Monday morning and had a visitor.

"Oh, hello, Wade." Ms. Majors set her coffee and books on the desk and sat down. "You startled me for a second. Did you need to talk to me about something?"

"Yes, ma'am." Wade pulled a chair next to her desk and sat down. "Something's been bothering me for a long time that I wanted to talk to you about." He looked at her with puppy-dog eyes. "And I also have a favor to ask."

Despite her professionalism, his athletic good looks were not lost on her. "Well, I'll certainly try to help you if I can, Wade. Tell me what's wrong."

~ * ~

Later that morning, Jeana took her seat in Psychology and got out her notes on behaviorism. Ms. Majors was going to assign partners for their project today, and Jeana already had an idea she hoped her partner would like.

"After a great deal of thought," Ms. Majors told the class, "I've decided to make your partner assignments alphabetically so as to be fair and avoid complaints. I won't allow any changes, so don't even ask."

Jeana closed her eyes. *Oh, no…*

Ms. Majors began calling out the pairs of names, and

when she got to *Jeana Russell and Wade Strickland*, Wade laughed and tugged on one of Jeana's curls.

"Looks like a sure A for the Wademan."

"I'll allow you some time at the end of the period every day this week to work with your partner," Ms. Majors said. "But you may also have to meet with each other on your own time."

When they paired up for the last fifteen minutes of class, Wade pulled his desk next to Jeana's and put his arm around her. "What time you want me to come over tonight, Jeana-baby?"

"Very funny." She moved his arm back to his lap. "I'm sure we can get everything done at school."

"Nah, you know I'm way too dumb," he said. "You gotta help me with everything, just like that time they made you tutor me in tenth grade."

Jeana told him her idea for the project that was based on Ivan Pavlov's conditioned reflex experiment with dogs. They would both choose a negative behavior—a bad habit or just something they wanted to avoid—and they'd wear rubber bands on their wrists at all times so that whenever they performed the behavior, they could snap their wrists with the rubber band to associate the action with pain. After charting the occurrences daily, they would make graphs to illustrate whether or not the behavior declined over the fixed time frame.

Wade's gaze never left her face as she talked. "Sometimes I forget how smart you are," he said when she finished. "That's a great idea, Jeana, but you always were good at planning stuff for us to do."

Jeana was instantly transported back to the day she'd shown him the secret code she made up for their club messages when they were ten, and her chest tightened with a pang of regret that so much had changed between them in the intervening years. An enormous lump appeared in her throat, and she was terrified that she was actually going to

21

cry.

"What's wrong?" he asked when she looked away.

"Nothing. I think there's something in my eye." The bell rang and she gathered her notes. "You need to think of a behavior tonight for the experiment so we can start tomorrow. I'll make the charts and bring you one."

"Okay," he said. "See you tomorrow, partner."

She nodded and said goodbye without looking at him.

Wade watched her walk out of the room, his clenched into fists on the desk in front of him. She hated him so much that he even upset her when he was trying to be nice. He should just stay the hell away from her.

But when he remembered the way her eyes looked when she talked about something that excited her and what it felt like to know you were the reason for her smile, he knew he couldn't leave her alone.

~ * ~

Jeana wasn't sure how Mickey would react to hearing that Wade was her partner, so she decided not to tell him while they were at school. He was always excited after the first practice of a new season, so she planned to go to his house when he got home and let him tell her all the boring details of basketball practice. Then he'd be in a good mood when she broke the news to him about Wade.

While she waited for Mickey to call, she did her homework and made the blank chart grids that she and Wade would use for their project. The phone rang a little after six, and she answered it with, "Hey, handsome!"

A pause, then: "How'd you know it was me, Redhot?"

"Wade? Why are you calling me?"

"I liked your first greeting a lot better."

"You know I thought you were Mickey."

"Can't see how you'd ever get us confused. I'm a helluva lot better than him. At everything." He laughed suggestively.

"What do you want, Wade?"

"I need you, Jeana."

"What?"

He laughed again. "I need you to help me think of something for the project. I can't come up with anything about me that needs to be changed."

She sighed. "This could've waited until tomorrow, you know."

"Hey, this is the first time I ever thought about school when I wasn't there. You should be proud of me."

"That's real dedication, Wade. I'm so impressed."

"What did you pick for your behavior?"

"I haven't decided yet," she said. "To tell the truth, I can't think of anything either."

"How about punishing yourself for thinking about Yankee-boy? That's a habit you sure as hell need to break."

"That will *never* happen."

"Hmm... it *is* hard to think of anything bad about you except your boyfriend. Do you still pop your knuckles?"

"Yes, unfortunately. That's actually a good idea."

"See, now you owe me. Think of something for me tonight, okay?"

"Okay," she said with another sigh. "I'll try to narrow the list down to under a hundred."

Mickey called a few minutes after she hung up with Wade. "Hey, baby. I just got home and I'm fixing to get in the shower. Want me to wait for you?"

She laughed. "You know better than to ask me something like that. What if I said yes?"

"I'd get an extra towel."

"Stop it, Mickey. Is your mom home?"

"Yeah. I guess she would've vetoed the shower-sharing idea anyway."

"Okay, I'll be there in about fifteen minutes, and I want you to tell me all about practice." She rolled her eyes and made a face.

Mickey took the news about Wade a lot better than

when they were sophomores and she had to tutor him in English. He didn't like the idea of her spending time alone with him, but he knew she didn't have a choice since Ms. Majors had already said no changes could be made. And he did make her promise to tell him immediately if Wade did anything out of line.

"He's not stupid, Mickey. He knows who I belong to." She pulled her necklace from inside her collar.

Mickey ran his finger over the engraved message. "It's warm from being inside your shirt. I'm jealous."

She put her arms around his neck and pulled him back on the couch. "Let's see if we can't warm you up a little too."

When Mickey walked her to her car before she left, he told her about the football banquet coming up on Sunday night. "It's at the Skyline Country Club. Would that be okay for a birthday date?"

"Of course, Mickey. You know I wouldn't miss seeing you get Defensive Player of the Year."

"I don't know about that." He flicked her earlobe. "Your partner had a good year too."

"Mickey, please." Jeana scowled at him. "You are *so* much better than him."

He scowled back at her. "And you are *so* biased, but I like it that way."

Before she went to sleep that night, Jeana lay awake thinking about the reaction she'd had to Wade in class that day, still baffled by what could have changed him so much from the boy she had once liked better than any other. The boy who'd patiently tried to teach her to whistle with her fingers like he did because he knew she'd always wanted to learn. And when she had finally given up and was depressed over her failure, he'd carved a whistle from a piece of driftwood and gave it to her to cheer her up.

Jeana was so used to Wade's obnoxiousness that she didn't know what to think now that it seemed he was making an effort to be nice. It had been a lot easier to tell herself that she hated him than it was to admit how much she missed the boy he used to be. When she'd heard the admiration in his voice that morning, it had made her want to ask him where he'd been.

Chapter Four

Wade tugged on Jeana's hair as he took his seat behind her in Psychology the next day.

"Did you think about me all night, Redhot?"

"No, it only took me about five seconds to think of something you need to stop doing." She handed him the chart she'd made along with a large rubber band.

"What'd you come up with?"

"The main thing you should quit is drinking." She gave him a disapproving look.

"Nah, I'm too good at it," he said. "That's my best talent."

She rolled her eyes. "Well, it wouldn't work anyway because it has to be something you do throughout the day, every day. So I guess you should use swearing."

"Hell, Jeana. It'll be damn hard to quit."

She tried not to smile. "Here, put on your rubber band and pop yourself twice for that. I'll show you how to mark it on the chart."

She came around beside his desk and leaned over to show him where to mark the time and number of behavior occurrences. Her hair fell next to his face, and she heard him breathe in deeply.

"What are you doing, Wade?" she said with a frown.

"Nothing." He turned his head away from her. "Your hair's in my face. I can't see what you're writing."

"Oh, sorry." She pulled it over her other shoulder. "If you don't remember to write it down every time, our data won't be valid."

"And we sure as hell don't want invalid data," he said, his gaze on the curve of her neck.

26

She snapped the rubber band on his wrist. "Mark your chart."

"Ow!" He rubbed his wrist. "You enjoyed that way too much."

"You have to make it hurt or it won't work." She folded her arms and sighed. "Are you going to take this seriously or not?"

"Don't worry, Redhot. I promise not to mess up your project. You can check my chart tomorrow, okay?"

"Okay. We'll collect the data all week and make the graphs over the weekend. I'll show you how to do it in class on Friday."

~ * ~

That night after supper, Jeana and Allison went to Bel Air Mall to buy dresses for the football banquet.

"How did you finally talk Billy Joe into going?" Jeana asked as they walked in the main entrance.

"I had to bribe him with brownies and an unspeakable act," Allison replied.

Jeana arched her eyebrow. "How unspeakable?"

"I have to wear a purple dress to the banquet."

Jeana winced and looked sympathetic. "Well, I'm glad you changed his mind. Why didn't he want to go in the first place?"

"He said the coaches never appreciated his kicking finesse, plus he hates the way Wade's dad acts like he's an NFL owner instead of the booster club president."

Jeana found a green dress at the Body Shop that she thought would light up Mickey's blue eyes. Allison found one purple possibility, but she said she'd bring Billy Joe back with her so she could try to talk him out of it before she bought it.

They agreed that no trip to the mall was complete without getting something from Orange Julius. Allison hurried to the restroom around the corner at Piccadilly Cafeteria while Jeana held their place in line to order. She

27

was waiting her turn, unconsciously popping her knuckles, when a hand wearing a diamond class ring reached around and snapped the rubber band on her wrist.

"You're a bad, bad girl, and you must be punished."

Jeana elbowed him. "You almost gave me a heart attack, Wade. What are you doing out here?"

He held up a bag from J Riggins. "Had to buy a dress shirt for the football banquet. I keep busting the seams on all of mine." He struck a bodybuilder pose and flexed his arms.

Jeana rolled her eyes and turned to order the drinks. "One Orange Julius and one lemonade, please."

"Who's the other one for?" Wade asked, leaning on the counter beside her. "Not *him* I hope."

"It's for Allison," Jeana said, opening her purse. "She went to the bathroom around the corner."

"DuBose's girl?" Wade pushed away her wallet and dropped a twenty on the counter. "I never could understand how you can be friends with her."

"What is that supposed to mean?"

"She doesn't know about you and him?"

"There's nothing to know, Wade." Jeana gave an exasperated sigh. "Billy Joe and I are just friends."

"Yeah, but he'd drop her in a second if he could have you."

"Why do you always have to be so mean?" She took the drinks and walked out into the mall.

"Jeana, wait." He grabbed his change and followed her. "I'm sorry. Here... you can pop my wrist to punish me." He held out his arm to her.

"Making fun of someone's feelings is not a joke, Wade, but I guess that's a lesson you never learned." She could tell he got the reference when he looked away.

"Are you ever gonna forgive me, Jeana?"

His words startled her, and she didn't say anything for a few seconds. Then she turned and looked him in the eyes.

"I don't know, Wade. Why don't you make me want to?"

Allison walked up before he could respond. "Hey, Wade. What's going on?"

He nodded at her. "Just keeping Jeana honest. If you see her popping her knuckles, make sure she snaps the rubber band on her wrist."

Jeana pointedly didn't tell him goodbye when they left. He watched them until they were out of sight, then he snapped the band on his wrist and walked away.

~ * ~

The rest of the week at school, Jeana only spoke to Wade about the experiment. Whenever he tried to engage her in conversation about anything else, she told him they didn't have time for his games. She reminded him on Thursday to make sure he brought his chart with him the next day so she could show him how to make his graph, but Friday morning he wasn't in class. She asked Ms. Majors for extra time since Wade was absent, but she told Jeana to contact him over the weekend to get everything finished.

Jeana was at a loss about what to do. She didn't want to see Wade alone away from school, but she also didn't want to compromise her grade.

"So you make a B on this project," Mickey said when she told him about it second period. "Will that be such a tragedy?"

Jeana looked horrified. "I've never made a B on anything."

He laughed and flicked her earlobe. "Then call him up and tell him to get his sorry butt over to your house tomorrow afternoon. I'll come over if you want me to."

Jeana shook her head. "You have practice, and you know what happened the last time you did that when I had to tutor him. He'd never cooperate if you were there. I'll tell him to meet me at the library if he's not still banned from it."

"Okay, great." Mickey pointed to the diagram of the

endocrine system they were labeling. "So quit frowning about it and show me which one of these things is the Island of Longhorns."

When she stopped laughing, she said, "It's the Islets of Langerhans, you big jock."

~ * ~

Wade was waiting by Jeana's locker when she went there before the next period.

"Where were you this morning?" she demanded. "We were supposed to make the graphs today."

He looked contrite. "I had car trouble and got here late. I'm sorry, Jeana. What are we gonna do?"

She slammed her locker. "We'll have to meet somewhere over the weekend to make your graph. I guess we can go to the library."

He shook his head. "They still won't let me in. Why don't I just come over to your house this afternoon? It's not like I don't know where you live."

She started to say something, but he took her hand.

"Jeana, I swear I didn't mean to disappoint you. Please let me make up for it." He was minus his usual smirk and actually looked sincere.

"Okay," she said. "Come over at four and bring your chart."

"I'll be there." He started to go then turned around. "*He* won't be there, will he?"

Jeana gave him an impatient look. "No, he has basketball practice. But we're going out tonight, so we have to be done before supper."

Chapter Five

Betty was surprised when Jeana told her that Wade was coming over, but she said she had always hoped he and Jeana could be friends again. She asked about his family when he arrived and sent her regards to his mother, then she left him alone with Jeana at the dining room table.

Jeana's graph showed a thirty-percent reduction in the negative behavior, and Wade's dropped by fifty percent. She showed him how to mark the grid and plot the points for the data, but she made him make the graph himself and could tell he was trying to do his best.

"You did a good job on it, Wade," she said when he finished. "It looks great."

"That's because you explain things better than any teacher I ever had. I told you that a long time ago." He looked proudly at the graph in his hands. "I can't believe I made this, but the real surprise is that I actually understand it."

"Why does that surprise you? You're supposed to understand it."

"Because I'm stupid, Jeana," he said. "You should know that by now."

She frowned at the matter-of-fact way he said it. "No you're not, Wade. You've done some stupid things, but there's nothing wrong with your intellect."

"I'm sure my dad would argue with you about that."

She was suddenly furious at the thought of his own father making him feel that way. "Then I wish he was here right now. I'd show him what it's like to lose an argument!"

Wade laughed. "Yeah, I'd pay big money to see that. Thanks, Jeana."

"I mean it, Wade." She put her hand on his arm and smiled at him. "Don't let him make you feel dumb, because you're *not*."

He stared at her a moment. "God, I've missed that smile."

There he was again—the Wade she'd grown up with. And she knew this was it. If she was ever going to find out what had changed him, it had to be now. She put her hand over his and looked into his eyes.

"Wade, do you remember when we were kids and we told each other our deepest, darkest secrets to bind the club members together?"

"Yeah," he said with a wry smile. "Your big secret was that you wanted to marry Captain Kirk."

She grimaced. "I forgot about that. Anyway, my point is that we trusted each other enough to tell those things. We knew our secrets were safe because we were friends." She squeezed his hand and looked at him earnestly. "Do you still trust me?"

"I want to," he said. "But don't you hate me, Jeana?"

"No, Wade. I hate some of the things you've done and don't understand you, but I don't hate you. Look, I'll make a deal with you." She held up her pinky finger the way they used to swear each other to secrecy. "I'll tell you a secret if you tell me one. Just like when we were kids."

She could tell he was wrestling with the idea, as if he wanted to confide in her but was too accustomed to shutting everyone out.

"Come on, Wade." She smiled at him again. "I promise I won't stick your finger and make it bleed this time."

"Okay," he said, hooking his finger with hers. "But we have to go to the clubhouse."

She drew back slightly. "You don't live there anymore, Wade. No one does right now, and it's probably locked."

"If nobody lives there it should be empty, so why would it be locked? And you know club secrets can only be told inside the clubhouse. You're the one who made that rule."

He seemed so much like his old self and she wanted to get through to him so bad that she agreed. She got a flashlight from the utility drawer in the kitchen, then they went out on the back porch.

"Is the board in the fence still loose?" he asked.

"I guess so, but you're too big to fit through it anymore."

"Maybe not," he said. "Come on."

He took her hand and went down the steps into the yard. They found the loose board in the privacy fence with some difficulty because of the growing darkness, and he swung it sideways on its single nail. Jeana fit through easily, but Wade had to suck in his stomach and get her to pull on his arm before he could squeeze through. They fell into the damp grass of his old back yard, their mingled laughter an echo from days long gone.

"God, it seems like forever since I was here," he said, looking around. "I don't remember the shed being so small." He checked the door and found it unlocked. "Gimme the flashlight and I'll make sure it's okay."

Alone with him in the shed, Jeana tried not to let him see her nervousness. How could she expect him to trust her if she wouldn't trust him? He found an old blanket in the corner and spread it on the floor, then they sat facing each other cross-legged with the flashlight aimed at them from where he propped it nearby.

"You first, Redhot." He hooked their fingers again. "It was your idea."

"Okay," she said, taking a deep breath. "I've never told anyone what you said about me to Jimbo that day in the sixth grade, and the reason I couldn't forgive you is…" She took another breath and forced herself to look in his eyes. "I thought you were the sweetest boy in the world until that day, and you broke my heart."

He looked stricken and wrapped her hand in both of his. "Jeana, I *swear* I'm sorry. I didn't mean it, it was just... when DuBose told me what you said, I got mad and tried to act like I didn't care anything about you. I told you how stupid I am!"

"What are you talking about?" Jeana's features converged in confusion. "What did Billy Joe tell you?"

"I went to see you the day before school started," he said. "I wanted to come see you sooner, but my dad wouldn't let me. You weren't home when I got there so I went over to DuBose's house. He told me you said I got stuck up after we moved and you hoped I never came back."

She shook her head and pulled her hand from his. "That's not true. Billy Joe wouldn't lie to you like that. I don't believe you."

"I swear to God, Jeana. He said you didn't think I was such hot stuff anymore, and he said you'd be his girl before the year was over. That's how I knew he loves you."

Could it be true? She remembered Billy Joe using the same words the day after Wade beat him up—accusing her of thinking Wade was *hot stuff* when they were kids.

"I never said those things, Wade. If Billy Joe told you that, it was because he knew I liked you and he was jealous. But that doesn't excuse what you did because you should've known me well enough not to believe it."

"I know—"

"And you *laughed* at me!" She hated the tears she felt on her cheeks, but she had to go on. "Did you know that for years I thought I was ugly because of what you said? That I thought I'd never be able to trust another boy after that, because *you* told me I was special"—she struck him on the chest with her open hand to emphasize her words—"and *you* made me feel pretty and said I was *your* girl, but you didn't mean any of it, did you, Wade? Because when we got back to school, I was just the weird nerd girl that

34

nobody could possibly ever like!"

He caught both her hands and held them to his heart. "No, I did mean all those things, Jeana. That's why I kept trying to tell you how sorry I was, but you wouldn't talk to me anymore. God, if you only knew how beautiful you are to me!"

She pulled her hands free and stared into her lap while she waited for her tears to stop. "Just forget it," she said finally. "It doesn't matter anymore. I just needed to tell you how I felt."

"Can you forgive me, Jeana?"

She hadn't realized how deeply it had affected her, but now that she'd told him how much his words had hurt her, she was tired of being mad about it. They had just been kids, after all, and it didn't seem quite so painful now that it was out in the open.

She looked up at him. "I'll forgive you if you promise to be that boy I liked again."

His face fell and he closed his eyes. "I don't think I can. Too much has changed."

"Like what?" When he only shook his head, she hooked his finger again. "Tell me what happened, Wade. It's your turn now. You have to tell me a secret."

"I can't, Jeana."

"Why not? I thought you trusted me, Wade. I promise to keep it just between us."

"You won't tell anyone? Not even him?"

"Not even Mickey."

He hesitated a second, then he said, "I do trust you, Jeana. Nobody else knows about this, not even my mother." He lowered his gaze and took a shaky breath. "My dad's been making me use steroids since the summer before the seventh grade. He said I didn't have enough talent to make it otherwise, and I was too stupid to do anything else."

"Oh my God!"

"I hated using them," he said, still not looking at her.

"They screwed up my head until I thought I was going crazy, and I stayed mad all the time and didn't know why. I tried to get him to let me stop a long time ago, but he said he had too much money invested in me to give it up. But I quit anyway, Jeana." He looked up at her finally. "I haven't used them for the last three months, I *swear*."

His eagerness for her to believe him made her eyes fill with tears. "How could he do that to you, Wade?"

"I used to tell myself he was doing it because he wanted to help me get better, but all he cares about is what people think of *him*—just like this thing." He held up his hand and fingered his class ring. "All I wanted was a traditional Vigor ring, but he said it would make him look cheap."

"But steroids could kill you, Wade. Doesn't he know that?"

He shrugged. "I guess he thought it was worth the risk."

It was Jeana's turn to wrap his hand in both of hers.

"He's a horrible, despicable man for doing that to you, Wade." She mustered the courage to go on. "Does he hit you too?"

"You figured that out, huh?" He looked ashamed to admit it. "Yeah, lotta good it does me to be big and strong. I'm still too much of a coward to stand up to him."

She tried to touch his face, but he turned away. "Wade, we've known each other all our lives. You can be yourself with me."

He looked at her again with tears in his eyes that he didn't try to hide. The tough, arrogant football player was gone, and he was just a boy whose father had always made him feel like he wasn't good enough to be loved. Jeana's heart went out to him, and she put her arms around his neck and pulled him to her.

"I'm so sorry he hurt you, Wade." She stroked his head while he cried against her neck. "And you did stand up to him. The drugs might have made you big and strong, but you stopped taking them because you have the kind of strength that only comes from your *heart*. You're so much stronger than he is, and you'll be a better man than he could ever hope to be."

"Nobody but you has ever thought there was anything good about me, Jeana. You've always been the only one." He pressed his face into her curls. "God, I love the way your hair smells. So sweet... just like you." His arms went around her too tightly. "I've been waiting so long for this, hoping you still cared about me."

She tried to pull away, but he wouldn't let her go. "Wade, don't misunder—"

"I couldn't get you out of my mind no matter how hard I tried! The booze didn't work, and all those other girls..." He held her head in his hands and pulled her face to his. "None of them were anything like you, Jeana. They couldn't make me feel the way I did when you smiled at me. When you were *my* girl, the way it's supposed to be. There's never been another girl for me after you!"

"Wade, stop..." She tried to shake her head and push his arms away, but he was incredibly strong.

"Why do I have to stop, Jeana? You know you'd still be mine if I hadn't moved. It isn't fair and it makes me crazy!"

"Wade, please..."

"Let me show you how I feel about you." He pulled her face closer. "I *love* you, Jeana. I've *always* loved you."

He kissed her and didn't seem to feel it when she pounded on his chest. He pushed her back until they were lying on the floor and she was trapped under him with his hands still holding her head.

"Let me go, Wade!" she said when she managed to pull her mouth away. "You have it all wrong."

"No I don't, Jeana! You're the only good thing I ever had, and I want you back!"

His fingers tangled in her hair as he covered her mouth again with his. There was no way she could push him off, so she knew her only chance to make him stop was to get him to listen to her. She worked one of her hands free and put it on his forehead so she could push his head back and make him look into her eyes.

"You're *hurting* me, Wade. I know you don't want to hurt me again."

It worked. He let her go and pulled her up beside him.

"I swear I never meant to hurt you the first time. I just don't know my own strength sometimes, and I'm so damn *stupid* that I waited until you were with him before I tried to get you back, and by then I didn't know how to be anybody but the *Wademan*." He pressed the heels of his hands to his eyes. "I hated myself for hurting you! Why do you think I wanted him to bash my face in?"

"Wade…"

He tried to kiss her again. When she wouldn't let him, he took her hand and kissed it instead.

"Can't you see how much I need you, Jeana? I don't want to be the Wademan anymore, I want to be the boy who fell in love with *you*." He picked up the flashlight and aimed it at the door. "The one who carved our initials in that heart over there and learned all the constellations from you. You're the only girl that's ever cared about *me* and not the football star or my dad's money or the 'Vette. You're the only girl I'm ever gonna love, and I know I can make you happy if you just give me the chance. I'll stop drinking, I'll study hard and go to college, I'll do *anything* to be good enough for you."

He got up on his knees and pulled her hand to his heart again.

"I might not be worth a damn at anything else, but I know I can be the best at loving you. Say you love me, Jeana. Please just let me hear you say it."

He looked at her with such desperate hope that she almost told him what he wanted to hear just so he wouldn't be hurt anymore. But she couldn't do that, because it would only make it harder for him when she told him the truth—

that she loved only Mickey. She put her hand on his face with tears running down her cheeks.

"I'm so sorry I misled you, Wade. I only meant to comfort you, as a friend."

"I don't want to be your *friend*—"

"But that's all we can be, because I love Mickey."

"Don't say that to me!" He covered his ears with his hands. "You're wrong. You just think you love him."

She took his hands down gently. "I'm more sure of it than anything I've ever known."

The muscles in his jaw began to twitch. "You're sleeping with him, aren't you? I've seen him with his hands all over you, feeling you up like he did that night in the parking lot!" His arm encircled her waist and jerked her against him. "I can give you that if it's what you want, and you'll like it a helluva lot more with me!"

"Stop it! Don't talk to me like that!"

"What if I decide to give it to you anyway? Who's gonna stop me?" The hand holding her jaw to make her look at him slid down her neck to the top of her breasts. "I can do things that'll make you forget you ever saw him. Things I've wanted to do to you for so long." He pulled her closer until their faces were almost touching. "I've been making love to you every night since I was thirteen. I want to see if it's as good as I dreamed."

His hand moved to her shirt buttons and began to undo them.

"Just relax, Jeana-baby. The Wademan knows how to give you what you need."

She didn't struggle or try to stop him because she wasn't afraid. She knew this was just his way of hiding his pain, so she looked into his eyes and made him be the boy they both wanted him to be.

"I would never have come here with the *Wademan*. Your name is Wade Anthony Strickland and you're the first boy I ever kissed. Your birthday is September 17, your

39

favorite color is yellow, you hate raisins and have a chickenpox scar behind your right ear, and you would never hurt me on purpose."

He stared back at her, his chest rising and falling as the smug look on his face slowly dissolved into one of utter disheartenment. He let her go and turned away, his voice barely audible when he spoke again.

"I guess you'll tell him all about this now."

"No, not everything. Didn't I promise to keep your secret?" She smiled when he looked at her. "Friends don't break promises."

"Tell him if you want to," he said. "Just do me a favor and don't stop him this time when he tries to kill me."

"Don't talk like that. It's not funny."

"I'm not trying to be funny!" He started to get up and shook off her hand when she held on to his arm. "Just leave me the hell alone, Jeana. I don't need your pity!"

"Wade, stop pushing everyone away. Quit acting like you don't care about anything and let somebody love you."

"But not you, right?" He didn't wait for an answer before standing up. "Come on, we better get outta here. You got a date to keep, remember?"

They left the shed and walked around the fence instead of going through it. He started to get in his car and Jeana stopped him.

"Wait, I'll go get your graph."

He was gone when she came back. She stood in the yard a moment, listening to the familiar sounds of the neighborhood she and Wade had grown up in together. The streetlights were on now, the signal that it was time to stop playing and go home. She wished things could still be that simple. How was she ever going to tell Mickey what she'd done?

She went inside and her mother told her that Mickey had called a few minutes earlier.

"Where were you, baby?" he asked when she called

40

him back. "Your mom didn't know."

"How fast can you get here, Mickey? I need your arms around me."

He was there in five minutes. She was waiting on the porch and went straight to his arms when he got out of the car.

"Jeana, tell me what's wrong." His voice betrayed how badly she'd scared him. "What did Wade do?"

"Not here, Mickey." She looked up at him and suddenly knew where they needed to go. "Take me back to center field."

Lying on the quilt in the haven of Mickey's arms, Jeana told him what happened. When she came to the part about the steroids, she told him that Wade had confided in her about something she'd promised to keep secret. Mickey didn't interrupt her while she talked, but she felt the tension in his body as he listened. His muscles were as taut as piano wires.

"Are you mad, Mickey?" she asked when she finished.

"I don't know," he said. "I hate the thought of him touching you, but at least you didn't get hurt."

"What are you going to do?"

He didn't say anything for several seconds, then he sighed. "It'd be easy for me to get mad and pound on him some more, but I don't see the point. He knows now that he'll never have you. That's gotta hurt a lot worse than anything I could do to him."

"Are you mad at me?"

He tilted up her face to make her look at him. "If you ever take chances like that again, I'll turn you over my knee."

She scoffed. "I'd like to see you try."

"You don't think I can do it?"

"Mickey, I said I'd *like* to see you try."

They both laughed, then he wrapped his arms around her again. "Why'd you want to come back here tonight,

Jeana?"

"I don't know. I just wanted to feel happy again, and the night we were here was the happiest I've ever been. So far at least."

"It won't be too much longer, baby," he said. "If I get to play baseball here at South, I should know within a year or so if any of the pros are interested in me. Then we can get married, and I'll make love to you every morning and every night and every other chance I get."

"Mmm… that sounds heavenly. But it's still so long to wait." She sat up suddenly and looked at him. "What if I got birth control pills, Mickey? I'll be eighteen in two days and can get them without my parents' permission."

"They're not guaranteed, Jeana. My mom was on them when she got pregnant."

"But they're a lot different now than they were nineteen years ago. Wait, I know!" She grinned at him. "What if I do a research paper on them and turn it in to you?"

He shook his head with a laugh. "You're beautiful and I love you, but you're such a nerd."

"You know what, Mickey? I *am*, and it doesn't bother me anymore." She stood and whirled around with her arms outstretched. "It's time I embraced my nerdiness!"

He watched her and laughed again. "How about embracing me instead?"

"You're the big jock. Why don't you catch me?"

She managed to avoid him twice before he did. He carried her back to the quilt, and since he was indeed a big jock, he demonstrated a few sports terms for her: forward pass, holding, and illegal use of the hands.

~ * ~

After Wade left Jeana's house, he picked up Jimbo and they bought some beer to take with them to Chickasabogue Creek. Jimbo had known for years how Wade felt about Jeana, but this was one of the rare occasions when he talked about her while he was sober.

"She wants us to be *friends*, Jimbo," Wade said as he opened the first beer. "How's that for a kick in the head?"

Jimbo chose his words carefully so Wade wouldn't get mad and shut down. "Gotta start somewhere, Wademan."

Wade shook his head. "I make a lousy friend."

"You don't hear me complaining, do you?"

"Because you know I'll kick your ass."

Jimbo laughed and opened his own beer. They sat in silence awhile, then Jimbo asked the question he'd never had the guts to ask before.

"Why *her*, Wademan? What makes her so special?"

Wade stared at the water through the windshield and didn't say anything for a long time. Jimbo wasn't about to push him and had decided he wasn't going to get an answer when he heard a heavy sigh on the other side of the car.

"Every tackle, every catch, every damn step I ever took on the football field was for her, but you know who she thought was hot stuff, Jimbo? The scrawny kid whose biggest claim to fame was doing handstands in the pool and whistling with his fingers. She's the best thing I ever had in my life, and the only time I ever felt even close to being a hero was because of the way she looked at me. And it didn't have anything to do with playing football or driving a Corvette. I've loved her since we were kids, and I'm never gonna stop."

Jimbo had no idea how to respond to that, so he didn't.

For the next half hour, Wade drank silently behind the wheel of the Corvette with the Eagles blasting from the stereo. But when Don Henley advised the "Desperado" to let somebody love him, Wade smashed the eject button with his fist and snatched the cassette from the slot. He ran to the water's edge and hurled the tape out into the creek.

"But not you, right?" Wade yelled into the darkness. "It's sure as hell not *you!*" He lost his balance and fell to his knees, pounding the sand with his fists until his anger dissolved into tears. "Why couldn't it be you, Jeana?"

43

Jimbo knew Wade would either drink himself unconscious or take them both to the brink of death driving the Corvette. Jimbo didn't feel like risking his life again tonight, so he took the keys from the ignition and grabbed a couple of beers, then he walked to a clearance in the tangle of kudzu vines about fifty yards away to wait for the Wademan to pass out.

Chapter Six

Jeana was in the porch swing the next afternoon when Billy Joe got home from work, so she called out and waved for him to come over.

"Are you and Allison going out tonight?" she asked when he came up the steps.

He grimaced. "Yeah, I lost a bet and have to take her to see *Blue Lagoon.*"

"Do you have a few minutes to talk to me?"

"Always," he said, sitting beside her. "What's up, kiddo?"

She picked up his hand and entwined their fingers. "Do you remember the summer Wade moved?"

"Sure. Why?"

"Did he come to see me the day before school started?"

Billy Joe blinked in obvious surprise. "So he finally told you. What brought up all that stuff?"

"Did you tell him I said he was stuck up, and that I didn't want to see him?"

"Yeah," he said, his brown eyes unapologetic. "I didn't want you to like him anymore. I knew he was bad news even then."

"That's not true, Billy Joe. He wasn't bad then, and what you said to him made him break my heart." She told him what happened the next day at school.

"Okay, maybe I shouldn't have lied to him, Jeana, but look what he did. Doesn't that prove I was right about him?" He pulled her hand to his heart. "You know I would never hurt you like that, no matter what I thought you'd said."

"I'm not mad at you, Billy Joe. I just want to know the

45

truth."

"Why does it matter now?"

"Because he did hurt me, and I needed to tell him so we could get past it. I knew the real Wade was still there somewhere inside him, and I wanted him to come back."

He searched her face anxiously. "Please tell me you're not letting him get to you again."

"Don't be silly. I just wanted to help him."

"Why? He doesn't deserve it after all the things he's done."

She turned around in the swing and put her hands on his shoulders. "Listen to me, Billy Joe. There are reasons he's like he is. His father is a horrible man, and you wouldn't believe the things he's done to Wade."

"Yeah? Well, maybe you shouldn't believe it either."

"You don't have to hate him, Billy Joe. He knows I love Mickey, and I don't think he'll cause any more problems. I just wanted to remember when we were kids without it hurting so much." She looked across the fence at Wade's old house. "I wanted my memories back."

He followed her gaze and sighed. "You liked him more than you liked me, didn't you?"

"Oh, Billy Joe." She leaned her forehead against his. "I was madly in love with Captain James Tiberius Kirk back then. You and Wade never came close to him in my heart."

He looked disgusted. "Kirk's a womanizer, you know. And he wears a rug now too."

"Don't bother," she said. "I got over him already."

He put his arm around her and leaned back in the swing with his legs stretched out in front of him. "If only there was a way to make Mickey look less than perfect to you."

"Don't even try."

"Let's see…" He fingered his chin. "There's the whole Yankee thing. You wouldn't want your kids exposed to *that*, would you?"

She laughed. "Stop it, Billy Joe."

"And he can't remember more than one line from any song, so don't expect him to ever sing to you or anything."

"Quit it!" She laughed harder.

"And he's not a very good speller either. He's got a *major* problem with double letters."

Jeana was laughing so hard that she couldn't speak, so she fell over in the swing and kicked him.

"But worst of all is what a lousy kisser he is," he said, grabbing her feet. "I can honestly say I'd rather kiss my grandma!"

~ * ~

Mickey arrived for their date at six. In his continuing search for some kind of sport Jeana would like, he'd talked her into going bowling. She was looking forward to it as much as a root canal.

"This could be the one to win her over," Mickey told Robert and Betty optimistically before he and Jeana left.

"I admire your persistence, Mickey." Robert patted his shoulder. "But I think you're in for more disappointment."

After they got in the Mustang, Jeana said, "I tried to get Billy Joe to bring Allison to the bowling gym after the movie, but he said they were going to the mall to get her dress. What's so funny?"

"It's called a bowling *alley*, Jeana."

"Well, ex*cuse* me." She made a face at him.

They arrived at Indian Lanes and were lucky enough to get a lane without having to wait very long. After renting their shoes—much to Jeana's repulsion—Mickey helped her find a ball that fit her hand and wasn't too heavy.

While she put on her shoes and waited for Mickey to come back with his own ball, Jeana heard high-pitched laughter and turned to see a group of teenagers coming in the door: Wade, Jimbo, Lamar, and Bubba, accompanied by four girls who—based on the amount of hairspray they used—had to be from Satsuma High School.

The whole group was loud and either drunk or high or

both, but the guy behind the counter didn't seem to care. He put their names on the waiting list for a pair of lanes and told them he'd call when he had something. They went in the game room to wait, and Jeana felt sure there would be trouble when Wade noticed her there with Mickey.

"Okay, let's get this over with so we can go do something fun," she said when Mickey came back.

"That's not a very good attitude, Jeana," he said. "C'mere and let me explain the concept to you."

Her eyebrow went up. "What concept?"

"You need to look at bowling in a geometrical sense," he said. "It's all about arcs and angles and the rotation of the ball."

"You mean you have to do *math* in this game?"

Mickey laughed. "Don't worry, baby. I'll explain it to you."

"Like I need your help." She gave him a shove.

He showed her the correct way to put her fingers in the holes and where to stand on the approach, then he demonstrated how she needed to push the ball out and let it swing back as she walked up to the foul line so that she'd get enough momentum to throw it. She made him go first so she could watch how he did it, and he got a strike.

"That's all there is to it?" she said. "You just hit them in the right spot and they all fall down?"

Mickey pulled her up from her seat. "Yeah, but it's not so easy to hit that spot every time, Jeana."

"You did it the first time."

"That was mostly luck." He picked up her ball for her. "Go ahead and try it, baby."

She did her best to remember everything he'd told her, but her ball fell into the gutter before it got halfway down the lane.

"Why do they have those *ditches* on the sides?" she asked. "That's not fair."

Mickey sighed and told her what she'd done wrong.

Standing behind her on the approach, he showed her how to follow through with her arm when she released the ball.

"That'll make the ball roll straighter so it won't go in the gutter," he said. "Well, maybe."

She tried again and came back with a big smile because she'd knocked down three pins. She continued to improve for the rest of the game, and when he asked her if she wanted to bowl another one, she grudgingly told him yes.

"You like it, don't you?"

She shrugged nonchalantly. "It's not as bad as I thought."

"Admit it, Jeana." He poked her in the ribs. "You like it."

"Okay, quit! I like it a little."

He tilted up her face to kiss her, and someone behind them said, "Well, ain't this *sweet*?"

They turned to see Wade standing by the table behind their lane with his arms draped across the shoulders of two of the girls.

Jeana held Mickey's hands tightly in hers. "Please try to ignore him."

Wade looked at her with heavy-lidded, bloodshot eyes. "You gonna make out with him on the pitcher's mound tomorrow night, Jeana?"

The girls with him giggled excessively, and Jeana's temper flared. "No, you've got it all wrong, Wade. We do it in center field."

Mickey bent his head to stifle a laugh, and Wade's face went a deep crimson.

"What's so funny, asshole? Don't you know where she was yesterday?"

"It won't work, Strickland," Mickey said. "I know about it already. Jeana told you the score, so deal with it."

"Why don't I just deal with *you*?"

Wade pushed the girls away from him and started down the raised platform toward Mickey. Jeana jumped up and

49

moved to get between them, but she stumbled on the edge of the step and fell with her hands out in front of her. Her fingers slipped through Wade's as he tried to catch her, and her head struck the edge of a table on her way down. She ended up on the floor at Wade's feet with blood oozing from a gash at the top of her forehead.

"Oh God, Jeana..." Wade fell to his knees and held her head in his hands. "I'm sorry—"

"Get away from her!" Mickey threw Wade aside and knelt over Jeana. "Can you hear me, baby? Open your eyes and look at me!"

He started to pick her up, but Wade stopped him with a hand on his shoulder. "Don't move her! Remember what Coach always told us about injuries on the field? I'll go call an ambulance!"

A woman in the crowd said she was a nurse and told Mickey to turn Jeana on her side and keep her head elevated. Somebody gave him their jacket to put under her head and somebody else gave the nurse a wet washcloth from the snack bar that she pressed to Jeana's forehead. Her eyes flickered open.

"Mickey..."

"I'm here, baby. Don't try to move." He pressed her hand to his lips. "I love you."

She smiled weakly and closed her eyes again.

Wade came back and knelt beside Mickey. "The ambulance will be here in a couple of minutes. Has she come around?"

"She just talked to me," Mickey said.

Wade stared at Jeana's blood on his hands. "I tried to catch her. I'm so sorry..."

Mickey looked at Wade's agonized face and said, "She's gonna be okay. Don't even think anything else."

They heard sirens approaching, and a few seconds later the paramedics rushed in and took over. They checked Jeana's vital signs, looked at her pupils, and bandaged her head. Although she was alert and responsive, they told Mickey that a doctor needed to examine her because she'd lost consciousness, so they were transporting her to Springhill Memorial Hospital.

"Can I ride with her in the ambulance?" Mickey asked as they lifted Jeana inside.

"No, you'll have to follow in your car," the attendant replied. "Has anyone called her parents?"

Mickey's hand went to his forehead. "I forgot about calling them."

"I'll go to her house and tell them," Wade said. "You stay with her, Mickey."

It wasn't until he was driving to the hospital behind the ambulance that Mickey realized this was the first time Wade had actually called him by his name.

~ * ~

Billy Joe was just getting home when he saw the Corvette pull up at Jeana's house and then saw Wade jump out and run up to the door. Billy Joe ran over to see what was wrong and insisted on going to the hospital with them. Wade followed the Russells in his car, and they all walked into the emergency room together. Mickey was sitting in the waiting area with his head in his hands.

"They wouldn't let me go back with her because I'm not family," he said.

Betty patted his arm. "I'll make them let you see her once we know what they're doing. Don't worry, Mickey."

The Russells spoke to the woman at the desk and found out they hadn't done anything to Jeana yet because they needed parental permission. Betty went back with the nurse while Robert filled out the papers. Mickey, Wade, and Billy Joe sat in the waiting area and alternated between staring at the floor and the ceiling.

After what seemed like an eternity to the three boys, Betty came out and told them Jeana's head CT looked good and she was going to be fine. She needed three stitches, but they were right at her hairline, so the scar probably wouldn't even show.

Betty took Mickey back with her to sit with Jeana while she got the stitches. Robert went to the cafeteria to get some coffee, so Wade and Billy Joe were left in the waiting area alone. They glanced at each other and then looked away, but after five minutes, Billy Joe broke the silence.

"Look, Strickland. I'm kinda low on gas, so if you're planning to smash my face again, could you do it while we're already here and save me the trip back?"

Wade snickered. "Why would I want to make you any uglier, DuBose?"

"I know you found out I lied to you the summer you moved," Billy Joe said. "Jeana never said you were stuck up. I was jealous because I knew she liked you better than me."

Wade sighed and leaned over with his hands clasped between his knees. "Yeah, I figured out a long time ago that you were lying about that. You can think of the last time I kicked your ass as payment for it, and we'll call it even."

Billy Joe's eyebrows went up. "Did you hit your head too?"

Wade rubbed his eyes wearily. "You didn't do nothing I wouldn't have done in your place, and it didn't work anyway. She still ended up with him."

They didn't talk anymore, and Billy Joe leaned back and closed his eyes. He had almost drifted off when Wade spoke again from right beside him, startling him awake.

"How can you watch them together? Doesn't it drive you crazy?"

Billy Joe blinked and shook his head to clear it. "You mean Jeana and Mickey?"

Wade nodded. "I know you love her too. How can you stand it?"

Billy Joe didn't even consider denying that he loved

her. He shrugged and said, "She loves him, and he makes her happy. As long as she's happy, I can live with it."

"Do you think he loves her as much as we do?"

"Wade, old buddy"—Billy Joe put a consoling hand on his shoulder—"I honestly believe he'd give his life for her. But don't get any ideas. You'd be the prime suspect."

Wade snorted a laugh. "What about you, dipshit? Don't tell me you never thought about bumping him off."

"Who me?" Billy Joe looked shocked. "Well, maybe once or twice. But that's all."

"You're still a goofball, DuBose." Wade shoved him and stood up. "I guess I'll go on home. Tell Jeana—"

"Tell me what?"

Mickey pushed Jeana's wheelchair over to where Wade and Billy Joe were sitting. Her head was bandaged and she looked a little paler than usual, but she was smiling.

Wade knelt in front of her and held both of her hands. "That I'm sorry this happened, and I'm so sorry I didn't catch you."

She squeezed his hands. "It's okay, Wade. I'm fine."

"Yeah, it's not your fault she's a klutz," Billy Joe said. "And why do you think you play linebacker, Wade? Coach knew you didn't have good hands."

Wade gave him a dark look. "It's not too late to change my mind about making you a patient here, DuBose."

As they were all leaving together, a police car pulled up and two patrolmen started into the emergency room. Billy Joe cupped his hands around his mouth and called out to them.

"She's over here, officers! And they're still on her feet!"

Jeana looked down and saw that she was still wearing the rented bowling shoes.

Chapter Seven

Sunday night when Mickey came to pick up Jeana for the football banquet, he whistled appreciatively when she walked into her living room to greet him.

"Notice anything different?" She smiled up at him and fluttered her eyelashes.

He inspected her face closely. "Um, you mean the three stitches in your forehead?"

"You know what I mean, Mickey. How do you like the bangs Allison cut for me to cover the stitches?"

"Oh, yeah…" He touched the wispy bangs and kissed her on the nose. "They're cute, but don't cut any more of your hair."

Betty took their picture before they left and told them not to be too late because they had school the next day. When they were in the car, Mickey said, "Now I can tell you what I really think about you in that dress. Can we just skip the banquet and go to center field?"

Jeana lifted her eyebrow. "I thought you wanted me to take it easy like the doctor said."

"I do, but I'm gonna have a hard time concentrating on anything but you tonight." He leaned over and kissed her. "Happy Birthday, baby. You get more beautiful every year."

She told him what she'd gotten from her family while they drove to the Country Club, then she asked him when she'd get his gift.

"You got a lot already, Jeana. Don't be greedy."

"Very funny."

He flicked her earlobe. "You know I like to make you wait. Don't you think anticipation adds to the gift?"

"No, I think you're just a sadist."

"Then that makes you a masochist," he said, "because you love me."

They met Marsha and Mickey's Aunt Robin in the Country Club parking lot, and they saved four places at their table for Billy Joe, Allison, and the DuBoses. Marsha and Robin excused themselves to go to the ladies' room before they sat down. Mickey went to speak to Coach Carter for a minute, so Jeana was left alone at the table. She felt a hand on her shoulder and turned to look as Wade sat down beside her.

"How's your head, Redhot?"

"It's fine," she replied. "Are the stitches very noticeable?"

He shook his head and touched her bangs. "Your hair's different, isn't it? I like it, and you look... even prettier than usual."

"Thank you, Wade. You look very handsome yourself." She fingered his sleeve. "The green in your new shirt matches your eyes. I'm glad you haven't busted the seams on it yet."

"I don't know." He flexed his right arm. "This one looks about ready to give. What do you think?"

She laughed. "Did you bring a date?"

"Yeah, but I can't remember her name."

She smacked his hand. "That's terrible, Wade. You need to wear a rubber band all the time so—"

"Be my guest." He held up his arm to show her the rubber band still on his wrist, and she snapped it.

"We'll make a choirboy out of you yet."

He took her hand and held it in both of his. "Remember the other day in the clubhouse when I said I didn't want to be your friend?" He looked up at her almost shyly. "Can I take it back?"

"I didn't believe you anyway."

"But if you change your mind and lose the Yankee..."

"Wade…"

He sighed. "I guess he's really a nice guy." Jeana nodded her agreement and he added, "Nice guys make me wanna puke."

They both laughed.

"Wade, I saw your car parked in front of Hamilton Elementary this morning on my way home from church. What were you doing there?"

He lifted one shoulder. "I like to go there sometimes and sit in the doorway by the cafeteria." He paused and gave her a wistful smile. "To remember the best day of my life."

Jeana felt her throat tighten. "That's one of my favorite memories too."

"Did you ever get over your fear of storms?"

"No, and nobody else knows about it, so you still can't tell."

He mimed zipping his lips, then he reached into his pocket. "I guess I better get back to my table. I just wanted to make sure you're okay and give you this. I've had it for a long time, but I added something new to it." He placed a small box in her hand, wrapped in white paper decorated with hand-drawn hearts and stars. "Happy Birthday, Redhot. I'm glad I can finally give this to you, but don't open it until you get home."

"Thank you, Wade." She leaned over and hugged him.

His arms stayed around her a couple of seconds longer after she let him go. He stood up and started to walk away, then he stopped and turned to look at her again.

"It was a pretty good idea, wasn't it, Jeana? The jokes I mean."

"It was a great idea, Wade, and it still works too." She smiled up at him. "Every time it storms, I think about knock-knock jokes and you."

The look on his face told her how much that meant to him. He touched her cheek and said, "See you later,

Redhot."

Mickey was on his way back to the table, so Jeana put the gift in her purse before he saw it. No sense putting a strain on his truce with Wade.

"I saw your visitor," Mickey said when he sat down. "What did he want?"

"He just came over to tell me Happy Birthday."

Mickey looked as if he were going to ask more, so Jeana was relieved when they were interrupted by Billy Joe.

"Oh, *man*," he said as he sat beside her. "The hospital must've caught your hair in the scissors when they did the sutures. Maybe you can sue."

Jeana hit him on the left arm and Allison—in all her purple splendor—hit him on the right.

Everyone at the table was introduced when Marsha and Robin came back. The people at the head table began taking their seats to start the banquet, then Mr. Strickland went to the podium to welcome everyone and announce that they would eat before beginning the program.

"What did you say to your coach?" Jeana asked Mickey as the food was served.

"He wanted us to tell him if any college recruiters had contacted us. I guess he's gonna say something about it tonight."

Jeana took the platter of rolls the waiter offered and looked at Mickey in surprise.

"Who's talked to you?"

"Alabama, Auburn, and Tennessee."

She frowned at him. "Mickey, you didn't tell me that."

"I didn't think it was important. You know I'm going to South, baby."

"I still like to know things like that. It's impressive for all of them to want you." She lowered her voice. "Of course, I know how they feel."

He laughed and flicked her earlobe. "I didn't get any

real offers. They just invited me to visit the campus and talk to the coaches."

"I got a call from Whatsamatta U," Billy Joe said, reaching for a roll. "I'm giving it some serious thought."

While the dessert was served, Mr. Strickland went back to the podium and made a grandiose speech about how much he'd enjoyed serving as Booster Club president for the past two years. Then he introduced the guest speaker, a "personal friend" and the Defensive Coordinator for the University of Alabama, Coach Henry Alexander.

Billy Joe leaned over to Mickey and whispered, "How much you think it cost him to buy this guy's friendship? Guess he's hoping to get an offer for Wade."

"They should want him," Mickey said. "He's a good linebacker and a hard hitter. I can personally vouch for that."

"Yeah, but I don't think he's got the grades for a Division One school."

Mrs. DuBose shushed them both and told them to pay attention.

Billy Joe scowled at her. "There's not gonna be a test on this stuff, Ma."

When Coach Alexander finished speaking, Coach Carter took the mic and introduced the players as they received their varsity letters. Then it was time for the special awards.

"Our next award is Defensive Player of the Year," Coach said. "This one was especially hard for me to decide this season. Our entire defense has been superlative for a couple of years now, but this year we had two of the finest linebackers I've ever coached."

Jeana squeezed Mickey's hand under the table, and he winked at her.

"In the end," Coach continued, "one factor tilted the scale in this young man's favor, and that was his remarkable ability to detect the slightest giveaway as to what play the offense is going to run. He's not only a hard-hitting linebacker, he's also a smart one. The Defensive Player of the Year is Mickey Royal."

Everyone except Mr. Strickland applauded as Mickey went up to accept the plaque. When he got back to the table, he handed the award to his mother and kissed her on the cheek. Coach Carter gave a couple of other awards, then it was time to announce the permanent team captains.

"I have to say I'm very pleased with the players' choices this year," Coach said. "Both of these young men are hard workers and have the strongest drive to win I've ever witnessed in high school players. In fact, it's so strong that they started out trying to kill each other in competition. But they learned to work together without too much animosity and set an example for the whole team as to the kind of work ethic it takes to win. Our permanent team captains for 1980-81 are Wade Strickland and Mickey Royal."

All the players stood and clapped as Mickey and Wade walked up to the podium. They both shook hands with Coach Carter and then—to everyone's complete amazement—they shook hands with each other. Coach Carter put a hand on their shoulders before they went back to their seats.

"I want to mention that both of these boys have been approached by college recruiters," Coach said. "Wade by Troy State and Livingston, and Mickey by Alabama, Auburn, and Tennessee."

As the room emptied after the banquet, Coach Alexander came over to Mickey and offered his hand. "I'm glad someone from recruiting has touched base with you already, son. From what Coach Carter said, it sounds like we'd be lucky to have you come to the University of Alabama."

"Thanks, Coach," Mickey said. "But my plans are to play baseball at South."

The coach looked surprised. "You'd rather go there than Alabama?"

"Yes, sir," Mickey replied. "My dad played there, so it's important to me."

"Well, I suppose I can understand that. Good luck to you, Mickey. Come see us in Tuscaloosa if you change your mind."

He turned to leave and was waylaid by Mr. Strickland. "I need a word with you in private, Henry."

When Marsha said goodbye to Mickey and Jeana in the parking lot, she kissed them both and dabbed at her eyes with a tissue. Jeana asked Mickey why she was crying when they got in the car.

"Who knows?" he said. "Could be anything."

Jeana thought there was something he wasn't telling her and was about to ask him about it when she realized she'd left her purse inside the Country Club, so they went back in to get it. When they came back to the car, she saw Wade's Corvette in the far corner of the parking lot beside his father's Cadillac. Wade and Mr. Strickland were standing between the vehicles, and she could hear their raised voices.

"What do you think that's about?" Mickey asked.

"I don't know," Jeana said. "But I'm sure it's nothing good."

"Well, I guess it's none of our business." Mickey opened the car door for her and they started to get in, but they stopped when the sound of a slap echoed across the parking lot. They turned to look and saw Wade lying back on the Corvette's hood with his hand to his mouth, his father shouting so loud now that both Mickey and Jeana could make out his words.

"All that money I spent to give you an edge and you still let that Royal boy show you up! Then you have the nerve to defend him to me? You're useless! Your grades are so bad Alabama won't take you no matter how much

60

money I donate! You make me *sick*."

Mickey looked at Jeana and she said, "Do something, Mickey."

He sprinted across the parking lot and reached them just as Mr. Strickland backhanded Wade again.

"Give me your keys!"

Mickey put a hand on the man's chest and pushed him away from Wade. "Don't hit him again."

"Get your hands off me, boy!" Strickland yelled. "Do you know who you're dealing with here?"

"Yes, sir," Mickey said. "And I'm not gonna let you hit him again."

Jeana ran to Wade and tried to help him up, but he pulled away from her and went around to the driver's side of the Corvette. When his father saw him, he tried to push past Mickey.

"Get away from that car! It doesn't belong to you anymore, you worthless piece of *shit!*"

The imprint of Jeana's hand appeared on Strickland's face, and all one hundred pounds of her blocked his path to Wade, her eyes full of green fire.

"Don't you *dare* talk to him like that! You're a vile, loathsome man, and Wade is worth a hundred of you!"

Strickland moved as if he meant to strike her, and Mickey threw him backward against the Cadillac. "Don't even think about putting your hands on her."

"You'll be sorry you did that, boy," Strickland said, straightening his tailored suit. "I'll have you arrested for assault, then we'll see how many of those schools want you."

"I think the police will also be interested in that *edge* you mentioned a few minutes ago," Jeana said. "What do you think, Mr. Strickland?"

He was visibly shocked by her words, but he immediately tried to cover it. "I don't know what the hell you're talking about, and neither do you, little girl. You need to mind your own damn business!"

"She knows, Dad," Wade said. "I told her, and I'll back her up if she wants me to. I told you I wasn't using any more steroids."

"*Shut your goddamn mouth!*" Strickland started toward Wade again. "I'll kill you, boy!"

"You're gonna have to get past me first," Mickey said as he moved in front of him. "And I don't think you can do it."

Strickland looked from Mickey to Jeana, and his expression suddenly changed. "Wait a minute. You're that little Russell girl who used to live next door." He turned to Wade with a mocking laugh. "You mean to tell me you let this boy better you in football, and he's got the girl you've been mooning over all these years too?" He looked gratified when Wade hung his head. "Didn't I tell you to forget about her the first time you came home whining about how she didn't like you anymore? I told you she'd never want a dumbass like you!"

"Yeah, you told me, Dad," Wade said. "You made sure I thought I wasn't good enough for her, because she scared the hell out of you, didn't she? You knew that if I had her, I wouldn't give a damn about any of the stuff that made you look like a big shot, and how would you control me then?"

"You ungrateful little punk! You're nothing but a—"

"Go to hell, Dad," Wade said. "You don't know anything about me."

Strickland's face was almost purple, and a vein pulsed noticeably in his right temple. "I know you'd better enjoy that car tonight, smartass, because you'll never see it again!" He started to walk off toward the Country Club but stopped and said, "See if you can keep from screwing up the car like you do everything else, boy. I want to at least get a decent price for it!"

Wade watched his father walk away, then he got in the Corvette and started the engine. Jeana ran to stop him before he could drive away.

"Please don't do anything crazy, Wade." She held on to his arm through the open window. "He probably didn't mean what he said."

He took her hand from his arm. "I guess I better do like he said and enjoy the 'Vette while I still got it." He looked up into the sky behind her with a mirthless laugh. "Hey, look. There's the North Star. The coolest girl in the world told me I could use it to find my way when I'm lost." His eyes locked with hers a second, then he pulled her face to his and kissed her softly on the lips, the way he'd kissed her when they were eleven. "Don't worry, Redhot. I'll be okay."

When Mickey walked up behind Jeana, Wade said, "I'm glad somebody finally stood up to him. God knows I could never do it." He put the car in gear and looked at Jeana again. "Take care of her, Mickey."

He put the Corvette in gear and drove away.

Chapter Eight

Mickey and Jeana didn't talk as they walked back to the Mustang, but when he opened the door for her to get in, she turned her face to his chest and started to cry.

"I feel so bad for him, Mickey."

He put his arms around her. "I know, baby. Me too."

"Thank you for helping him. You were wonderful as always."

"You were pretty feisty yourself. I bet that jerk's jaw is gonna be sore tomorrow." He felt her arm for a muscle. "I didn't know you packed a punch like that."

"Let's go, Mickey. I'm sick of this place." They got in the car, and when they pulled out of the parking lot, she asked him where they were going.

"I thought we'd go to the Gulf," he said.

"Tonight?"

"Sure, baby. The quilt's in the trunk. What else do we need?"

They were in Gulf Shores an hour later. Mickey's aunt and uncle owned a beach house a couple of miles down Fort Morgan Road, so they parked there and walked to the private beach nearby. Lying in each other's arms under the diamond-encrusted sky, with the surf as their background music, they talked about their future.

"I finally made a decision about my major," Jeana said. "I want to teach."

"That's great, baby. What made up your mind for you?"

She hesitated a second before answering. "It was something Wade said actually. He used to tell me all the time when we were kids that I should be a teacher, and when we were working on the graphs for our project, he told me I made it easy for him to understand. I liked the feeling I got from watching him take pride in what he was doing."

"Do they have a good College of Education at Troy State?"

"What difference does that make? I'm not going there."

"Jeana, it doesn't make any sense—"

"We've already had this conversation, Mickey. I'm not leaving."

"You know it would kill me too, but—"

She cut off his words with a kiss. He kept trying to talk at first, but she quickly drew him into it. He gave up and kissed her back, rolling over so that he was lying on top of her. Jeana loved to feel the sinewy curves and rigid planes of the muscles in his arms and back. She ran her hands over them while they kissed, something that never failed to excite them both.

They had kept the pact they'd made as sophomores not to make love, but not without a few close calls. Jeana knew her weaknesses so they usually tried to avoid too much temptation. But it was hard to resist the myriad sensations they'd learned to give and receive with their hands, and they got carried away sometimes. Mickey was usually the one to stop and take a breather before they went too far. This time it was Jeana.

"Time out, Mickey," she said, sitting up breathlessly. "I want my birthday present now."

"Uh-oh." He stared at her a second, then he jumped up and ran toward the car, calling to her over his shoulder. "I'll be right back!" He returned empty handed a few minutes later and said, "Did I give you the keys when we got here, Jeana? They're not in my pocket or the ignition or the trunk."

"No, I haven't seen them."

"Oh, great. I must've dropped them out here somewhere."

They both felt around in the sand on their hands and knees. After a few minutes of unsuccessful searching, Mickey picked up the quilt so Jeana could look under it.

"Hey, I found something," she said, "but it's not the keys."

"What is it, baby?"

She stood up and turned so the moonlight shone on the object in her hand. "It's one of those plastic containers from a bubble gum machine, and there's something in it." She opened it and peered at the contents. "It's a toy ring and a note or something, but it's too dark for me to read it."

Mickey tilted up her face with his finger. "It says *One precious jewel for another.*"

Jeana's eyes widened as she looked closer at the ring in her hand—a solitary diamond.

"Oh, Mickey…"

He took the ring and slipped it onto her finger, then he dropped to one knee and looked up at her.

"Jeana Lee Russell, I've loved you since the first time I saw you smile when I was eleven years old. I love everything about you—your curls that surround us when you're in my arms, the way you laugh like a lumberjack and cock your eyebrow at me, your amazing intelligence, and your total lack of athletic ability. You're everything I've ever wanted and my every dream come true. I promise I'll always take care of you, I'll do my best to make you happy, and I'll never stop loving you. Will you marry me?"

She was crying, so it was a few seconds before she could speak. She didn't want Mickey to think she was hesitating out of doubt, so she threw her arms around him and knocked him over backward.

"Yes, I'll marry you, Mickey! I love you so much I need another chamber in my heart just to hold it." She kissed him to seal the promise, and neither of them cared that they were lying in the sand.

Mickey lifted her hand to his lips and kissed the ring.

"This means you'll be mine always and forever, like our song."

"Yes, Mickey. Always, forever, endlessly, perpetually, infinitely, ceaselessly, incessantly, boundlessly, eternally... I can go on if you want me to."

He laughed. "I believe you, baby."

"Is this why your mom was crying when she told us goodbye?"

"Yeah, she's been weepy ever since I told her I was gonna ask you tonight."

Jeana sat up and looked at the sand covering them both. "Mickey, I have an idea."

"Oh, God," he said. "Any idea that makes that eyebrow go up is bound to be trouble."

She stood up and grasped the hem of her dress to pull it over her head.

"What are you doing, Jeana?" Mickey looked wary, but interested.

"We need to wash off this sand." She grabbed his hand and pulled him up with her. "Take off your clothes, Mickey. Let's go skinny dipping."

"Jeana, it's *November*. The water will be freezing."

"It's not cold tonight." She started taking off her pantyhose. "Come on, Mickey. It's my birthday and I want to swim with you in our birthday suits."

She began unbuttoning his shirt and he laughed. "You've lost your mind, Jeana."

"You're right, it's called *prenuptial insanity*. Now hurry up and help me."

She had all his shirt buttons undone and was working on his pants. Mickey shook his head in amusement, but his fingers began to unhook her bra and take it off. The blue of his eyes intensified, and Jeana had to remind him of what he was supposed to be doing. She pulled his T-shirt over his head and threw it aside, his pants slid down to his ankles, and a moment later they faced each other wearing

67

nothing but their smiles.

"Ready, Mickey?"

"Definitely," he said, his gaze moving over her moonlit body. "Oh, you mean to swim? I guess so."

She laughed and took his hand as they ran down to the water. The air temperature was about sixty-five degrees— not that unusual for an autumn night on the Gulf Coast— but the water temperature was close to fifty. The cold shocked them when they ran into the surf, but it wasn't quite so bad after a few minutes. They played in the waves like children but couldn't keep their hands off each other for long. Soon they were standing in chest-high water, kissing through chattering teeth.

Mickey carried her out of the water thirty minutes later. They wrapped up in the quilt together, shivering and giggling for as long as they dared to be that close to each other naked, then they shook the sand from their scattered clothing and reluctantly got dressed.

"Now wasn't it a good idea?" Jeana asked as they walked back to the car.

"I think we've got more sand on us now than we did before, but it was fun." He flicked her earlobe. "You are something else."

"You know what I am, Mickey? *Engaged.* An event like that just seemed to require nudity." She held out her hand and admired the way the diamond sparkled in the moonlight.

Mickey laughed. "You're gonna get me in so much trouble one of these days."

Chapter Nine

Takeoff initiated as soon as the Corvette's tires hit Kali Oka's pavement. All systems were go. Flying already with not even a quarter mile gone.

Wade ran his hand lovingly over the dash. "This is it, baby. Time to give it all we got, pedal to the metal and all that shit." He laughed and watched the speedometer needle move steadily to the right. "The old man's counting on me to screw up again, and I sure as hell wouldn't wanna disappoint him."

The headlights sliced a path in the dark, the scenery flying past as indistinguishable shadows. The only break in the blackness came from an occasional streetlight on the few side roads, and the North Star shining brighter than all the others around it in the sky overhead.

"He's really pissed at me this time," Wade said. "He'll be hell bent on making me pay, and we both know he's always had a talent for hitting me where it hurts the most. But I'm not gonna let him win this time, baby. No sir, he's gonna have to go to Plan B."

The needle hit seventy and Wade smiled. The split pine he'd always used as the point of no return was long gone— taken with the thousands of other trees felled by Hurricane Frederick the year before—but that was okay. Wade was pretty sure he'd be well over the record when he reached the curve.

"Nope, not gonna let him take you this time, baby. Me and you gotta stick together. Can't let him bust us up." He pushed a cassette into the slot, and the guitar solo at the end of "Free Bird" soared out of the speakers.

The speedometer read seventy-eight.

"Gonna be airborne soon!" Wade shouted over the music. "Gonna look down on the old man and just laugh my ass off." His hands caressed the steering wheel. "It's always been you and me, baby. True love, just like Jeana said."

As soon as he said her name, his smile disappeared and tears rolled down his cheeks, but he swiped them away and looked at the speedometer again. Coming up on eighty-five and the music was accelerating along with the 'Vette.

"Don't get sidetracked now, dumbass! Gotta stay focused. Can't think about Jeana and how she looked at me tonight, or the way she told the old man off, or how it felt when she hugged me after I gave her the—"

His eyes widened as a thought occurred to him, and he took his foot off the accelerator at the same instant the headlights reflected off the warning signs. What the hell was wrong with him? He stomped the brake, causing the rear end to fishtail just enough to put the driver's side to the fore when the Corvette took flight into the curve.

Just before impact with the tenacious scrub oak that had managed to escape Frederick's wrath, Wade had just long enough to whisper, "I'm sorry, Redhot. I didn't mean to spoil your birthday."

Chapter Ten

It was almost one o'clock when Jeana and Mickey pulled up at her house, so they were surprised to see Billy Joe and Allison sitting in the porch swing.

"Hey, what are y'all—" Jeana froze when she saw their faces. "What's wrong, Billy Joe?"

He met her at the steps and took her hands. "You know Allison's brother is a paramedic, right?"

Jeana nodded. "What is it? Tell me!"

"When I took Allison home a little while ago, Danny was just coming back from a call out on Kali Oka Road." Billy Joe paused and looked from Mickey back to Jeana. "He said a guy in a yellow Corvette didn't make the curve and wrapped it around a tree."

"Oh, God…" Jeana turned to Mickey and he put his arms around her.

"Danny told us they airlifted him to USA Medical Center," Allison said. "We were waiting for y'all so we could all go down there. Billy Joe already told your parents."

They went to the emergency room first and found out that Wade had been rushed to surgery. All they were told about his condition was that it was critical. They found the surgery waiting room, and Wade's family was already there. His mother and Sissy were huddled together on one of the couches, and his father was standing by the wall staring into a Styrofoam cup. Jimbo was across the room in the corner.

"Hey, man," Billy Joe said when they walked over to Jimbo. "Any word yet?"

He shook his head. "He's been in there for over an hour

71

and nobody's come out to say anything. How'd y'all know he was here?"

Billy Joe told him about Allison's brother, and Jeana sat down beside him.

"What was he doing, Jimbo?" she said. "Did you see him after the banquet?"

"Yeah, he told me to take his date to my house and wait for him because his dad was pissed about something." Jimbo shot a look of pure hatred at Mr. Strickland. "When he got there, he asked me to take her home for him."

"Was he drinking?" Jeana asked.

"No, that's the weird thing about it. He was stone sober, but I knew something was bad wrong. It was like..." He ran a hand through his hair and shook his head. "I don't know. When I looked at his eyes, it was like nobody was in there. And I found this in my car after he left."

He pulled something from his jacket pocket and held it out to Jeana. She looked at the folded piece of paper with the rubber band she had given Wade wrapped around it, and her heart lurched in her chest.

"What is it, Jimbo?"

"I couldn't make any sense of it, but it has your name on it."

She unfolded it and drew a choked breath when she saw that it was written in the code she had made up so long ago. She read it silently through her tears.

My sweet Jeana,

Thanksf orw haty ous aida boutm et om ydad. Youa ret heo nlyo new hoe verm adem ef eell ikeI wasw ortha nything. Iw ass ol uckyt oh avey ouf ora littlew hilea ndt hatw ast heh appiestt imeo fm yl ife. Ih opey oub elievet hatI nevers toppedl ovingy ou.

72

Ik nowM ickeyw illt akec areo fy oub uti fy oue verg etf rightenedi na stormj ustc losey oure yesa ndy ou'llf eelm ya rmsa roundy ou. Iw ishw eh adt riedt her ubberb anda longt imea go. Keepi tt or ememberm e.

Love, Wade

P.S. Pleaset ellm ym othera ndm ys istert hatI lovet hem.

Jeana was sobbing when she finished, and Mickey pulled her into his arms. When the others tried to question her, he held up his hand to stop them and led her away.

"What is it, baby? Can you tell me?"

"He did it on purpose, Mickey. He wrote this to say goodbye."

Mr. Strickland spoke loudly from across the room. "Why are you kids here? You all need to go home."

"Why don't *you* leave?" Jimbo said. "You sure as hell don't care anything about him!"

"Shut your mouth, punk!" Strickland said. "Or I'll shut it for you!"

"For God's sake, Chuck!" Mrs. Strickland cried. "They're Wade's friends. Don't make this any worse." She started to sob, and Sissy hugged her with eyes that pleaded with her father.

Mr. Strickland glared at Jimbo a moment longer, then he threw his cup in the trash and walked out into the hall. Jeana and Mickey went back to sit with the others. Ten minutes later, Allison was asleep with her head on Billy Joe's leg.

"She's usually out by eight-thirty," Billy Joe told Jimbo, tucking a lock of hair behind Allison's ear. "She was lucky to hold out this long."

"It was good of y'all to come," Jimbo said. "I know you had problems with Wade in the past."

"He was my best friend before he was yours," Billy Joe said with a catch in his voice. "We all want to see him pull through this."

"I went looking for him out at Chickasabogue, and I knew it was him as soon as I heard the sirens over on Kali Oka. He's been flirting with that curve ever since he got the 'Vette." Jimbo dropped his head into his hands.

"Hang in there, man," Billy Joe said.

Jimbo looked up at Jeana with her head on Mickey's shoulder and lowered his voice. "I wish Wade knew she was here. I never saw anybody have it so bad for a girl."

Billy Joe looked at her too. "Yeah, she's hard to get over."

Mr. Strickland came back in the room but didn't speak to anyone. Another thirty minutes crawled by before the door opened and a doctor wearing scrubs came in. He spoke to the Stricklands in such hushed tones that Jeana and the others had to cross the room to hear what he was saying.

"...couldn't repair the damage to his heart, and we lost him. I'm very sorry."

Mrs. Strickland started screaming *no* and Sissy covered her face with her hands, but Mr. Strickland didn't say anything. He just looked at the doctor with his mouth pressed into a hard line.

Jimbo staggered out into the hall and stood there a few seconds before an anguished cry erupted from him as he slammed his fist into the wall next to the door. Billy Joe came out and found him with his face pressed into his arm, his bloody fist still weakly pounding. For once in his life, Billy Joe was at a total loss for words.

While all this was going on, Jeana stood silently beside Mickey, his arm around her with a dazed look of shock and disbelief on his face. All of a sudden, Jeana turned and looked up at him with eyes that were dry and much too bright.

"Wade will need a new shirt now, Mickey," she said. "He just bought the one he's wearing because he didn't have another dress shirt. I have to go tell his mother."

She started toward Mrs. Strickland, but Mickey caught her hand and pulled her back.

"Not now, baby."

"You don't understand, Mickey." Jeana's eyes were wide and still completely dry. "It was his only dress shirt. I have to tell her now so she'll have time to find another green one. To match his eyes."

She tried to walk away again, but Mickey put his arms around her and held her against his chest. "Jeana, you're upset right now and don't know what you're doing."

She tried to pull free but he wouldn't let her go, so she looked up at him plaintively. "But it was the only one he had, Mickey. He *told* me…"

Her voice broke and she closed her eyes, her tears finally coming in a torrent that filled the hospital's deserted corridors with the echoes of her sobs.

~ * ~

When they got to Jeana's house, Mickey went in with her because she was still too much in shock to talk. She clung to Mickey the whole time he told her parents about Wade, and Betty had to coax her to let him go. After Mickey left, Betty helped her get undressed and commented on all the sand in her clothes.

"We went to the Gulf after the banquet." Jeana held up her hand so her mother could see her ring. "Mickey proposed to me, Mama."

Despite her own grief, Betty couldn't hide her delight. "Honey, you know how much your daddy and I love Mickey. We couldn't be happier for you."

"Oh, Mama." Jeana started to cry again. "How can the

happiest day of my life also be the saddest? I just got Wade back as a friend, and now he's gone!"

"I know, baby." Betty put her arms around Jeana and rocked her. "I wish there was something I could say to make it not hurt so bad, but only time can do that."

~ * ~

Jimbo was late for the funeral when it was held two days later. He'd held his own memorial service at Chickasabogue Creek, and it had taken him longer than he expected to get drunk enough for the Wademan to appreciate it as a tribute. Then he'd had to drink some more for his own sake.

When he got to Radney Funeral Home, the cars were already pulling out for the drive to Forest Lawn Cemetery. No one seemed to notice the Camaro at the end of the procession that drifted off the road a couple of times. Jimbo was supposed to be one of the pallbearers, but he guessed they'd found someone to replace him because he watched six solemn-faced young men lift the expensive casket from the hearse. He recognized Lamar, Bubba, Billy Joe, and Mickey among them. Jimbo waited until everyone had gathered around the gravesite before he got out of his car, stopping to put on his suit jacket and straighten his tie before going over to his best friend's grave.

Everyone was standing except Wade's family, who were seated in folding chairs beside the casket. Sissy stared blankly, her tears leaving pale streaks in the makeup on her cheeks. Wade's grandparents sat close together with their arms around each other, and his mother wept into a handkerchief trimmed with French lace. Mr. Strickland sat stoically beside his wife, offering her no comfort at all. They all faced Jimbo as he walked up, but they paid him no attention and neither did anyone else.

The minister was quoting scripture from Psalms. *"The sorrows of death compassed me, and the pains of Hell got hold upon me: I found trouble and sorrow. Then called I upon the name of the Lord—"*

"You're the one who better call on the Lord, you sonofabitch!" Jimbo pointed his father's .44 caliber handgun at Mr. Strickland. "And I hope He sends you straight to Hell where you belong!"

Everyone looked at Jimbo and uttered a collective gasp at the sight of the gun. Screams pierced the air as people scrambled in every direction to get out of the line of fire, but Mr. Strickland didn't move. He stared at Jimbo and actually looked pleased to see him.

"Go ahead and pull the trigger, boy," Strickland said with a mocking smile. "I don't think you've got the balls."

"Shut up, you bastard!" Jimbo said as he cocked the gun. "You're the reason he's gone, and I'm gonna make you pay for all the shit you did to him!"

"Don't do it, Jimbo." Billy Joe stepped in front of Mr. Strickland and held up his hands. "It won't change anything."

"Get outta the way, DuBose!" Jimbo waved the gun at him and wiped his eyes to clear his vision. "I gotta do this for the Wademan."

"Mind your own business, son," Strickland said to Billy Joe. "Can't you see the boy's on a mission?" He sneered at Jimbo again. "How 'bout it, punk? You gonna choke like you always did in football?"

"Shoot him, Jimbo," Lamar said.

Jimbo moved around Billy Joe to aim at Strickland again. "There was only two things in this world Wade ever gave a damn about—what you thought about him, and Jeana. At least he knew she cared about him. All he ever got from you was your belt or the back of your hand!"

At those words, Mrs. Strickland fainted into Sissy's lap and Jimbo lowered the gun slightly while his attention was on her. Mickey grabbed him from behind, coming down hard on his arm and squeezing his wrist until he dropped the gun. Billy Joe and Bubba ran over and helped Mickey hold Jimbo, who struggled madly to pick up the gun again.

"Lemme go!" he cried. "That sonofabitch has to pay!"

"He'll pay for it," Billy Joe said. "But not this way."

Jimbo gave up and slumped against them, and the minister helped the boys lead him away.

Mr. Strickland still hadn't moved. He stood with his head down and his eyes closed while Mrs. DuBose attended to his wife beside him. Most of the crowd had already left or were leaving, so no one but Lamar saw Strickland walk over to the gun. He picked it up and studied it in his hand a few seconds, then he looked around and spotted Lamar staring at him with obvious contempt. Strickland proffered the gun, his eyebrows lifted slightly as if in question: *How about you?*

Lamar's face didn't change as he extended his middle finger in silent disdain.

Strickland smiled and raised the gun to his own temple. The sun glinted off the diamonds in Wade's class ring on the hand holding the gun and reflected in green eyes that were the same shade as his son's. He continued to look at Lamar and read his lips as Lamar mouthed the words: *Do it.*

He pulled the trigger.

Chapter Eleven

A month later, most of Wade's classmates had recovered from the shock of his death, but his friends and family hadn't fared quite as well. His mother and sister struggled to deal with their double loss combined with the guilt they felt over not doing anything to stop Wade's abuse, and Sissy spent more time at the Russells' house than she did her own. She seemed to draw comfort from her longstanding friendship with Shelly and the happy memories she had from when they had lived next door.

Despite what Wade had written in the note he left, Jeana couldn't help feeling that she had contributed to his misery, so her grief was compounded by guilt of her own. Why hadn't she listened to him when he'd tried to talk to her all those times in the sixth grade? And when she'd finally listened and he opened his heart to her in the shed, why had she smothered all his hope that she could ever love him? Would it have made a difference if he'd believed there was still a chance that she might ever feel differently about him? Maybe given him a reason to put up with his father until he could've found someone else to love? The questions haunted Jeana day and night.

The week before Christmas, she pulled into the parking lot at Vigor and her gaze still turned to the end of the lot where Wade had always parked the Corvette. She supposed she was doing a little better. At least she didn't cry this time.

"Hey, baby," Mickey said when she got into the Mustang with him. "Last day of school before Christmas. Are you excited?"

"Not really. I wish they let us have Christmas parties

79

like we did in elementary school."

"What a coinkydink." He reached over and flicked her earlobe. "Aunt Robin is having a Christmas party tomorrow night and wants me to bring you so you can meet your future in-laws."

"Okay, that sounds like fun." Jeana hoped her smile didn't look as forced as it felt. She really did want to go, but it was hard to let herself feel happy anymore. At least Mickey didn't appear to notice.

"I want you to meet somebody else tomorrow night too," he said. "Her name's Miranda Wells, and her parents were Mom and Dad's best friends when we lived here before. They moved to Pensacola the year after we left." He glanced sideways at Jeana and added, "She's the first girl I ever kissed."

Jeana's lukewarm interest began to boil. Her eyebrow went up and she looked at him without a trace of amusement.

"And you think I want to meet her *why?*"

"Because, baby." He looked surprised. "I thought it would be cool for the first girl I ever kissed to meet the last girl I'll ever kiss."

She smiled reluctantly. "You set me up for that, didn't you?"

He squeezed her cheeks together and kissed her. "I knew you'd fall for it."

"So why will this Melinda person be at the party if she lives in Pensacola?"

"It's Miranda, not Melinda. She and her mother are coming to pick up my mom for Rick's wedding. He's Miranda's older brother."

The bell rang and they went inside. Jeana no longer had Ms. Majors for first period. She hadn't been able to look at the empty seat behind hers without breaking down, so she'd dropped Psychology at the quarter break and changed to Mythology. When she got to Biology class second period,

Billy Joe sat down beside her and put his arm around her shoulders.

"What are you doing, Billy Joe?" she said. "See all this red hair? Allison's a blonde, remember?"

"I know exactly who you are," he said. "I'm giving you moral support in your time of crisis because I'm such a devoted friend."

Her forehead wrinkled. "What crisis?"

"I heard about Mick's other woman." He pulled her next to him. "I'm here for ya, kiddo."

She pushed him away. "Go back to your table. You're not funny."

"But I'm on *your* side, Jeana." He slapped his hands down on the table. "Just because Mickey is actually friends with someone who openly yearns for you, he thinks he can expect you to make polite conversation with this hussy for a few hours? The nerve of the guy!"

She looked to make sure Allison hadn't heard him and whispered, "Don't ever let her hear you say anything like that. It would hurt her feelings, and she's my best friend."

"She knows I'm just kidding, and I thought I was your best friend."

"Then why do you torment me?"

He tweaked her chin. "Because you're so cute when you're mad."

Mickey arrived and Jeana gestured at Billy Joe. "Evict him please."

"Stop teasing her, Billy Joe," Mickey said. "It's my turn." When Jeana didn't smile, he added, "Don't be mad, baby."

"Why did you tell him about your old girlfriend, Mickey? You know he loves to irritate me."

"She's not my old girlfriend, Jeana. Just an old friend."

"Then why did you kiss her? Do you kiss all your friends?" She turned her back to him when he laughed.

"Actually, she kissed me, and we were only six at the

time." He put her in a bear hug from behind and whispered in her ear. "And it didn't make me see fireworks like when I kiss you."

She looked up at him and finally smiled. "You're such a smooth talker. Lucky for me you don't lie. You'd probably be good at it."

School dismissed early and there was no basketball practice, so Mickey followed Jeana home then they went to the mall to finish their Christmas shopping. When they were done he asked her if she wanted to get an Orange Julius, and Jeana immediately remembered seeing Wade there the week before he died. Her eyes filled with tears that she hurried to hide from Mickey. As wonderful as he was, she didn't expect him to understand why she still thought about Wade so often.

While Mickey stood in line to order, Jeana saved them one of the small tables for two and thought about what Billy Joe had said earlier. He was right, Mickey never acted jealous about anything even though he had plenty of reasons to. Like the rubber band she still wore on her wrist all the time. He didn't even mind that. She watched him walk to the table with their drinks and decided she would try to be nice to this Miranda if that's what he wanted.

"Lemonade for you, orange for me," he said.

"I love you, Mickey." She leaned across the table and gave him an emphatic kiss that surprised him.

"Man, I gotta buy you lemonade more often."

She blew the paper from her straw at him. "So when are Melissa and her mother coming to get your mom?"

"Jeana, it's *Miranda*. They're coming tomorrow afternoon and going back to Pensacola after the party. The wedding is Saturday night."

"How will your mom get back home?"

"She wants me to pick her up Sunday afternoon."

One of Jeana's eyebrows moved skyward. "So... you'll have the house all to yourself this weekend?"

He stopped in mid-slurp. "Uh-oh. I know that look."

Jeana ran her fingers up his forearm. "Mickey, how would you like for me to give you your Christmas present Saturday night?"

He shivered. "Don't do this to me in public, Jeana."

~ * ~

She borrowed one of Shelly's dresses for the Christmas party, a black crushed velvet with a slit in the back that revealed the seam in her black stockings. She also let Shelly pull up her hair on one side with a rhinestone-studded comb and line her eyes with a brown pencil. The girl staring back at Jeana from her dresser mirror looked almost like a stranger to her, but that was okay. Maybe she could enjoy herself without feeling guilty if she pretended she wasn't the girl who had broken Wade's heart.

After Shelly left, Jeana searched the top of her closet for the small evening bag she'd taken to the football banquet and felt a square object inside—the birthday gift Wade had given her! With everything that happened that night, she'd forgotten all about it. Grief descended on her like a shroud, and she fell to her knees with the small package clutched in her trembling hands. She carefully tore off the paper Wade had decorated and opened the little box to reveal a gold key chain with a small picture frame attached.

The picture was from a strip of four taken in the photo booth at Gaylord's department store in Chickasaw. Jeana had one of the other pictures, but she'd hidden it away with her other memories a long time ago. This pose showed Jeana with Wade and Billy Joe, their faces pressed together so the three of them could fit into the picture, all of them laughing because Jeana was squeezed between the two boys. Tears dropped onto her hand as she ran her finger over the words engraved on the frame—*Friends Forever*.

"I miss you, Wade."

She started to put the key chain back, then her heart

leapt when she saw a folded piece of notebook paper in the bottom of the box. Mrs. Langston's handwriting jumped out at her from the top of the page as she unfolded Wade's poem from their sophomore English class.

The Big Lie

Everyone's impressed with the Big Shot
Wants to be your friend
What a tough guy, what a joke
It's all just pretend

Gotta keep up the act
For the old man's image
Can't let them see it's all a lie
In an easy to swallow size

You remember the last time you were happy
You see a girl with red hair and laughing eyes
Smiling at you
But you screwed that up too

Too stupid to know what a treasure you lost
Until you see her smile
At someone else
And you can only blame yourself

They can keep the applause
And the plastic friends with extended hands
They can have it all for just one more time to see
Her smile and know it's only for me

At the bottom of the page, Wade had written *Happy Birthday Redhot. Thank you for smiling at me again.*

"Oh, Wade..." Jeana held the paper to her heart. "I'm sorry it took me so long."

Chapter Twelve

Jeana knew by the look on Mickey's face when he picked her up that she had succeeded in hiding the evidence of her earlier tears. She turned around so he could get the total effect, then she took his hands.

"Do I look okay, Mickey?"

"For a valedictorian, you sure ask dumb questions sometimes," he said. "You look gorgeous, baby. In fact, I don't think I can take you around my cousin looking like this."

She laughed. "Why not?"

He shook his head and frowned. "He thinks he's a real lady killer. I knew he'd flirt with you, but he's gonna flip when he sees you in that dress. I might have to lay him out."

"Don't worry." Jeana pulled her necklace from inside her collar. "I'll make sure he knows that I belong to Mickey."

His dimples appeared and he bent to whisper in her ear. "The only time you looked more beautiful was on the beach in the moonlight."

"And nobody but you will ever see me like that," she whispered back, running her hand over his chest. "Maybe I need to worry about Marissa seeing you in this maroon sweater. The velour really shows off your muscles."

He sighed. "Her name's Miranda, and you know you don't need to worry about anybody, Jeana."

On the drive to the party, Mickey told her that his aunt and uncle, Robin and Ken Randall, lived in a restored antebellum home on Dauphin Street in Mobile with their three children—Ty, who was the same age as Mickey and played football and baseball for UMS Preparatory School, thirteen-year-old Jeremy, and a four-year-old daughter named Susannah. Mickey said he and Ty got along okay, although they tended to compete with each other in everything.

When they turned down a driveway lined with oak trees draped in Spanish moss and lit up with hundreds of tiny white lights, Jeana's face wore a look of growing enchantment. As soon as the house became visible at the end of the drive, her hands went to her cheeks.

"Oh my gosh, Mickey! You didn't tell me we were coming to a scene from *Gone With the Wind.*"

He had to keep tugging on her hand to keep her moving as they walked up to the house, because she was captivated by everything she saw—the topiary bushes, the fountain, the gazebo, and the wishing well. When they finally got to the front door, Mickey stopped before ringing the bell and turned to Jeana.

"Oh, I almost forgot. If Ty offers to give you a tour of the house, say no."

She frowned at him. "But I want to see all of it, Mickey."

"Then I'll show it to you. I'm serious, Jeana. He's a wolf."

The door was answered by a handsome young man with dark hair and equally dark eyes that lit up at the sight of Jeana.

"How's it going, Ty?" Mickey said. "This is my fiancée, Jeana Russell."

Ty took the hand Jeana offered and tucked it into the crook of his arm. "Mickey, you *dog.* No wonder you haven't brought her over before." His gaze took in every detail of Jeana's appearance. "I'm Ty Randall, Mickey's much-better-looking and extremely-more-talented cousin."

"Nice to meet you, Ty." Jeana tried not to laugh at Mickey gagging himself with his finger behind his cousin.

"My mother gave me explicit instructions to bring you out to the back verandah as soon as you arrived."

Ty led them out of the entry hall through a wide set of louvered doors and into an area crowned with a magnificent chandelier at the bottom of a curved staircase. As they walked through a large parlor, he pointed out several articles to Jeana and told her they had belonged to the house's original owner.

"I'll have to give you a tour later on," he said. "Mickey can find something else to do."

"She only takes tours with me," Mickey said from behind them.

Ty stopped and gave Jeana a coaxing look. "Mickey doesn't know squat about the house's history. Don't you want me to show it to you?"

Jeana smiled. "I wouldn't dare take you away from your other female guests, Ty. It might cause a riot. And I'm sure Mickey will make up for his lack of historical knowledge somehow. He hasn't disappointed me yet."

"Suit yourself." Ty gave Mickey a dirty look for laughing before turning on the charm again for Jeana. "But I'll have to get at least one dance with you before the night's over. It's a house rule."

When they reached the entrance to the verandah that spread across the entire back side of the house, Robin came over and took Jeana to be introduced to the family—Ty's father and two siblings, Mickey's Uncle Dave and Aunt Cathy, and his grandparents, Mr. and Mrs. Tanner.

Jeana was a hit with everyone except Susannah, who told Jeana huffily that Mickey was going to marry *her*. Jeana spent the next half hour getting to know everyone and didn't see Mickey at all after Susannah confiscated him to go see her new kittens.

Jeremy brought her some punch and a plate of food, then he gazed adoringly at her while Mickey's grandfather talked to her about teaching. A retired high school history teacher, Mr. Tanner's gruff old face softened when he found out that Jeana planned to major in education, and he made her sit beside him and talk shop.

She looked up from Mr. Tanner's story about a parent who came after him with a board for teaching his class the "Yankee version" of the Civil War and saw Mickey walk in with Marsha and her guests. A pretty girl with long black hair was holding his hand.

Jeana's anger hit her like an acute allergic reaction. Her heart pounded in her ears, she felt a rush of heat spread over her entire body, and just like the time she'd seen Tiffany hanging on Mickey's arm at the football game, everything seemed to be tinted red. She tried to focus on Mr. Tanner's words, but she found it impossible to think of anything but murder.

"Jeremy," she said, "will you get me some more punch, please?"

"Sure, Jeana," he said, jumping up. "Anything else I can get for you?"

"Not right now, but thanks." She saw Mickey approaching and wondered how she could be polite to this girl when she wanted to break her fingers for holding Mickey's hand. Doing her best to keep her voice even, she turned back to Mickey's grandfather and smiled. "Tell me more about when they first integrated the schools, Mr. Tanner. It's fascinating."

He beamed at the request, but Mickey interrupted them. "I need to borrow Jeana for a little while, Grandpa."

"Maybe she doesn't want to go with you, boy," Mr. Tanner said. "Always ask a lady. Don't assume."

"Yes, sir." Mickey suppressed a smile. "Excuse me, Jeana. Will you come with me to meet someone?"

Jeremy came back with her punch and blushed when Jeana told him he was sweet. Stalling in an effort to control the anger she knew was unreasonable, she took a couple of sips before answering Mickey.

"Well, I'm really enjoying the company of these handsome gentlemen, but I guess I can tear myself away for a little while." She set her cup on a coaster and asked Jeremy to watch it for her.

Mickey put his arm around her as they walked away. "I thought you were gonna turn me down for a second there, baby."

"Mickey, I need to talk to you before—"

"Here she is!" Marsha took Jeana's hand and pulled her toward the dark-haired girl and her mother. "This is Mickey's fiancée, Jeana."

"It's nice to meet you," Jeana said, holding out her hand to the woman.

"Marsha's told us so many nice things about you, Jeana," she said. "I'm Lisa Wells, and this is my daughter, Miranda."

As soon as their eyes met, Jeana knew this girl didn't like her and thought *Well, right back at you, Pocahontas!*

Miranda gave her a condescending smile. "Yes, Marsha told us you had red hair like hers." She turned to lay a hand with long fuchsia nails on Mickey's chest. "I hope you don't have one of those Odysseus complexes, Mickey Ray."

Jeana's eyebrow went up along with her ire. "I think you must mean an *Oedipus* complex, unless you think Mickey has a problem finding his way home after wars."

Mickey's laugh died when he saw the look that passed between the two girls. "Mom, I had to pry Jeana away from Grandpa and Jeremy. I warned her about Ty, but I didn't know I'd have to worry about them too."

"Do you know Mickey's cousin Ty?" Jeana asked Miranda. "I'm sure you could persuade him to give you a tour of this beautiful house. Mickey's giving me one."

Miranda ignored her and turned to Mickey. "Introduce me to this cousin of yours, Mickey Ray. If he's anything like you, I'm sure I'll like him."

"There's Ty." Marsha waved at him across the room. "Come on, Miranda. I'll introduce you."

Jeana pulled Mickey over to the corner as soon as Marsha and her guests walked away. "I can't do this, Mickey. I'm not wonderful and understanding like you."

He looked down at her in amusement. "What are you talking about, Jeana?"

"If I have to listen to her call you *Mickey Ray* one more time, I'm gonna yank that black hair of hers right out of her head!"

Mickey laughed and put his arms around her. "Don't be silly, baby."

"It's *not* silly." She pulled away from him. "I'm warning you, Mickey. I can't handle watching her make eyes at you. I might do something drastic."

He searched her face a moment, then he took her hand and led her back inside the house. "Come on. We need to take that tour I promised you."

"I don't want to do it now, Mickey. I'm too mad to enjoy it."

"Trust me, Jeana. It'll make you feel better."

They made their way through the house to the central hall, then he took her up the circular staircase. When they passed several rooms without even going in, Jeana said, "We're sure skipping a lot on this tour. Maybe I should let Ty take me after all."

Mickey scoffed. "Yeah, like I'd let that happen. Besides, you'll like the room I'm looking for a lot better than those." He stopped at a set of huge double doors. "This is the one."

She followed him into an immense room lined with shelves of books that rose all the way to the ceiling. A ladder on rollers for access to the top shelves stood by one of the windows, and the room was furnished with three sofas upholstered in red and gold brocade. Jeana's eyes lost their angry green and virtually sparkled as she looked around the room. She went over to one of the shelves labeled CLASSICS and read some of the titles aloud.

"*Of Mice and Men, To Kill a Mockingbird, The Catcher in the Rye, Little Women*—that's my very favorite book, Mickey! I could stay here forever."

"Sorry," he said, taking her hand again. "You're coming with me."

He led her around the end of the last row toward another door that was barely discernible in the wall. After opening the door and pulling Jeana in with him, he locked it behind them. The only furniture was a single overstuffed chair with a small table and lamp beside it. The room had a fireplace and a hearth with a rug, but no windows.

"What is this place?" Jeana asked.

"The man who built this house was named Beauregard Manning," Mickey said. "He had this alcove made into a private reading room so he could come here with his Dalmatian named Magnolia and hide from everyone in the house."

Jeana put her hands on her hips and scowled at him. "I thought Ty said you didn't know any of the house's history."

"Ty's full of crap. My mom loves this story. She's told it to me dozens of times."

Jeana smiled. "Then tell me more, Mr. Handsome Tour Guide. Why did he want to hide from everyone?"

"Well, even though he denied it, rumor had it that he was homosexual and only married for the sake of appearances. The servants said that whenever the missus was feeling romantic, old Beau would come here and hide from her."

"How sad for both of them," Jeana said, running her hands over the carved mantelpiece. "But what made everyone think he was gay if he denied it?"

"Look at the carvings on the mantel."

She stopped to peer closely at the figures in the wood.

"Oh my Lord, they're all naked men!"

"Okay, that's enough looking," he said, pulling her to him. "I'm starting to get jealous."

She put her arms around his neck. "Mickey, I've seen you naked. You don't need to be jealous of *anyone*." She laughed when he blushed.

"I knew you'd like coming here," he said. "But I really just wanted a place where I could hold you."

"Don't just hold me. I need you to kiss me. Right now." He did as he was told, and she returned the kiss fervently. "You belong to *me*, Mickey, and I'm not any good at sharing."

"Who said anything about sharing, baby? You know you're the only girl for me."

She put her head on his chest. "I wish I could be understanding like you are about this kind of thing, but I'm not. I can't help it."

"We can leave if you want to, Jeana."

"No, I enjoyed talking to your grandfather, and I promised Jeremy a dance. I don't want to leave, I just don't want to see *her*."

"You never stop surprising me." He tilted up her face with a finger under her chin. "You're gonna yank out her hair, baby? I didn't know you were a scrapper."

She looked embarrassed. "It's not funny, Mickey. I don't know what happens to me. When I saw her holding your hand, I was so mad I couldn't see straight."

"Jeana, listen to me," he said, looking into her eyes. "I love you and I'm gonna marry you. You know that. If you feel yourself getting mad, just look at your ring. That's my promise that I'll always love you and *only* you."

They came out of the library just as Ty and Miranda exited the room across the hall.

"Hey, no fair sneaking off with her," Ty said, taking Jeana's arm. "Grandpa told me to bring her back. You get her all the time, you lucky cuss."

Miranda slipped her hand into Mickey's. "You can finish my tour, Mickey Ray."

He glanced at Jeana and moved Miranda's hand to his arm. Jeana rolled her eyes and twisted the ring on her finger as Ty led her downstairs. But when they reached the bottom and he turned in the opposite direction of the verandah, Jeana stopped walking.

"Where are you taking me, Ty?"

"Don't I get a chance to talk to you like the rest of the family?" he asked.

"I don't think Mickey would like this."

"Too bad," he said. "Let him entertain Miss Artificial for a while."

A smile spread slowly across Jeana's face as she took his arm again. "You just earned yourself a chat."

They went out the front entrance and crossed the lawn to the wrought iron gazebo situated next to an enormous magnolia tree. When they were seated in the swing inside the gazebo, Ty put his arm around Jeana and she moved it back to his lap.

"Why don't you tell me about the house now?" she said.

He gave her a well-practiced recitation about how the house had been built in 1860 by the notorious Beauregard Manning, who had made his fortune because of Mobile's crucial position as a cotton port. The house was built in the Greek Revival style popular for the era, with six Doric columns across the front verandah and ceilings that were sixteen feet high. The floors were tongue-and-groove cypress, and the slide-by windows had jib doors that could be opened for access to the wing porches.

Jeana was truly impressed when he finished his spiel. "You really know your Southern architecture, Ty. Have you thought about becoming an architect yourself?"

He shrugged with a laugh. "I really only learned that stuff to impress girls who come to see the house." He noticed the rubber band on her wrist and touched it. "This is an odd fashion accessory."

The smile on her face disappeared, and she lowered her gaze. "I wear it to remember a friend who died in a car accident last month."

"Oh, yeah. I heard about that on the news. Didn't he do it over some girl?"

Jeana's head jerked up. "Where did you hear that?"

He seemed surprised by her reaction. "I dated a girl from Vigor who went out with him once. She said he got drunk on their date and kept talking about some girl with red hair—" He stopped when he saw the look on Jeana's face. "Oh, shit. I'm sorry."

She shook her head and started to cry. "It's not true."

"Jeana, I didn't know." He put his arm around her again. "Man, that's gotta be tough for Mickey."

"What do you mean by that?"

"I know I'd hate it if I had to compete with the memory of a guy who killed himself over my girl."

She pushed him away from her and got up. "What a horrible, insensitive thing to say!" She ran out of the gazebo with him calling after her that he was sorry. Mickey was just coming into the entry hall when she went in the front door, so she ran to him and buried her face in his chest.

"Jeana, what's wrong?" He led her into the parlor and closed the door. "What happened, baby?"

"Ty said something cruel about Wade. I changed my mind, Mickey. I do want to go home!"

The door opened and Miranda came into the room. "Oh, there you are, Mickey Ray. I see you told her you're coming to the wedding with us. Don't you think she's overreacting?"

Jeana looked up at Mickey in tearful confusion. "What is she talking about?"

"I was on my way to find you so I could ask you about

it," he said.

She pulled away from him and ran out of the room.

"Jeana, wait!" Mickey started to follow her but Miranda stepped in front of him and held on to his arm.

"She'll get over it if you leave her alone. Come dance with me."

"No, I have to go talk to her! Get out of the way." He moved Miranda aside and almost bumped into his mother coming in the door.

"I've been looking all over for you, Mickey," Marsha said. "Take Jeana home and go get your clothes. We'll leave from here when you get back."

"I'm not going, Mom," he said. "Jeana's upset about something, and we had plans for tomorrow night anyway."

"Can't you postpone them for one night?" Marsha asked. "I'm sure Jeana would understand."

He shook his head. "She might've understood if I'd gotten a chance to talk to her about it before Miranda told her I was going, but now she's upset and I'm not gonna leave her."

Marsha sighed. "Okay, baby. You know I can't bear to see that look in your eyes. Go find Jeana. I'll see you Sunday afternoon."

"I love you, Mom." He kissed her and hurried out of the room.

"You shouldn't let her manipulate him like that," Miranda said.

Marsha frowned. "You don't know what you're talking about, Miranda. Did you see his face? He loves that girl the way Stephen loved me. If she's upset, there's nothing in this world or any other that could keep Mickey away from her."

Chapter Thirteen

The Mustang was the only place Jeana could think of to go. The emotional upheaval that had started with finding Wade's gift and poem finally overwhelmed her, and Mickey found her sobbing with her face in her hands.

He opened the passenger door and pulled her into his arms. "Please don't cry, Jeana. I'm not going anywhere."

"Then why did she say you were going to Pensacola with them?"

"One of the groomsmen got sick and won't be there for the wedding tomorrow. Lisa asked me to fill in, so I told her I'd talk to you about it."

Jeana looked up at him, still confused. "But what about our plans for tomorrow night?"

"I thought we could just postpone them for a day."

"You know I wanted us to be alone when I give you your present. Tomorrow night is our only chance for that."

Mickey sighed. "Being alone with you at my house isn't such a good idea, Jeana. You know what you do to me. We're gonna get in trouble if we keep fooling around."

"*Mickey...*" She drew back as if she'd been slapped. "You sound like I'm a bad habit you're trying to break."

"You know that's not what I meant." He tried to hold her hands, but she backed away from him even more.

"And if the things we've done are just *fooling around* to you, then you're right. We shouldn't do them anymore. I thought they meant as much to you as they do to me, but I guess I was wrong!"

"Jeana, I didn't mean it like that!"

"Take me home, Mickey. I don't want to be with you anymore tonight." She got in the car and locked the door.

He went around to the driver's side and got in too. "I'll take you home, but we're not leaving things this way."

She stared out the window until they got to Chickasaw. When they got off the interstate, she told him to take her to Allison's house. She didn't want her parents asking why she was upset.

"Come back after you call your mom," he said when they pulled into Allison's driveway. "We have to get this straightened out."

"Go home, Mickey. No—go to Pensacola and walk Miranda down the aisle!"

She got out and slammed the door, but he jumped out of the car and followed her up the sidewalk. "I'm not going anywhere until you talk to me!"

"Just leave me alone, Mickey!"

Allison opened the door and looked at them both in surprise. "What's wrong?"

"Is it okay if I spend the night?" Jeana asked.

"Sure, but—"

Jeana stalked past her. "Mickey's leaving."

"No I'm *not*." He followed Jeana inside but stopped to answer Allison's baffled look. "She's mad over a stupid misunderstanding and won't talk to me about it."

Allison told him her parents were at a Christmas party, so it was okay for him to go after Jeana. He found her in Allison's room on the phone with her mother.

"Come back outside and talk to me, Jeana," he said when she hung up. "Right now."

"I don't want to talk anymore. I don't like the things you've already said." She knew she was going to cry again and tried to leave the room, but he caught her from behind and put his arms around her.

"Let me go, Mickey."

"No, I love you too much."

"You shouldn't love me, Mickey! I'll only get you in trouble like you said."

He turned her around to face him. "Don't *ever* say that, Jeana. I'll always love you."

She wouldn't look at him, so he picked her up and carried her to the front door, heedless of her protests.

"What are you doing, Mickey?" Allison said as she followed them outside. "Where are you taking her?"

"To my house," he replied without stopping. "I'll bring her back after we get this settled."

Jeana gave up struggling. "Don't worry, Allison. We can't stay there long because we'll be alone. He doesn't trust me enough for that."

When they parked in his driveway, he said, "Are you coming in voluntarily, or do I need to carry you?"

"I can walk," she said, staring straight ahead.

Inside the house, she sat on the couch and snatched the comb from her hair, then she threw it across the room and shook out her curls. So much for being someone else tonight.

Mickey sat beside her and took her hand. "How could you think I don't want to be alone with you, Jeana?"

"You said it wasn't a good idea, didn't you? Like there's something bad about me that you should avoid!"

"Jeana—"

"That's how it made me feel, Mickey. Whether you meant it that way or not!" She pulled her hand free and walked to the other side of the room. "All I planned to do tomorrow night was cook for you. I wanted to fix supper for the two of us and give you your Christmas present."

Mickey hung his head. "I'm sorry, Jeana."

"You should be, because you were ready to just cancel our plans so you could spend the weekend with *her* hanging all over you! And the times we've been the closest to each other—the times you know are so special to me—you called them *fooling around*. Like they don't mean anything! I never thought you'd ever say anything to hurt me, Mickey. But you *did*."

He looked at her as if he were in physical pain. He closed his eyes, and tears ran down his cheeks. "Jeana, I'm *sorry*. I'd rather die than hurt you—"

"Don't say that!" She ran to him and shook him by the shoulders. "Don't *ever* talk about dying, Mickey! Take it back—take it back this second!"

"Baby, stop..."

He stood and tried to hold her, but she beat on his chest with her fists. He managed to catch her hands and pin her arms against him, but she shook her head frantically until her eyes fluttered and she went limp in his arms. He carried her to the couch, and when he realized that she'd fainted, he lay his head on her chest and sobbed.

"Oh, God, what did I do!"

When Jeana opened her eyes a moment later and saw him in tears, her own hysterics fled and she put her arms around him. "I'm so sorry, Mickey. I didn't mean to make you cry."

He looked up at her with bewildered blue eyes. "What happened to us tonight, Jeana? I don't understand any of this!"

"It's all my fault," she said. "I don't know what's wrong with me."

"I wish we'd never gone to that stupid party!" he said. "I barely got to see you, then I said all the wrong things and made you mad at me, but the worst part was when you told me not to love you." He held her head in his hands and looked into her eyes. "That's like telling me not to breathe, Jeana. Why would you ever say something like that?"

"Because every boy who loves me gets hurt, Mickey. Billy Joe got beat up because of me, and look what happened to Wade." She tried to cover her face with her hands, but he pulled them away.

"That wasn't your fault, Jeana!"

"Yes it was. I hurt him just as much as his father—"

"It wasn't your fault!" His fist struck the coffee table,

and she could tell from the way his whole body trembled that he was fighting hard to maintain control. When he looked at her again, he said, "Maybe he loved you, Jeana, but you weren't supposed to be with him because you're *mine*. I'm sorry he's gone, but I'm *not* sorry he lost you, and I'm not gonna lose you because of what he did!"

"I don't know why either one of you loves me. I don't deserve it."

"Stop talking like that!"

"It's the truth, Mickey. Why did I have to be so heartless and stay mad at him for so long? He tried to apologize to me when we were kids but I wouldn't let him. I can't stop thinking that he'd still be alive if I'd just forgiven him sooner."

"And then you would've been with him when I met you." He grabbed her by the shoulders. "Is that what you wish, Jeana? That you were with him right now instead of me?"

The doubt and torment on his face were like a blow to her heart. She'd been wrong—Mickey had clearly noticed her lingering thoughts of Wade after all.

She put her hands on his cheeks. "No, of course not, Mickey. You're the only one I love."

"Then why is he always here between us? I'm sick of it, Jeana!" He leaned her back on the couch and covered her body with his. "I won't share you with Wade Strickland now any more than I would when he was here. You're *mine*, and I want him out of your head!"

He kissed her so hard that she had to push him away to catch her breath, and his hands were on her body with an urgency she'd never felt before. She tried to keep her thoughts rational in the wake of the volcano he was stirring inside her.

"Mickey, slow down. We have to be sensible."

"Don't argue with me this time, Jeana. I'm tired of being sensible. I want to make love to the girl I'm gonna marry."

Her half-hearted protests were silenced by his mouth on hers and the things he was doing with his hands. When his fingers touched the rubber band on her wrist, he took it off her arm and threw it aside.

"That has to go. Tonight there's only me and you, Jeana. I don't want you to think about anything or anybody else. The rest of the world doesn't exist, do you hear me?"

"Yes, Mickey. Just you and me."

He stood and pulled her up with him. "Come to my room with me so I can show you how much I love you."

She wanted Mickey to make love to her more than anything in the world, but she had to give him one last chance to stop. "Don't do this because of the way I acted tonight, Mickey. Don't do it unless it's what you really want."

He put her hand on the indisputable proof of his desire. "I want you so bad it hurts."

He carried her to his room, his eyes locked with hers. When they were standing face-to-face beside his bed, he started to take off her dress and stopped her when she tried to help.

"Let me do it, baby. I've done it so many times in my dreams."

The blue of his eyes deepened with each article of her clothing that he removed, and she loved the way he was looking at her as if she were a delicacy he wanted to devour. Never had she felt so beautiful.

"Don't ever doubt that I'm yours," she said, lifting his hands to her breasts. "Every part of me."

"Mine," he whispered as his hands slid over her body. "All mine."

"Yes, and you're mine, Mickey. We belong to each other, and I want to see all of you too."

When all his clothes were shed, she marveled at how someone so absolutely male could be so beautiful. Now that she didn't have to worry about restraint, she reveled in the glorious lines of his body, exploring every swell and valley of his muscles with both her eyes and her hands, until they were both breathless with their desire for each other.

With her own love reflected in the miracle that was Mickey's eyes, Jeana lay beside him on his bed, and although they had both been awaiting this night for two years, they refused to rush. Neither of them wanted their first time to be the frantic, mindless pursuit of physical gratification common among their peers. This wasn't just sex for them, it was the consummation of their love, and they wanted to savor every look, every caress, and every sensation as their bodies were finally united the way their hearts had been for so long.

Finally, when they couldn't bear to wait one second longer, Mickey moved on top of her and looked into her eyes. "I want to be inside you now, Jeana."

She was unafraid because of her total love and trust in him, and her inherent sexuality made her naturally uninhibited. She sensed his fear of hurting her and tried to reassure him, guiding and urging him with her hands until he gave up and sank into the silken inferno they made between them. When she cried out as he pushed past the initial resistance, he grasped her face in his hands.

"I hurt you…"

"No, Mickey." She covered his hands with hers and kissed him. "That wasn't pain you heard in my voice."

He smiled, and they began to move together in a rhythm that came naturally to them both, as if their bodies were perfectly matched components of a finely-tuned machine. But the sublime sensations were soon too much for him, and his body was shaken as his ecstasy overtook him.

"I'm sorry, baby. I couldn't stop."

"Shh…" She pushed the hair from his eyes. "It's okay,

Mickey. I'm not going anywhere, and we have all night."

They were novices finding their way only by instinct and their love for each other, but they were also both overachievers used to excelling at whatever they did, and this was no exception. They taught each other and learned quickly.

Just before dawn, they made love a third time. Mickey was able to go much slower, so this time when he reached the point where he was unable to stop, Jeana didn't want him to. With her body arched to receive him clear to her soul and her fingers entrenched in his back, she clutched him in desperation and cried out his name.

"Oh, *Mickey*..."

Afterward, they lay in each other's arms with their faces touching while their hearts and their breathing slowed to normal. One of his fingers traced the shape of her ear, and she had her hands in his hair.

"Did I make you feel good, baby?"

"Better than good, Mickey. Divine."

"I liked it when you said my name."

She smiled blissfully. "So did I."

"I knew making love to you would be incredible, but my dreams didn't even come close to the real thing. I wish we could stay here forever, Jeana."

"Me too, but at least I can stay and sleep in your arms tonight."

"I want to tell you something before we go to sleep, baby. Something I've never told anyone."

She pulled back so she could see his face. "What is it, Mickey?"

"Remember when I had the fight with Wade, and you told me it scared you to see how mad I got?"

She nodded. "It's not like that happens all the time."

"I know, but it did happen before. Before my dad was able to stop drinking for good, this guy in Washington called him a sorry drunk and I..." He paused, and she could see how difficult this was for him. "I almost killed him, Jeana. I used to think maybe God was punishing me for my temper, and that was why I lost my dad. I was afraid I was always gonna lose the things I loved the most. That's why I kept trying to do everything better than anybody else—like maybe it would make up for being such a failure at controlling my temper. But I was always scared it wasn't enough." He ran his fingertips over her face and kissed her. "You're the reason I don't think that anymore, Jeana. I know God must really love me, because He gave me you."

"And you'll always have me," she said. "We'll have each other."

"My Jeana... I love you more than anything in the world."

"I love you too, Mickey. You *are* my world."

They fell asleep still wrapped up in each other. And when they awoke, Mickey's name echoed through the house again.

Chapter Fourteen

Mickey and Jeana got to Allison's house around mid-morning to find Billy Joe there showing off his new paint job on the El Camino. Metallic yellow flames now blazed atop the purple paint from the front bumper to the doors.

"Gee, I feel underdressed," Billy Joe said when Jeana got out of the Mustang wearing the black velvet dress.

She looked sheepishly at Allison. "Do you have something I can change into?"

Allison grabbed her arm and hauled her into the house. "Why didn't you call and tell me you weren't coming back?"

"I didn't know until it was too late to call," Jeana said. "I'm sorry."

"What happened?"

The dreamy smile on Jeana's face answered the question, and Allison squealed.

"Shh!" Jeana smothered a laugh. "The boys will hear you."

"You have to tell me *everything*," Allison whispered.

"All I can tell you is that it was the most wonderful night of my life, and I love Mickey more than ever."

When they got back outside after Jeana changed, Billy Joe stopped her as she started to put her clothes in the Mustang. "Wait, why don't you just ride home with me and save Mickey the trip?"

"I don't want to ride in that thing." Jeana wrinkled her nose at the El Camino. "But I will if Mickey wants me to."

"I am kinda tired." Mickey smiled sleepily at her. "And Coach called practice this afternoon because he got us in

McGill's tournament next week."

"Okay." She tiptoed to put her arms around his neck and give him a kiss. "Go take a nap and call me when you get home from practice."

"What are you gonna cook for us tonight?"

"It's a surprise."

Billy Joe pretended to play "Taps" on an imaginary bugle. "Been nice knowing you, Mick," he said with a salute. "Gonna miss ya, buddy."

"Don't laugh, Mickey," Jeana said. "It just encourages him."

On the drive home, Billy Joe surprised her when he pulled into the parking lot at Hamilton Elementary and turned off the car.

"Why are we stopping here?" Jeana asked.

Billy Joe stared at his hands on the steering wheel and sighed. "Please tell me you're on the pill."

"What are you talking about, Billy Joe?"

"Don't play dumb, Jeana. It doesn't work for a valedictorian. I know you spent the night with Mickey, and I want to know if you used protection."

"Did Mickey say anything to you?"

He scowled at her. "You know he wouldn't do that. How stupid do you think I am, Jeana? You show up wearing last night's clothes, and both of you look like you didn't sleep more than a couple hours. It's not hard to figure out."

She couldn't seem to meet his gaze. "It's none of your business, Billy Joe."

"How can you say that to me? You've been my business for eighteen years."

She stared out the window. "I'm sorry, but this isn't something we can talk about."

He turned her face around with his finger. "Just tell me the truth, Jeana."

But she didn't tell him the truth. Because she didn't

want him to be mad at Mickey, she lied to him.

"Yes, we used protection."

"Good." He let out a relieved sigh and started the car again. "So, is he better than me?"

"You idiot. How would I know?"

"Wanna find out?"

"Billy Joe DuBose!"

"Come on, Jeana." He rubbed his shoulder where she'd punched him. "You know I still carry a torch for you. Where do you think the flames on the car come from?"

~ * ~

After taking a nap of her own, Jeana made a blueberry icebox cheesecake to take with her to Mickey's for dessert. She also planned to make bayou shrimp gumbo and got some last-minute tips from her mother.

"I wish you'd give me exact amounts for the ingredients, Mama. I don't know how much a pinch or a dash is." Jeana was taking notes, of course. "Didn't you write down the recipe when you got it from Leanna's mama?"

"Good cooks don't measure and go by recipes," Betty said. "You have to use your instinct."

"I don't have any instinct, Mama. I need instructions!"

Betty patted her cheek. "You'll do fine, honey. Gumbo is all in the *roux*, and I showed you how to make it. Besides, Mickey's eaten here enough for me to know he's not a picky eater."

Jeana looked offended. "Oh, so you mean he'll eat it even if I mess it up?"

"You sure are touchy today," Betty said. "You must not have gotten enough sleep. Did you and Allison stay up all night talking?"

"I have to get ready to go." Jeana left the kitchen in a hurry.

She stayed in the shower too long because she was daydreaming about the one she and Mickey had shared that morning. Laughing at the butterflies she felt in her stomach every time she thought about him, Jeana dressed in jeans and a blue sweater that was Mickey's favorite.

She couldn't wait to see him again, and she was also excited about giving him his Christmas present. She'd had to save her babysitting money for months and drive all the way to a flea market in Biloxi to buy it from a man who'd smelled like Bengay and called her *girlie*, but she'd managed to purchase Mickey Mantle's 1962 Topps baseball card. She couldn't wait to see Mickey's face when she gave it to him.

Billy Joe was just getting to work when Jeana stopped at Delchamps for gumbo filé on the way to Mickey's house.

"Hey, Jeana!" he shouted across the parking lot. "I called ahead and got 'em to fix a care package of antacids for Mick. It's at register four with your name on it."

"Ha-ha, you're just so funny, Billy Joe. When do you go on tour?"

He put his arm around her as they walked through the automatic doors. "Bad news, kiddo. Mickey really sucked at practice today. When Coach found out who'd sapped all his strength, he put you on his shit list. If we lose Tuesday night, he's gonna have your legs broken."

"Oh, shut up." She pushed him and started to walk away, but he grabbed her hand and pulled her back. "Aren't you late for work? Put on that fashionable blue vest and go stock some canned goods."

"One more thing," he said. "You need to get some ointment for those scratches on Mickey's back. And try to take it easy on him, you big brute."

~ * ~

Jeana looked through the screen door when she got to Mickey's and could see him asleep on the couch. She went in quietly and put the food in the kitchen before waking him with a kiss. He smiled without opening his eyes and pulled her down on top of him.

"We gotta be careful," he whispered. "My girlfriend's coming over and she might yank out your hair."

"You're not any funnier than Billy Joe," she said. "Didn't you get to take a nap before you went to practice?"

"No, I had an errand to run and it took longer than I expected."

She folded her hands on his chest and propped her chin on them. "What kind of errand?"

"I figured since we were gonna be here alone tonight, I probably—okay, make that *definitely*—would want to make love to you again, so we needed to be prepared this time."

"Oh. But why did it take longer than you thought?"

"Well, I went to Eckerd's in Chickasaw, but the lady behind the counter goes to my church."

She giggled. "Did she see you looking at them?"

"No, I left as soon as I saw her. So then I went to Eckerd's in Saraland, but Coach Tucker's wife was there waiting for a prescription, and she starts *talking* to me." He reached in his pocket. "Here, I bought some Chap Stick."

She took it and laughed again. "Did you give up?"

"Are you kidding?" He looked incredulous. "But I had to go all the way to the store on Dauphin Street before I could buy any. Then I got to thinking that I might have the same problem next time, so I bought three boxes."

"Mickey, you didn't!"

He grinned. "I did. The old guy behind the counter shook my hand before I left."

Jeana covered her face and they both laughed.

"Um, Mickey," she said, "you smell kind of... pungent. You didn't take a shower when you got home from practice?"

He raised one of his eyebrows with his finger. "No, I was waiting for you."

"Okay," she said with a smile. "But I need to put the food on first if we're going to eat tonight. Go back to sleep until I get it started."

"I don't think I can sleep anymore," he said with a yawn, "but I'll try."

When she checked on him five minutes later, he was snoring. She got the gumbo in the pot to simmer and made some rice to go with it, but Mickey wasn't on the couch when she went to wake him. She found him asleep on his bed wearing only a towel, his hair wet from the shower. He smelled like Ivory soap and strawberry shampoo, and his skin glowed from the scrubbing she now knew firsthand that he gave it when he showered.

Careful not to wake him, she sat beside him on the bed so she could look at him uninterrupted. She couldn't imagine ever seeing anything so perfectly beautiful as the sight of his sleeping face, and she wished she could lock the image away in her mind for safekeeping.

She hadn't thought it possible to love Mickey any more than she already did, but now she knew what it meant to love someone body and soul. All the epic loves she'd read about and envied so much when she was growing up had nothing over her love for Mickey, and she believed with all her heart that he loved her just as much. She nestled into the delicious warmth of his arms and woke an hour later with him kissing her neck.

"Are you ready to eat now?" she asked.

He put his head inside her sweater and said something about working up an appetite.

While they were still catching their breath after the first time, Jeana moved on top of him with her legs straddling his hips.

Mickey's eyebrows went up in amused surprise. "You really do have a problem with patience, Jeana."

"Yes I do. But I'm pretty sure I can speed things up a little."

Her fingers brushed the muscles of his arms and chest with feathery little teases, a mischievous smile playing on her lips as she looked into the blue depths of his eyes and watched his lids grow heavy. But when he lifted his hands to touch her breasts, she grabbed his wrists and pushed his arms down beside his head.

"You're tied up," she whispered against his lips. "Lie still while I have my way with you."

His dimples appeared. "Yes, ma'am. But I need a few more minutes to recover."

"No, I don't think you do, Mickey." Her hand drifted to where her hips moved against his in a delicious rhythm. "I told you a long time ago not to challenge me."

His eyes rolled back in his head. "Be gentle with me, baby."

"Not a chance."

They were both ravenous by the time they finally ate. The gumbo was a big success, and Mickey ate three pieces of cheesecake. After they washed the dishes together, she asked him if he was ready to get his Christmas present.

"Last night and tonight are all the present I need," he said, pulling her to his lap as he sat on the couch. "And I don't have yours yet."

"I don't care about that. I went to a lot of trouble to get this for you, so you're taking it, buster." She poked him in the chest and gave him the small package.

"Okay, if you insist." He tore off the paper, and his reaction didn't disappoint her. "Oh, man... you shouldn't have spent this much on me, baby, but it's great."

"And guess what else," she said. "The man I bought it from said Mickey Mantle will be at Springdale Plaza next month. Maybe you can get it autographed."

His eyes were like blue saucers. "The Mick's coming to Mobile?"

Jeana nodded. "The card man showed me a list of his upcoming appearances in a magazine."

"Thank you for everything, baby." He wrapped his arms around her. "This is so great."

Her gaze fell on the rubber band he'd taken off her arm

the night before that was lying on the coffee table. She picked it up and put it in her pocket.

"You can wear that again if you want to, Jeana. I was just upset last night and didn't want you wearing it when we made love."

She shook her head. "I don't need to wear it to remember Wade, and you were right about him being there between us. I'll never forget him, but I have to let him go." She told him about finding Wade's poem, and he was furious when she told him what Ty had said to her at the party.

"He's a fool for repeating that garbage to you! Think about it, Jeana. Nobody who loved you enough to write something like that would kill himself to hurt you. And you can't help it that every guy you get close to falls in love with you. I'm just the lucky one you picked to love back."

"I didn't have any choice about that, Mickey. The first time you kissed me, I knew you were my destiny."

He kissed her then flicked her ear. "These last two nights have been the happiest of my life, baby."

She walked her fingers across his chest. "You mean you're not sorry you didn't go to Pensacola, *Mickey Ray?*"

He pinned her down on the couch. "Maybe I need to show you how much I'm not sorry."

She laughed. "Maybe you need to show me twice."

~ * ~

While Mickey was gone to pick up his mom the next afternoon, Jimbo paid Jeana a surprise visit and asked her to come out on the porch to talk to him for a few minutes.

"I know we've never really been friends." Jimbo rubbed his palms on his jeans as they sat in the swing. "But I listened to Wade talk about you so many times, it feels like I know you better than I do."

Jeana put her hand on his arm. "He must have trusted you a lot, Jimbo. You were a good friend to him."

"I used to wonder what it was about you that got to him

112

so bad." He looked at her apologetically. "That doesn't mean I don't think you're pretty, because I do—"

"It's okay, Jimbo. I know what you mean."

"Anyway, I thought you should know that he told me before the football banquet that you were friends again, and it was the first time in years that I'd seen him really happy about anything."

"I just wish we'd had more time…" She broke off, and he put his arm around her. "Can I tell you a secret, Jimbo?"

"Sure."

"When I first saw you with the gun at Wade's funeral, I almost asked you to let me do it."

His eyebrows went up. "For real?"

She nodded and told him about the scene with Wade's father after the banquet. "He was an evil man, and I wanted to make him pay too."

"You really slapped the SOB?" Jimbo sounded impressed.

"Yes, and it felt good too." She gave him a big smile. "*Damn* good."

He looked at her as if he'd never really seen her before. "No wonder Wade couldn't get over you, Jeana. When you smile, it makes a guy want to do whatever it takes to see that smile again."

"Thank you, Jimbo." She smiled again and hugged him. "That's one of the sweetest things anyone has ever said to me."

"I don't know why I waited so long to come see you, but I know the Wademan wanted me to." He looked a little embarrassed. "I had a dream about him last night, and he told me to get my lazy ass over here."

Jeana laughed. "That sounds like Wade. Thank you, Jimbo."

She went to her room after he left and got down the shoe box from the top of her closet where she'd put Wade's poem. She read it again and knew Jimbo was right. When she'd talked to him before the banquet that night, it *had* seemed as though he'd come to terms with their relationship and truly wanted them to be friends. He really had been happy, until his father had hurt him again.

As she was putting the poem back in the box, she got an idea. She went out to her back porch and reached under the bottom step to find the wooden box Wade had made for them to use as their club mailbox. After stopping in the kitchen for a can of furniture polish and a dusting cloth, she took all of them back to her room. When the box had been lovingly rubbed to an amber glow, she put in all her keepsakes from Wade—his poem, the rubber band, the whistle he'd carved for her the summer they were ten, their Mystery Master contracts with the bloody fingerprints under their signatures, the book of knock-knock jokes, the star wheel, the picture keychain, the hand-decorated wrapping papers, the note he left her the day of their first kiss, and the one he left her the night he died.

"Thank you, Wade." She held the box to her heart. "Thank you for all these things, and thank you for sending Jimbo to tell me it wasn't my fault. I can finally believe it now."

Chapter Fifteen

The following Tuesday, Jeana and Allison went to Vigor's basketball game in the tournament at McGill-Toolen High School. While the teams were warming up, Jeana saw Katrina and Darryl enter the gym, so she waved them over.

"Hey, girl," Katrina said as they climbed the bleachers. "Is that pretty boyfriend of yours gonna show us something tonight?"

"I sure hope so," Jeana said. "I don't want my legs broken."

Katrina frowned. "Say what?"

"Never mind." Jeana laughed and introduced them to Allison.

Katrina looked closely at Allison's eyes. "Funny, you don't look crazy. How do you put up with that fool DuBose?"

Darryl scowled at her. "Don't be talking about my man like that. Show a brother some respect, woman."

Katrina rolled her eyes. "Why don't you stop tripping and go get us a drink?"

"I'll go with you, Darryl," Allison said. "It's nice to find somebody else who appreciates Billy Joe."

Darryl took her hand to help her down the bleachers, and Billy Joe yelled at them from the court.

"Get your hands off my girl, Darryl! She don't go for black guys anyway!"

"Oh, yeah?" Darryl yelled back. "Then why does her boyfriend have that sad little wannabe 'fro?"

Jeana noticed Katrina wasn't laughing and asked her what was wrong.

"I was gonna call you before school started back," Katrina said, "but I guess I might as well tell you now. I'm dropping out."

"What are you talking about? You can't quit school. You're sure to get a music scholarship."

Katrina picked at the hem of her jacket. "I'm pregnant. I found out last week."

"Oh, no." Jeana took her hand. "But you don't have to quit school. Other girls have kept going when they were pregnant."

Katrina shook her head. "I'm not gonna have people laughing and talking about me like I'm trash. Some girls might not care, but I do."

"What did Darryl say?"

"Before or after he passed out?"

Jeana laughed. "Seriously, Katrina."

"Oh, after he cussed and threatened to sue the company that made the rubbers, he said he loved me and he'd stick by me."

A seed of fear sprouted in Jeana's stomach. "You used a condom every time?"

"Yeah, ain't that a bitch?"

"Are you going to get married?"

"Not right now. I love Darryl, but one of us needs to finish school and get a decent job. And I know my mama won't kick me out. She'll yell and probably swear she's gonna castrate Darryl, but she'll take care of us." Katrina put a hand on her stomach affectionately. "She always said she wanted a bunch of grandbabies."

Jeana put an arm around her friend. "Well, you'd better call me if there's anything you need. You know I'll do whatever I can to help."

"Thanks, Jeana." Katrina wiped her eyes and they hugged each other.

~ * ~

Mickey scored twenty-seven points and got nine rebounds

to help Vigor win 76-68. Billy Joe fouled out early in the fourth quarter, but he made twelve points and got four rebounds, so they were both in high spirits after the game.

"You wanna go get something to eat?" Mickey asked while they waited for the girls to come out of the restroom.

"Can't," Billy Joe replied. "Al promised to attack me if I made it to the fourth quarter before I fouled out." He put a hand on Mickey's shoulder. "It means a lot to her. You understand, Mick."

"Sure, buddy." Mickey laughed.

After Billy Joe and Allison left, Jeana gave Mickey a kiss for playing a great game.

"I'm getting a lot better at understanding it too," she said proudly. "I can tell when somebody travels now."

"That's really good, baby. Pretty soon you'll be giving the referees a hard time." He flicked her earlobe and pulled her closer. "You wanna go somewhere and give me the rest of my reward?"

Jeana's smile faded, and she told him about Katrina. "It scares me, Mickey. They never did it unprotected and she still got pregnant. We didn't use anything Friday."

"I know we took a big chance, but I don't regret it. It was worth it to be with you."

"I'm not sorry either, Mickey. This weekend was ours and it was wonderful, but we can't just forget about all our plans now."

"I know, but—"

She put her hands on his cheeks. "Mickey, listen to me. All you have to do is get your scholarship and wow them enough to get some scout to notice you, then you get a contract offer, I get to marry a major-league ballplayer, and we can make love as much as we want."

"That's all there is to it, huh?"

She nodded. "We just have to be smart and stick to the plan."

"But that man at the drug store is gonna be *so*

disappointed when I don't come back." Mickey made a sad face. "I was his hero."

"He'll get over it. And you'll still be my hero."

"Katrina's news must've really shook you up, baby."

"It did, Mickey. The same thing could happen to us if we're not careful. I just hope it's not already too late."

"When will you know?"

"In about two weeks."

Mickey sighed and held her tighter. "I know you're right, but I don't know how I'm gonna survive without you now, Jeana. I'm pretty sure this qualifies as cruel and unusual punishment. Give me a taste of paradise and then take it away from me."

She frowned. "It won't be any easier for me, you know. And at least you can use the old standby and think about baseball."

He scoffed. "That might've worked if we hadn't made love in center field the other night. How am I ever gonna play there now?"

~ * ~

They went back to school two weeks later on January 5. Mickey greeted Jeana in the parking lot with a kiss and an anxious look.

"Anything?" he asked.

"Not yet, but I won't be late until Wednesday."

"Any symptoms?"

"My heart rate is up and I feel lightheaded." She put a hand on her forehead. "Oh, wait. I always feel that way around you."

Mickey scowled. "I'm gonna have to keep you away from Billy Joe. He's starting to rub off on you."

Jeana truly wasn't worried because she'd actually been having her usual monthly symptoms: breast tenderness and a slight backache. She thought she'd be able to allay Mickey's concerns soon, but by Friday she wasn't so sure. Her periods were usually regular, and she'd never been more than three days late before. When Mickey picked her up for their date Friday night to go watch the Jags play Auburn, the anxiety showed on both their faces.

"Try not to worry, baby." He held her hand while he drove. "That could even be what's wrong."

"We have to be realistic, Mickey. If I don't start by next Wednesday, I should get a test done so we'll know for sure."

She went to see him Tuesday night to tell him she'd found a clinic that did pregnancy tests for ten dollars without an appointment. Marsha was at one of her Narcotics Anonymous meetings, so Mickey and Jeana were alone at his house. She was lying on the couch with her head in his lap.

"I'm going to the clinic tomorrow right after school," she said.

"Can't you wait until I get home from practice so I can go with you?"

"They'd be closed by then."

"I don't want you to go alone, Jeana. I'll skip practice."

She gave him a shocked look. "You've never missed practice in your life, and I'm not going to be the reason you miss your first one. I'll be fine, Mickey."

He fingered her earlobe. "But what if they tell you it's positive? You won't have anyone there with you."

She put her arm across her eyes. "It's not like it'll be a big surprise. I've just about gotten used to the idea already."

"Jeana…" He took a shaky breath. "What if they talk to you about an abortion? What will you tell them?"

She moved her arm and saw the fear in his eyes. "Mickey, what are you thinking? You know I'd never do that." She sat up and put her arms around him.

"I don't know what I'm thinking anymore. I only know I love you and wish you could stay in my arms forever."

"I know. I'm not scared when you're holding me."

119

What started out as a comforting hug changed rapidly when his hands started to drift over her body and he began kissing her neck.

"Let me make love to you, Jeana."

"Mickey…"

"It won't matter if you're already pregnant, and it should be safe right now if you're not. Please, baby. I need you to get through this."

"What if your mom comes home?"

"Her meeting won't be over until nine. That gives us at least two hours." His hands slipped inside her shirt. "Don't you want me too, baby?"

Looking into those blue wonders he had for eyes, she was helpless to resist. They went to his room and forgot their worries for the next hour. Mickey fell asleep afterward and Jeana was afraid she'd doze off too and Marsha would find them that way, so she took her clothes with her into the bathroom to get dressed. She came running out a minute later and jumped on top of him.

"Mickey, wake up! *I'm not pregnant!*" She bounced on him until he opened his eyes.

It took him a second to comprehend, then he grabbed her and they rolled over, laughing and kissing. "I told you not to worry, baby."

"Now we can do everything we planned, and we'll be incredibly happy the way I always knew we'd be!" Her glee affected her aim when she threw her arms around him, so he ended up in an exuberant headlock.

"As much as I like getting hugged like this," he said, "if you don't put on more than those little blue panties, we're gonna have another problem when my mom gets home."

Jeana slept better that night than she had in two weeks, but she was surprised in the morning when there was barely anything on her tampon. She thought she remembered other times when she'd had a couple of light days at the beginning of her period, so she told herself not to worry.

She didn't say anything to Mickey about it when she got to school. Besides being a distasteful subject, she didn't want to worry him unnecessarily. They'd both been scared for the past week, and she never wanted to see that frightened look on his face again.

Right before the Christmas holidays, Mr. Brownlee had given them a list of topics for doing a research paper for Biology, and it was time to make their decisions. When Jeana chose "Special Health Concerns for Teenage Pregnancies," Mickey asked her why she'd picked that topic. She told him it was so she could tell Katrina anything she needed to know about.

When she got home from school that afternoon and her sanitary pad was barely soiled, she still refused to think negatively. It had to be just a light period. After all, her body had gone through some major changes lately. She kept telling herself there was nothing to worry about for the next two days, until the spotting disappeared altogether.

While researching her paper at the library, she checked several gynecological reference books for articles about changes in menstrual flow, and she was encouraged to read that a woman's periods could undergo changes after she became sexually active. That had to be what was going on with hers, and she wasn't going to be active anymore. Not after this close call.

Mickey took her bowling again on Friday night so she could use one of her Christmas presents: her very own bowling shoes so she wouldn't have to wear—or steal—the rented ones. On the way home, she talked him into stopping at McDonald's for sundaes.

"Something happened at school today," Jeana said while they ate their ice cream in the car. "I was in the bathroom after third period and Tiffany came in throwing up. She told me she's pregnant."

Mickey looked surprised. "I always heard she was only a tea—" He broke off when he saw the frown Jeana was giving him. "I mean, whose baby is it?"

"She said it's Bubba's," Jeana replied. "You know there's never been any love lost between Tiffany and me, but she was really beating herself up about it. I guess I wanted her to know I understood how she felt because it could happen to anyone, so I told her about our scare. She must've been desperate for somebody to talk to, because she started telling me all about how Bubba swore he loved her just to get her to sleep with him, and now he won't believe it's his baby even though he's the only one she's ever been with." Jeana stirred her sundae and sighed. "She's heartbroken and scared to death."

"Man, that's rough," Mickey said. "What's she gonna do?"

"She doesn't know yet. I feel so bad for her and other girls who've been lied to and then deserted." She reached over and held Mickey's hand. "I know how lucky I am to have a wonderful guy like you, but it really made me stop and think about how close we came to having our lives changed forever. What if I'd been pregnant, Mickey? Would you still go to college and play baseball?"

"I don't see how I could," he said. "I'd have to get a full-time job to support us because I couldn't stand it if we had to borrow money from anybody."

"I could've worked so you could stay in school."

He shook his head. "I'd never risk your health like that. Nothing's more important to me than you, Jeana."

She gave him the rest of her sundae and sighed. "Well, we were incredibly lucky this time, and I don't want to push it. We absolutely can't take any more chances."

"I know, but it's gonna be hard." He gave her a look that affirmed the double meaning. "I was late for fifth period today because I was daydreaming about you in English and couldn't get out of my seat when the bell rang."

Jeana laughed. "We'll just have to make sure we don't

get the opportunity, like not being alone at your house anymore."

"Yeah, I don't think my mom will let that happen anyway." He fingered the steering wheel and avoided her gaze. "She kinda knows about us."

"What do you mean she *kinda* knows?"

He looked at her helplessly. "She asked me and I had to tell the truth."

"Mickey! What did she ask you?"

"She wanted to know why I suddenly started washing my own sheets. I tried to dodge that question, but then she just came out and asked me. I couldn't *lie*, baby."

She covered her eyes with her hands. "Oh, God. What does she think about me now?" She glared at him when he laughed.

"Don't be silly, Jeana. She thinks you love her son—the one you're engaged to, remember?"

"She wasn't mad?"

"More like concerned. She told me the whole story again about what happened to her and Dad, and she said she hoped me and you would use more restraint than they did."

"Well, you be sure to tell her we're going to be models of restraint from now on." She whacked him on the shoulder. "And why did you let her see you washing your sheets, you big jock?"

He pulled her over to his side of the car. "You just think you're *so* smart, don't you?"

"That's because I am!" She squealed and tried to escape the Finger Brothers.

"Oh, yeah?" he said. "Then why haven't you noticed that you're missing the pantyhose you wore to the Christmas party? Mom found them hanging from the bat of my Leading Hitter trophy on top of my bookcase. How was I supposed to explain *that*, Miss Valedictorian?"

Chapter Sixteen

M ickey Mantle came to Gayfers department store in Springdale Plaza the last week in January. Jeana and Mickey took the baseball card to get it autographed, and Mickey got to shake Mr. Mantle's hand. He told Jeana he just wished his dad could've been there too.

Jeana didn't think about her period until it was time for it again, around February 10. She didn't say anything to Mickey because she felt like a fool for not knowing whether or not she'd had a period the month before. When she was ten days late, she went to the women's clinic for a pregnancy test. While she sat alone and frightened in an exam room cold enough for meat storage, a somber lab technician told her that her test was positive and she could pay at the cashier's window on her way out. She stopped one of the nurses in the hall to ask her some questions, but the nurse told her to make an appointment for abortion counseling.

"No, you don't understand," Jeana said, her voice rising with her panic level. "I just have a few questions about my test. Can't you help me?"

"I'm sorry," the nurse replied. "I'm very busy, and counseling isn't part of my job description."

Jeana went back into the exam room to get her things and ended up crying into her hands, longing for Mickey. She didn't hear the door open and was startled when she felt a consoling hand on her back and looked up into green eyes that reminded her of Wade's.

"Are you in pain, Miss?" the young doctor asked.

Jeana shook her head. "I can't get anyone to answer my questions."

"I'd be happy to talk to you." He pulled a rolling stool in front of her and handed her a tissue as he sat down. "My name's Dr. Harper. What questions do you have?"

She told him about the light period she'd had the previous month. He said it had probably not been a period at all and that many women experienced spotting in the early months of pregnancy around the time of their regular periods. He told her that a doctor would need to examine her in order to get a more accurate due date, but she was probably about ten weeks pregnant.

"Are you here alone, Jeana?" he asked. "I can see you're upset over this news. Do you need to speak to one of the counselors?"

"No, I was just confused, but you answered my questions. My fiancé would be with me if he knew I was here." She wiped her eyes with the tissue. "I don't know how to tell him. I feel so stupid for the mistake last month and making him think we didn't have anything to worry about."

"You shouldn't feel that way. It's a common mistake women much older than you have also made." He patted her hand. "So you're going to have the baby?"

"Yes."

He wrote something on a prescription pad. "Here's the name of an obstetrician who's very good at managing teenage pregnancies. You should make an appointment to begin your prenatal care, and you definitely need to get your vitamins started as soon as possible."

She looked at the paper he'd given her. "Can you give me a prescription for the vitamins? I'm not sure when I'll be able to see a doctor because my parents don't know yet either."

"I'll write you the prescription, but if you don't go to this doctor, you should at least see one at the Board of Health clinic."

"I will. Thank you, Dr. Harper."

When she got home, Jeana didn't want to do anything but sleep, so she told her mother she had a stomach virus and slept for two hours. When she woke up, she stared at the ceiling and wondered how she was going to tell Mickey. He'd started baseball practice two weeks earlier and always called her when he got home, so when she saw that it was after seven o'clock, she knew she'd missed his call.

"Your mom told me you were sick," Mickey said when she called him back. "What's wrong, baby?"

"It's okay, I feel better now. Will you come get me?"

"You know I will, but are you sure you feel like it? You sound tired."

"I'll be fine as soon as I'm with you, Mickey."

"Okay, I'll be right there. I've got some news to tell you."

I've got some for you too.

When Mickey got there ten minutes later, he said, "Where do you want to go?"

"Just somewhere we can be alone and talk."

"We can go to my house. Mom's not home tonight." He saw her look at him and added, "I promise to be good."

"I guess it'll be okay," she said. It wasn't like they could get in any more trouble than they were in already. Her fear dissipated a little as soon as they got to his house and she was in his arms, but she still dreaded seeing the worry reappear on his face when she told him.

"What's wrong, baby? Do you feel sick again?"

She shook her head. "You said you had something to tell me. What is it?"

"The baseball coach from South came to Vigor today."

She sat up to look at him, and he had a big smile on his face. "Why was he there, Mickey?"

"To get a copy of our schedule from Coach Creel. He said he heard we had a couple of good prospects that he wanted to see in action."

126

"Did he say anything to you?"

His smile widened. "He told me he'd be talking to me after the Satsuma game next week."

She threw her arms around his neck. "Oh, I knew you'd get your scholarship!"

"Unless I really screw up and he changes his mind," Mickey said. "Maybe you shouldn't come to that game, baby. I have trouble concentrating with you around."

Her smile disappeared. She couldn't tell him she was pregnant now. It could make him lose his scholarship.

"I won't go if you think I shouldn't," she said. "I don't want anything to mess this up for you."

He scoffed. "I was only kidding. You know I always want you at my games." He lifted her chin and kissed her. "Who's my inspiration?"

She put her head on his chest. "Whatever you say, Mickey. I just want you to play your best so you can make your dreams come true."

"You already did that, Jeana." He wrapped his arms around her. "Everything else is just a bonus."

She told him she was feeling bad again so he'd take her home. She went to bed early but lay awake wondering what she should do. After running all the possibilities through her head, she decided she'd wait until Mickey got his scholarship before she told him she was pregnant. Maybe that way she could persuade him to stay in school after he knew. She could deal with it by herself for a couple of weeks. Especially since it was all her fault.

~ * ~

Three weeks later, when Coach Laird told Mickey that he definitely wanted him to play at the University of South Alabama, Jeana balked again at telling Mickey she was pregnant, this time because she didn't want to spoil his happiness over his scholarship and ruin his last year of high school baseball for him. He should at least get to enjoy his success for a little while before she took it all away from him.

Despite daily bouts of fatigue, she managed to march in all the Mardi Gras parades without any problems. Her morning sickness was only mild nausea, so no one seemed to notice that she was just skipping breakfast. Her valedictorian mentality and the research she'd done on teenage pregnancies also served her well. She got the prescription filled for the prenatal vitamins and supplemented them with what she knew teenagers needed in additional amounts. Her blood type was A-positive, so she didn't have to worry about the Rh factor. And to keep off extra weight without sacrificing any nutrients, she cut out all soft drinks and drank lots of water. So far, she hadn't gained a pound.

Focusing on all these things kept her from facing the inevitable: when she told Mickey she was pregnant, all his dreams would come to an end because of her, and she was terrified that he would end up hating her because of it. Although she kept telling herself that she could persuade him to stay in college, she secretly knew he wouldn't do it. Her time was running out. She would have to tell him soon.

~ * ~

The first day of April, Allison bounded into Jeana's room after school and sat on the bed with barely contained excitement.

"Did you get your class rank from the counselors today?" she asked.

"Sure," Jeana replied. "Mine was first and Mickey's was seventy-fifth. Why?"

Allison was practically glowing. "When they gave me mine, they also gave me a letter from Troy State about their summer basketball program for scholarship winners!"

"You didn't tell me you got a scholarship to Troy State," Jeana said.

"I didn't know!" Allison laughed and grabbed Jeana's hands. "Coach Perkins was supposed to give me my letter, but she forgot. Can you believe it?"

"That's wonderful!" Jeana said. "Are you going to do their summer program?"

Allison nodded. "All I have to do is take at least one class and I can start receiving my housing money in May. The rest of the time I can spend at basketball clinics."

"Oh, I'm so happy for you!"

They hugged each other, then Allison gave her a sly look. "You know, Jeana, they have a summer program in the College of Education too. We could be roomies if you took your scholarship."

The realization that what Allison had just suggested would be the answer to her problem hit Jeana like a bucket of ice water, and she froze as she quickly ran the details through her head to see if it could work.

"Jeana, what's wrong?"

Allison would have to know the truth in order for the plan to work, so Jeana took a deep breath and just blurted it. "Allison, I'm pregnant. Mickey doesn't know yet and I don't want him to find out. You just gave me an idea about how to keep it from him, but I'll need your help."

Allison stared at her a few seconds then laughed nervously. "This is an April Fool's joke, right?"

"I wish it was, but it's true." Jeana got the receipt for the pregnancy test from her purse and handed it to Allison.

Allison gaped at her when she saw the date on the receipt. "You've known since *February?* God, Jeana, why didn't you tell me?" She pulled her into a tearful hug. "And why don't you want Mickey to know?"

Jeana wiped her eyes. "Because he'll give up his scholarship and take some horrible job at one of the paper mills or the shipyard so we can get married right away. He'll end up miserable, and I can't let that happen to him, Allison. I just *can't*. He'd hate me for it, and I'd hate myself."

"Mickey wouldn't blame you, Jeana. He had just as

much to do with this as you."

"No, it's my fault. He told me when we were sixteen that we had to wait until we were married. If it hadn't been for me scaring him with my big emotional scene the night of the Christmas party, we wouldn't have done it unprotected."

"How long do you think you can keep it from him?"

"A lot longer now that you gave me the idea to take my scholarship and go to Troy as soon as we graduate. If he doesn't find out until after he's already playing baseball at South, maybe he won't drop out of school."

"But he'll know when he sees you in another month or so. Everyone will."

Jeana got up and started to pace. "I won't come home after I start to show."

"What about when Mickey comes to Troy? You know he will."

"I don't have everything figured out yet," Jeana said. "But I'll think of something."

Allison sighed. "I don't see how this will ever work, and I really think you should tell Mickey the truth, but I have to admit I'm glad you're coming with me."

"Me too. It's so good to have someone to talk to about all of it." Jeana sat beside Allison on the bed and hugged her again.

"No one knows but us?"

Jeana shook her head. "Shelly couldn't keep a secret if her life depended on it, and I know my mama and daddy and Billy Joe would tell Mickey if they knew."

"Billy Joe!" Allison's eyes widened. "How are you gonna keep it from *him* when he comes to see me in Troy?"

"Maybe between the two of us, we can threaten him enough to make him keep his big mouth shut."

Allison looked skeptical. "In the immortal words of Scooby Doo—Rotsa Ruck."

~ * ~

130

The Russells were surprised but pleased when Jeana told them about the change in her college plans. The guidance counselors at Vigor helped her make all the arrangements to start the summer semester on scholarship at Troy State, beginning the end of May.

Jeana didn't know what to expect when she told Mickey. He'd been trying to get her to do this for a long time, but since she'd always insisted that she'd never consider it, she was afraid he'd be suspicious about her sudden change of heart. She invited him to come eat supper with her family and took him out to sit in the porch swing afterward.

"I've got something to tell you, Mickey." She sat on her heels facing him and held his hand in both of hers. "I've been thinking about it for a long time, but I didn't want to say anything until I'd made up my mind." She took a deep breath. "I'm going to take the scholarship to Troy State."

He was clearly surprised. "That's great, baby, but what changed your mind?"

"Several things," she said, unable to look him in the eyes. "Allison's going there and we can be roommates, plus I found out that Troy offers a couple of education classes I want to take that aren't offered at South. And I can take them at Troy in the summer semester."

"Oh." He looked even more surprised. "So you'll be going sometime this summer?"

This was the hardest part.

"I'll be leaving right after graduation, Mickey."

He'd never been able to hide his feelings from her, and his face plainly showed his distress. "God, that's barely a month from now."

"I know, but if I start classes now and take some every summer, I can get finished sooner and come back for good."

"You'll come home on the weekends though, won't you?"

"I'll come when I can, but it's a four hour drive and I'll have homework. I might not be able to come very much." She hated the anguish that was already in his eyes. "Please don't look at me like that, Mickey."

"I'm sorry, baby. It's just hard to think about you leaving me so soon."

"Don't say it like that. I'm leaving home, I'm not leaving *you*."

"There's no way I can go all summer without seeing you," he said. "I'll just have to come to Troy every weekend."

That was the last thing she wanted, but she wasn't going to argue with him about it now. "Sure, you and Billy Joe can both visit."

She walked him to the car before he left. When he held her against him, she worried that he would feel the slight rounding of her stomach that she'd detected in the past few days, but he was apparently too distraught to notice anything.

"Tell me you'll always love me, Jeana."

It had been a long time since he'd needed to be reassured like that. She sighed and put her arms around him. "Of course I'll always love you, Mickey. You're supposed to know that already."

He buried his face in her hair and nuzzled her neck. "Let me make love to you again before you leave me."

If she hadn't been afraid he'd notice the change in her figure, she would've told him to take her somewhere that second. She closed her eyes and remembered the incomparable feeling of lying beside Mickey in his bed with their bodies and their hearts entangled. She wanted desperately to tell him yes, but she knew she couldn't risk it.

"We can't, Mickey. Remember how scared we were in January?"

"I'm scared now. Scared I'll lose you."

132

"You won't lose me, Mickey. I promise."

Before the summer was over, she would regret making him that promise.

Chapter Seventeen

The next few weeks were filled with prom, exams, graduation activities, and preparations for moving. Jeana and Allison went to Troy with their mothers the last weekend in April and found a furnished two-bedroom apartment to rent. They paid the deposit and told the landlord they would be moving in about May 10, the weekend after graduation.

Allison's mother was a humorless woman who seemed to distrust her daughter for no apparent reason. She lectured Allison and Jeana about being responsible and not allowing any boys to visit, especially that "wild-haired, impertinent Billy Joe." Jeana had a hard time holding her tongue, but since she was moving to avoid seeing the boys in the first place, she didn't see the logic in defending their right to visit. Betty, however, told Mrs. White in no uncertain terms that she would trust either Mickey or Billy Joe with her daughter's life, and they were both like sons to her.

As graduation drew nearer, the activities increased to an exhausting level. Jeana had a clarinet solo in the musical prelude to Commencement, so she had band practice daily. She had to write and memorize her valedictory address, and she and Allison were busy buying things they needed for their apartment.

Mickey felt positively neglected. Two days before graduation, he came over to see Jeana and walked dolefully to his car after Betty told him she'd gone to the mall with Allison to look for some inexpensive flatware. Billy Joe saw him as he was leaving and crossed the street to talk to him.

"I don't like it either, Mick. They're not nearly as

devastated about leaving us as they should be."

Mickey barely managed a smile. "Guess we'd better get used to being on our own, huh?"

"Wanna go cruising in the El Camino?"

"No, I'd be afraid of who we might attract."

Billy Joe laughed and sat on the Mustang's hood. "Cheer up, Mick. Jeana's just caught up in the excitement of graduation and moving right now."

"Yeah, I know. I just miss her already, and she's not even gone yet." Mickey picked up a rock and chunked it into the yard next door.

"Trust me, they'll be homesick in no time and coming home every weekend," Billy Joe said. "And we'll be going to Troy a lot, at least until my folks make me sell my soul to International Paper Company."

"You're not going to school anywhere?"

"Nah, I can't find one that offers a degree in gigolo."

Another weak smile. "I guess I'll go home and call Jeana later. See you tomorrow, buddy."

Billy Joe stood in the yard and shook his head as he watched Mickey drive away. "That's one pitiful Yankee."

~ * ~

When Jeana got home an hour later, Billy Joe accosted her as she took the bags from the back seat of her VW Beetle.

"Hey, there was some guy here to see you earlier," he said. "He kinda looked like Mickey, except for the big hole where his heart should be."

She gave him an impatient look. "What are you babbling about now, Billy Joe?"

"Look, I know you're busy being deliriously happy about leaving and all, but do you think you could spare a few minutes a day to pretend like you're gonna miss him just a little?"

"Don't be ridiculous. He knows I'll miss him." She closed the car door and started up the steps, but he took the bags from her and blocked her path.

135

"I'm serious, Jeana. I've never seen him look so down before."

"He's just bored," she said, reaching for the bags.

He scowled at her. "What's wrong with you? This is Mickey we're talking about."

"*Fine.* I'll talk to him about it." She snatched the bags and shouldered him aside. "Now leave me alone."

"What the hell is going on with you, Jeana?"

She wheeled around and shouted at him. "Do you have any idea how many things I have to worry about right now? I just want to get all this over with so I can go to Troy, and I don't need a guilt trip from you!"

She stormed through the house to her room where she threw the bags on the floor then sat on her bed and immediately started to cry. It was so hard to keep avoiding Mickey when all she wanted was to be in his arms. She knew he was upset, but when he looked at her with those blue eyes of his and talked about how much he wanted to make love to her, it took all her willpower to keep from telling him to take her to his room, lock the door and throw away the key.

The phone rang, and she knew it would be Mickey before she even picked it up.

"I came over earlier," he said. "Why didn't you tell me you were going to the mall?"

She sighed. "I didn't think you'd want to go look for dishes with us, Mickey."

"I just wanted to see you. We only have a few more days before you leave me."

"I wish you'd stop saying that. You're the main one who wanted me to go, remember?"

"Yeah, in the fall. I didn't know you'd be gone all summer."

"But this way I'll get through sooner. Try to think of it that way, okay?" When he didn't answer, she said, "Mickey, please don't be like this."

"I can't help it, Jeana. I miss you."

"Okay, Mickey. You win." She couldn't bear to hear him sounding so bereft. "Come to my window in about forty-five minutes."

She put on an oversized nightshirt and a pair of flannel pajama pants, hoping Mickey wouldn't notice her thickening waistline through all the clothes. She heard him tapping on her window ten minutes before he was supposed to be there.

"I couldn't wait any longer," he said as he climbed in. He immediately pulled her into his arms and kissed her. "It feels like I'm drowning and your lips are my lifeline."

She held his face in her hands. "You know I don't want to leave you, Mickey. How could you ever think that?"

"The thought of you being so far away makes me crazy, Jeana. You were right all along. I don't think I can do it."

"We don't have a choice now."

"Yes we do. I won't go to South. I'll go to Troy with you and get a job."

"No you won't, Mickey. You have to play baseball like you promised your dad."

"But, Jeana—"

"That promise you made is important to both of us, and I'm not going to let you break it because of me."

He closed his eyes and held her tight. "I know you're right. I'm just gonna miss you so much, baby." When he let her go, he noticed her clothes. "What happened to those cute little pajamas you used to wear?"

She shrugged. "I get cold at night sometimes."

He sat on the bed and pulled her down beside him. "You need me to keep you warm, and I just need you period." He lay back on the bed and lifted her on top of him.

"No, Mickey. We have an agreement, remember?"

"That was before I knew you were leaving me." His hands caressed the curve of her back inside the nightshirt and pulled her against him. "I want you so much I'm going out of my mind, Jeana."

Her heart was pounding and she didn't know if it was more from fear or from longing for him. "You know I want you too, Mickey, but we can't."

"Please, baby. It's the only way I can survive without you."

His hands moved to her breasts, and she was quickly lost in the heat she'd always felt at his touch. She let him put her hand inside his jeans and watched as his eyes got the drowsy look she loved, but she stopped him when he started to slide down her pajama pants.

"Just with my hand, Mickey. You like that."

"No, I want to make love to you, Jeana. I need to hear you say my name and tell me you love me."

"We can't..."

"Yes we can, baby. I brought a rubber." He reached in his pocket for it, and she almost laughed.

"Well, you certainly had high hopes for this visit."

"I told you I'm going crazy, Jeana. Making love to you is all I can think about anymore."

He was kissing her neck again and weakening her fragile restraint, so she switched her tactics to a stall.

"Stop, Mickey. Not now and not here." She sat up and straightened her clothes.

"Then when? Thursday night after graduation?"

"We're going out to eat with Billy Joe and Allison then."

"I mean afterward. We can go to Aunt Robin's beach house. Ty can get me the key."

"Mickey, we shouldn't—"

"I know we shouldn't, but we are. Now come back here and at least let me hold you." He pulled her down beside him again.

"You sure are bossy all of a sudden." She snuggled into his arms. "I wouldn't let you get away with it if I didn't love you so much."

She held on to him while she still could, thinking how ironic it was that after tempting Mickey so many times in the past, she was the one who now had to be strong enough to say no.

Chapter Eighteen

Jeana regretted yelling at Billy Joe, so she took him a peace offering the next day.

"I should be offended that you think you can still appease me with mere cookies," he said as he ate the fifth one. "Don't you have anything more to offer?"

"I have some gum in my pocket." She dunked a cookie in his milk and took a bite. "Besides, when have we ever had a problem that cookies couldn't solve? Oh, and in case you were wondering, I talked to Mickey last night. He feels better now."

"Good." Billy Joe produced a loud burp and got a dark look. "Did you and Al get extra dishes and stuff for when me and Mick come to see you in Troy?"

"I don't know if y'all should visit," she said. "Allison's mother warned us about you two shady characters—especially you. What's her problem anyway?"

He shrugged. "She thinks I have no future. And she's jealous of my hair."

"What *are* your plans for the future? I know you don't want to work at the paper mill." She rested her chin in her hand and watched him finish the cookies.

"Oh, I'll find a rich widow looking for a young stud to keep her company and get her to buy me a studio in Paris." He gazed off into the distance. "I'll paint naked all day and make love all night."

Jeana laughed. "I can picture you doing that."

"So you do fantasize about me. I *knew* it."

"Would you be serious for a minute? You have so much talent and I don't want to see you waste it. What about taking art classes somewhere?"

He shook his head. "I'm too fond of eating to be an artist. I'll probably end up working at IP until I die, like my old man."

"Well, you at least have to promise you'll paint a picture of me someday." She put her hand on his and squeezed. "I love all the sketches you've given me, but I want one that everyone can see."

He smiled and touched her chin. "Okay, I promise."

~ * ~

"Ty's coming over to bring me the key tonight," Mickey said when he called Jeana after lunch. "He wants you to be here so he can apologize for what he said at the party, but I told him you were too busy getting ready for graduation. I don't want him upsetting you again."

"I do need to practice my speech a little more," she said.

"You're still not gonna let me hear it before tomorrow night?"

"Nope. And remember to get there early so you can hear my solo. We start playing at six-fifteen, and my song is first."

"I won't miss it, baby."

"Why didn't you wake me when you left last night? I wanted to kiss you goodbye."

"If you'd kissed me goodbye, I wouldn't have been able to leave. I can't wait until tomorrow night, Jeana."

His voice had that same husky quality it got when he murmured to her while they made love, and a shiver ran up the length of her spine.

"I can't wait either, Mickey."

She couldn't help it. She needed him the way her heart needed its next beat.

~ * ~

She woke at four-thirty the next morning and needed to use the bathroom, something she had to do with increasing frequency these days. When she got back to her room, she

141

took off all her clothes and stood in front of the full-length mirror on her closet door, trying to see if there was any chance Mickey wouldn't be able to tell the difference in her body.

Her stomach definitely had a roundness to it that she could see, but she wasn't sure Mickey would notice that. Her stomach wasn't one of his favorite body parts, but her breasts definitely were. She'd been overflowing the cups of her regular bras for the last two weeks and had just bought a bigger one at the mall the other night.

She turned sideways and stuck out her chest. Oh, yeah, Mickey would notice these babies for sure, but maybe he'd be too enraptured with them to ask any questions. She started to giggle and was afraid she'd wake up her family, so she got dressed and went out to sit in the swing and practice her speech.

A breeze stirred the bushes beside the porch and carried the heady scent of gardenias to the swing, reminding her of another morning a long time ago. She'd awakened early the day she started middle school and had come out to sit in the swing and savor the exhilaration she felt every time she thought about seeing Wade again.

She realized guiltily that she hadn't thought about him since she'd found out she was pregnant. She pulled up her legs and rested her forehead on her knees as she tried to envision his face, and she was surprised that the image in her mind was of Wade as an innocent boy of eleven, with green eyes that showed only how much he liked her and had no trace yet of the pain his father would cause him. Tears dropped onto her legs as she remembered his poem, and she knew she had to make an addition to her speech.

~ * ~

Vigor's graduation was held at the Mobile Municipal Auditorium and was scheduled to begin at seven. Jeana warmed up with the band at five forty-five and saw Mickey wave to her from the lobby where the graduates were lining up for the Processional. Promptly at six-fifteen, the band played "Morning, Noon and Night," and Jeana performed her solo flawlessly.

Mickey was waiting for her in the hall after she put on her cap and gown. He pulled her away from the other graduates, an anxious expression on his face. "I have to tell you something, baby."

Before he could say anything else, Katrina's boyfriend Darryl interrupted them wearing a big grin.

"I need a favor, Jeana. Can you keep your speech short so we can blow this joint? I got a beautiful woman ready to have a baby, and she don't like to be kept waiting."

"Darryl, that's wonderful!" Jeana said. "Do you think it will be tonight?"

"If Katrina has any say in it. She's been trying for two days but the doctor keeps sending her home. One more time and she's gonna slap him upside the head."

Jeana laughed. "Be sure to call me when the baby gets here so I can go see them."

"I'll do that," Darryl said.

Mickey held out his hand. "Good luck, man. Take care of that family you're getting."

"Thanks, Mickey. Gonna do my best."

After Darryl walked away, Mickey shook his head. "Poor guy. He's scared to death."

"Why do you say that?" Jeana asked. "He didn't look scared, just excited."

"His hand was all sweaty when I shook it," Mickey said. "I can understand why. It's gotta be scary knowing you're gonna have two people depending totally on you to take care of them."

"It's not all the man's responsibility," Jeana said, a little knot forming in her stomach. "Women are supposed to be equal partners in a relationship. Don't be so chauvinistic, Mickey."

He put his arms around her. "You're so cute when

you're being a feminist. It makes me want to kiss you." He tried, but she pushed him away and laughed.

It was time to line up for the Processional, so they didn't get a chance to talk anymore. A few minutes later, accompanied by the familiar strains of "Pomp and Circumstance," Jeana led her class down the auditorium's center aisle. Once she was seated on the stage with the other honor graduates, she searched the faces of her classmates and located Mickey so she could look at him when it was time to give her speech.

"Dr. Butler, Dr. Hawkins, Mr. Davis and administrators, guests, parents, faculty, and fellow classmates: tonight has been the goal of this group of young people since we first entered Vigor High School in 1977. Now that we have made it to this threshold to the rest of our lives, we should pause and examine our priorities, for these are the guidelines by which we will mold our futures.

"As you decide which path you will take after graduation, you must be certain you are striving for your own goals and not just what is expected of you. Don't let anyone make you think you must always follow the traditional course. Find something you love and work hard until you have it mastered, because real success is loving what you do. Cling tightly to your dreams, and never let anyone take them from you."

Jeana continued with more of the obligatory axioms and platitudes usually heard at Commencement, then she spoke from her heart.

"I'd like to take advantage of having my classmates as a captive audience and share what I feel are the most important things I've learned from high school in addition to academics. Everyone at Vigor knows about racial diversity, and I always liked to believe I was such an open-minded, liberal thinker. But I discovered that I was guilty of some prejudices and misconceptions common between groups other than the races. Whether we are scholars, athletes, musicians, activists, or socialites, we think we know people because of what they do and with whom they associate, but we're often wrong in our assumptions. We shouldn't stereotype people because of their talents and interests any more than we should because of their race.

"I've learned that people are like diamonds, multifaceted and flawed, but intrinsically valuable. Athletes aren't just strong, swift, and agile. They can also be brilliant and sensitive. Many of them are held in high esteem because of the strength in their arms and legs, but I've learned that they can also possess amazing strength of character. I can honestly say that the finest athlete I know is also the finest person I know."

She smiled at Mickey and pulled her earlobe, then she looked at Billy Joe.

"I've also learned how priceless true friendship is and what it means to have a friend who loves you and cares about your happiness even more than they do their own. Someone who will always be there for you no matter what, and upon whom you know you can always depend. These are the people we must hold on to all our lives, because they are much too precious to ever let go.

"Finally, I've learned that you should never give up on a friend, even if they've hurt you. Some people use bravado and anger to hide their own pain. Tell them if they've hurt you and then forgive them. Don't waste time that can never be retrieved, because they could leave you forever, and then all you can do is miss them."

Jeana paused and closed her eyes.

"Wade Anthony Strickland, although you did your best to hide it, I know you had a heart as big as your muscles and a poet's soul. Everybody knew you were big and strong and struck terror in the hearts of running backs, but I know you were good at remembering birthdays, whistling with your fingers, making a frightened ten-year-old girl feel safe and protected, and being strong when it counted the most.

You gave me some of my happiest memories, and I'll never forget you. I'll hear your voice in the rain and see your eyes in the greens of the pines, and I want you to know that the smile I wear when I think of your face… is only for you."

It was several seconds before she could go on, and sniffling could be heard throughout the auditorium.

"As valedictorian of the class of 1981, I truly wish the best in life for all my classmates. And I hope that from this day forward, whenever anyone asks you where you went to school, you will hold your head high and be proud to say that you graduated from Vigor High School. And so, fellow graduates, I leave you with three things to remember: who you are, what it is that you want out of life, and whence you came. Thank you."

At the end of the ceremony, as they sang the "Alma Mater" with their index fingers held high, Jeana was struck by the realization that a part of her life had just ended, and she couldn't stop her tears. She'd known many of the people in the audience since kindergarten, and she knew she would never see some of them again after this night. The thought made her feel profoundly sad.

Chapter Nineteen

After they turned in their robes, Mickey and Jeana found their families in the throngs of proud relatives filling the auditorium lobby. Sissy was there with Shelly, and she pulled Jeana aside.

"Thank you for what you said about Wade. I know why he loved you so much, Jeana."

Jeana hugged her. "I meant every word of it, Sissy. He'll be in my heart forever."

Mickey's grandfather gave Jeana a hearty hug and gave Mickey a stern look. "This is a mighty special young lady you have here, boy. See that you remember it."

"Don't worry, Grandpa." Mickey put his arm around Jeana. "I know how lucky I am."

"You sure are," Ty said, shaking Mickey's hand. "Mind if I kiss the valedictorian?"

Mickey looked at him without smiling. "That's not a tradition like kissing the bride. Stick to a handshake."

Many rolls of film later, after all the relatives had departed, Mickey took Jeana's hand and led her to the parking lot. "I need to talk to you about something before we meet Allison and Billy Joe at the restaurant." When they were in the Mustang, he leaned over to kiss her. "First I want to tell you how proud of you I am. What you said in your speech really made me feel good."

"You know I meant it, Mickey. I'm proud of you too."

He stared at his hands on the steering wheel and chewed his lip. "Jeana, Coach Laird at South called this afternoon to tell me about a 19-and-under baseball team that travels to tournaments in the summer. He said he encourages his recruits to play on teams like that, so he gave my number to the team's manager. He called me right after I hung up with Coach."

"That sounds wonderful, Mickey," she said. "Why do you look like it's bad news?"

"Because the first tournament is this weekend in Memphis, and we're supposed to leave tonight."

"Oh."

"I wouldn't normally get to play since I haven't been to practice or anything yet, but a bunch of the other players graduate this weekend and can't make the trip. That's why he asked me to go and fill in." He took her hand, and his eyes searched her face anxiously. "I don't have to go, baby. I'll stay if you want me to."

She squeezed his hand and tried not to let him see how relieved she was. "Of course I want you to stay, Mickey, but I can't be selfish like that. Will we still be able to go out and eat tonight?"

"Yeah, we don't have to meet and load the bus at Springdale Plaza until eleven."

She put her hand under his chin. "Don't look so guilty, Mickey. You're not deserting me. I'm the one leaving town next week."

"I know, and I wanted to spend tonight with you in my arms." He closed his eyes and leaned his head back on the seat.

"I wanted it too," she said, "but you know we shouldn't have been doing it anyway. Playing on this team will be good for you, Mickey. You needed something to keep you busy this summer while I'm gone. Do you want me to go with you to meet the bus?"

He nodded as he started the car. "I don't wanna leave the Mustang in the parking lot all weekend, so I need you to drive it home for me."

"You mean I actually get to *drive* this hot rod?" She slapped her hand to her heart in feigned shock, then she threw her arm around his neck. "So... how fast will this baby go?"

Mickey scowled at her. "Try to keep it under eighty, Mustang Sally."

They met Billy Joe and Allison at Pier 4 Seafood Restaurant on the causeway, where they had a gorgeous view from their table of the city's skyline and the moon on Mobile Bay. Their dinner was in honor of more than just graduation since Allison's birthday was May 11 and the girls would be in Troy then, so they were celebrating her birthday while they were all still together. When they ordered their food and Jeana declined anything but water to drink, Mickey asked her about it.

"Soft drinks are just empty calories," she said. "I don't need all that sugar."

Billy Joe nodded. "Yeah, I noticed you're getting kinda hefty." He frowned when Allison whacked him on the arm. "What? She's the one who brought it up."

"Don't pay him any attention, baby," Mickey whispered. "You look beautiful, and if you've gotten any bigger, it's in all the right places."

Jeana gave Billy Joe a murderous look and made a mental note to leave some food on her plate, even though she was starving. Mickey told them about the summer baseball team, and Billy Joe wanted to know if he'd still be able to help move the girls to Troy on Sunday.

"We're coming back after the last game on Saturday," Mickey said. "I hope it'll be the finals, but I still should be back by Sunday morning."

It was almost ten when the two couples said goodbye in the parking lot. Mickey had his bag with him and they had some time to kill before meeting the team, so he and Jeana drove to a spot off the causeway where fishermen launched their boats. They got their trusty quilt from the trunk and spread it on the ground, the only light coming from the Battleship U.S.S. Alabama docked in the bay nearby.

"I hope there won't be any girls traveling with this

team," Jeana said when she was lying in Mickey's arms.

"Don't be silly, Jeana," he said. "They'll be waiting for us in every city, not traveling with us."

She grabbed him roughly by the collar. "Don't make me have to follow you and yank out somebody's hair."

He pulled her tightly against him. "Don't make me have to whup-up on any college boys in Troy."

"Okay, it's a deal."

They laughed, and he wrapped his arms around her. "How am I gonna survive without being able to hold you like this every day?"

"You'll still be holding me in my dreams, Mickey."

He nuzzled her ear and whispered, "The first chance I get to come for a visit, I'm gonna make love to you all night long, just like our first time. I want to hear you say my name over and over and over…"

She gave a shuddery laugh. "Mmm, what a delicious image. I can't wait for you to love me again, Mickey."

She was telling the truth, it was just that she knew it would be a lot longer than he thought before they could be together. His leaving town had saved her this time, but there was no way he could see her in a couple of weeks and not know she was pregnant. She didn't know how she would do it, but she had to find some way to put him off.

When they got to Springdale Plaza, Mickey put his bag on the bus and came back to tell Jeana goodbye.

"I'll call you tomorrow night when we get back to the hotel after the last game," he said as he put his arms around her. "I love you, Jeana."

"I love you too, Mickey. Hit a homerun for me." She put her arms around his neck to kiss him and was startled by a ticklish fluttering in her stomach that made her utter an involuntary "Oh!"

Mickey's forehead creased. "What's wrong, Jeana?"

She froze a moment then felt it again. *Oh, God, that was the baby moving!* Tears rolled down her cheeks as she

150

looked into Mickey's eyes and longed to tell him what she'd felt.

"I'm just going to miss you, Mickey. Be careful and hurry home."

She sat in the car and waited for the bus to pull away, wondering if her tears were from anguish or happiness. She'd just felt her baby move for the first time. Until that moment, she had only thought of it as her unplanned pregnancy, but it was a *baby*—hers and Mickey's. The indisputable proof of a life inside her that she and Mickey had created with their love filled her with immense joy, and not being able to share it with him was excruciating.

"This is our baby, Mickey," she said as she waved at the departing bus with tears streaming down her face. "It's alive and moving, and I promise I'll take good care of it."

After she got home and was in her bed, she lay in the dark hoping to feel the fluttery movement again. That night and every night for the rest of her pregnancy, she went to sleep with her hand on her baby.

~ * ~

Mickey called late Friday night to tell Jeana they'd won their first two games. He played center field and went 3-for-4 and 1-for-2, the one hit in the second game the homerun she had requested. She had to smile at the excitement she heard in his voice when he told her he'd be pitching on Saturday. He loved baseball so much that she was almost jealous.

Darryl called on Saturday morning with the news that Katrina had just delivered an eight-pound, five-ounce baby girl.

"You should see her, Jeana." He sounded proud enough to bust. "She's almost as pretty as her mama."

Jeana told him she'd be down to see them later in the afternoon, then she spent the morning getting everything ready for transport to Troy the next day in her Volkswagen and Billy Joe's El Camino. Allison's car was already in

Troy because her parents had made a trip with some of her things a few days earlier and left it there. Jeana walked into Katrina's hospital room at three o'clock with a balloon bouquet and a dress for the baby.

"I went by the nursery to see her," Jeana said. "She's so beautiful."

"You won't get any argument from me on that." Katrina looked happy but exhausted.

"What are you naming her?" Jeana asked.

"Sheniqua LaKeesha Hudson." Katrina paused then laughed at Jeana's expression. "Girl, you're so gullible. We're naming her Valerie Annette after her two grandmamas."

"Very funny." Jeana rolled her eyes. "Where's the proud papa right now?"

Katrina's smile disappeared. "We had a big fight this morning because my uncle got him a job interview at Bender shipyard. Darryl says he doesn't want to work there, but that's the only job he could get right now that would pay enough for us to get married and get a place of our own." Her eyes filled with tears. "I thought he'd be happy about it, but he said it feels like everybody's deciding his whole life for him."

"He's probably just overwhelmed right now," Jeana said. "I could tell how happy he was about the baby when he called me. Don't worry, he'll come around."

"I don't care if he does or not." Katrina wiped the tears from her cheeks. "The way he's acting, he probably thinks I got pregnant just to trap him. I don't need him doing me any favors, and I told him so. That's when he got mad and left."

Jeana knew her friend too well to buy the callous act. "He'll be back. You know he loves you, don't you?"

Katrina sniffed and nodded. "Yeah, and I love him too, Jeana. That's why I don't want to force him into marriage and kill our chances of being happy down the road."

"I understand." Jeana squeezed her hand. "Believe me, I really do."

Darryl walked into the room just then, wearing a three-piece suit and a sheepish look.

"You think this'll be okay to wear for the interview?"

Katrina started to cry again, and Darryl sat on the side of the bed and put his arms around her. Jeana decided it was time to leave and didn't think the new parents would mind. In fact, she didn't think they'd even notice she was gone.

~ * ~

The Russells took their daughters to Godfather's Pizza in Saraland for the last night their family would all be together. When they got home, Billy Joe came over and sat on the porch with Jeana and Shelly.

"How did anybody else get any pizza with Jeana there?" he asked.

"Shut up, Billy Joe." Jeana had forced herself to stop at three slices and elbowed him sharply. "Haven't you figured out yet that a girl's weight isn't a subject to joke about?"

"I didn't say you looked *bad*," he said. "I always thought you were too skinny anyway. You're finally getting a few curves."

Shelly laughed. "Look who's calling somebody skinny."

He stood up to flex his chest and shoulder muscles. "I'll have you know I'm a lean, mean love machine. If I was any sexier, you'd both be at my mercy."

Jeana and Shelly looked at each other and busted out laughing.

"You're gonna make me wet my pants," Shelly said as she got up. "See you later, *stud*."

Billy Joe sat down in the swing again beside Jeana. "Any word from Mick?"

"They won their first two games and he was supposed to pitch today," she said. "I'm so glad he's playing with

153

this team. He needed something to keep him busy this summer so you won't get him in trouble cruising around in your hideous car." She jumped up and pulled on his hand. "Hey, let's go get a sundae!"

"Okay, but you have to ride in my hideous car, 'cause I ain't folding myself into that insect you drive."

"You don't have to," she said with a grin. "I have a Mustang."

They ate their sundaes in the parking lot at McDonald's. As Jeana took the last bite of hers, Billy Joe said, "Well, this is a first. I can't believe you didn't want me to finish yours for you."

"I just had a crav—" She looked at him with an uneasy smile. "I mean, I've just been dying for some ice cream lately." She fumbled in her purse for the keys and hoped she hadn't made him suspicious.

"Wait a second before we go." He took the keys from her and held her hand. "I wanna tell you something while we're alone." He didn't look at her and almost seemed embarrassed—a rarity for him.

"What is it, Billy Joe?"

He rubbed the back of her hand with his thumb. "I know I'm always teasing you about being a know-it-all, but I wanted to be sure you know that I'm really proud of you for being valedictorian. And just like you said in your speech, you *can* always depend on me no matter what."

"I know that, Billy Joe. I'm so lucky to have you."

"I'm gonna miss you like hell, Jeana. I've seen you every day for the last eighteen years, and it's gonna be so weird for you to be somewhere else." He looked up at her finally, and his sweet brown eyes were brimming with tears.

She put her hand on his cheek. "I'll miss you too."

"I know you love Mickey and you're gonna get married and all," he said, "but just this once… could you kiss me goodbye?"

154

She could see how hard it was for him to ask her, and also how much he was hoping she would say yes. So she pulled his face to hers and kissed him, and not just a kiss between friends. A *real* kiss. Just this once.

Chapter Twenty

Mickey called a little after nine Sunday morning. When Jeana went to pick him up, she wheeled into the parking lot at about thirty miles per hour and parked near the crowd milling around the bus. Mickey watched her get out with a look of surprise on his face and started to circle the Mustang.

"What are you doing, Mickey?" she said. "Get over here and kiss me!"

"After the way you cruised in here, I figured I'd better check for dents."

She put her hands on her hips. "I was just in a hurry to see you."

"In that case I'll forgive you." He dropped his bag and put his arms around her.

Mickey's coach, a stocky young man named Brett, walked up while they were kissing. "You think the other guys would play like you if a gorgeous redhead welcomed them home like that, Mickey?"

"I don't know," he replied, "but they'll have to find their own redhead because this one's all mine."

On the way home to Chickasaw, Mickey held Jeana's hand while he drove. "Don't you want to know if we won the tournament, baby?"

"They had you didn't they?" she said.

His dimples appeared. "You know, I'm really gonna hate it when you finally discover that I'm not the World's Greatest Athlete."

"That's never going to happen, Mickey. So did you win?"

"Yes, but we lost our first game yesterday and had to

156

play five straight to come back through the loser's bracket. The last game was over around midnight, and we won 2-0 with yours truly on the mound."

"I knew you made the difference for them. Did you like playing with this team?"

He nodded. "Yeah, the other guys are great, and everybody played hard. We should be able to win a lot of games this summer. And guess what Brett told me, baby."

"What?" She smiled at the little-boy-in-a-toy-store excitement on his face.

"Pro scouts come to these tournaments sometimes!"

Jeana was truly thrilled about that. "Oh, Mickey, that's wonderful! Someone is bound to notice you. Be sure to smile a lot."

He laughed and flicked her ear. "I don't want 'em to ask me out."

"Don't laugh at me, Mickey. You have to get their attention so they'll see how talented you are."

He dropped her off at her house and went home to take a shower before he went back to help with the move to Troy. Marsha hadn't left for church yet, so he told her about his games.

"We still need a few more players," he said. "Especially a second baseman. I'm gonna call Ty and see if he wants to play."

"I like it when you and Ty do things together," Marsha said. "Robin thinks you're a good influence on him. He's always been so girl crazy."

"I'm girl crazy too, Mom." Mickey kissed her cheek. "But only for one girl."

He called Ty before he got in the shower. Ty said it sounded like fun and he'd be there for practice on Monday.

"So you were gone all weekend, Mickey?"

"Yeah, we just got back this morning."

"Is everything still cool between you and Jeana?"

"Of course. Why would ask that?"

"I really wish I didn't have to tell you this, Cuz, but I saw something last night I think you should know about."

"What are you talking about, Ty?"

"I met this girl at your graduation—cute little cheerleader named Sissy. We went out last night."

"Great, I'm happy for you," Mickey said. "But why do I need to know about it?"

"That's not the thing. After I took her home last night, I passed by McDonald's in Chickasaw and saw your Mustang in the parking lot."

"So? Jeana had it while I was gone."

"Well, I thought it was you so I stopped to say hello to my favorite cousin and his beautiful girlfriend."

"If you upset her again, I swear I'm gonna kick your—"

"I didn't even talk to her!" Ty said. "I left before she saw me."

"Why?"

"Because she was in your car kissing some guy with curly hair."

Mickey laughed. "Let me guess, a blond afro?"

"You think it's funny?"

"It had to be Billy Joe. He's a good friend to both of us."

"So you let him go around kissing her? Man, if you're that generous with your friends, what will you let your cousin do?"

"Watch it, Ty. They don't usually kiss each other, but I'm sure it was innocent. I trust both of them."

"I don't know, Mickey. It looked like a pretty hot lip lock to me. I think you should keep an eye on this Billy Joe."

Standing in the shower with the hot water beating down on the back of his neck, Mickey couldn't help wondering about what Ty had seen. He did trust both of them, but now that he thought about it, Jeana had been acting funny ever since she'd decided to take her scholarship to Troy. And of course, he also knew Billy Joe had always loved Jeana too.

"Stop being ridiculous." Mickey turned to let the water hit him in the face and wash away any foolish doubts he had about the girl he loved and his best friend.

~ * ~

The foursome met later at Jeana's to get everything loaded before they left for Troy.

"We should make up some signals in case we need to stop for something," Jeana said as they were getting in the cars.

"Okay, pay attention," Billy Joe told her. "If I scratch my head and rub my nose, it means a bathroom stop. But if I touch my ear before I rub my nose, it means low fuel so we have to stop at a gas station. And if I blink twice after I touch my ear, it means I can't *believe* Jeana wants to eat again!"

He hid behind Mickey when she tried to punch him, so she punched Mickey instead. "What did I tell you about laughing at him?"

The Russells came out to say goodbye, then Billy Joe told everybody they needed to get on the road because he had to be at work by eleven for inventory. Jeana noticed the odd look on Mickey's face and asked him what was wrong when they got in the car.

"I didn't know Billy Joe had to work tonight," he said. "I thought we were gonna stay over."

"I wish you could, but it doesn't make sense to take three cars, Mickey."

He leaned his head back and closed his eyes. "It's like we're hexed or something. We'll never get to be together."

"Yes we will," she said. "We just have to remember how to be patient."

"It's a lot harder to be patient now that I know exactly what I'm having to wait for."

They stopped for lunch in Greenville, and Jeana got a Big Mac, a large order of fries, a vanilla shake, and a hot apple pie. Mickey gaped at her when she finished ordering.

"Where are you gonna put all that food, baby?"

"I probably won't eat it all." She traded looks with Allison. "We can eat the rest in the car later."

She ate everything except two bites of the apple pie that she grudgingly saved for Mickey. And although she used the restroom right before they left, she had to go again thirty minutes later and bought a bag of cookies at the 7-Eleven when they stopped.

They pulled up in front of the apartment just after three. Jeana and Allison gave the boys the grand tour: kitchen, living room, two bedrooms, and the bathroom that Jeana needed to use again. As soon as the cars were unloaded, Mickey motioned for Jeana to follow him to her bedroom.

"What's wrong, Mickey?"

He closed and locked the door, then he sat on the bed and pulled her to his lap. "We have about three hours before me and Billy Joe have to leave." He started to unbutton her shirt and she stopped him.

"No, Mickey. We can't."

"Why not, Jeana?"

"Billy Joe and Allison are in the next room. What would they think?"

He looked pained. "Oh, I don't know... maybe that we love each other?"

"I can't do it," she said, shaking her head. "Especially not with Billy Joe here."

"Gimme a break, Jeana." Mickey fell back on the bed and closed his eyes. "He's a big boy. He can handle it. And it's not like we'll have that many chances to be together anymore, you know."

She stood up and folded her arms. "Mickey Ray Royal, I can't believe you're acting this way after telling me no for two years!"

He opened one eye and peered at her. "I guess we finally made it to our traditional roles after all, huh?" He sat up and reached for her hand. "I'm sorry, baby. I'm suffering from Jeana withdrawal and it makes me act crazy."

"I forgive you." She kissed him then pulled him to his feet. "Come on. Allison and I need you to move some heavy stuff for us."

"I always knew you were only using me for my muscles." He followed her dolefully to the living room where he and Billy Joe spent the next hour arranging and rearranging the sparse furniture under the girls' direction.

"Okay, that's it," Billy Joe said finally, dropping to the couch. "This is exactly like we had it forty-five minutes ago. I'm not moving another thing."

"Okay," Allison said. "I guess we can leave it like this until the first time you visit."

"Trying to talk me out of coming back, huh?" Billy Joe pulled her down on the couch beside him.

"Hey, why don't we get a pizza before y'all leave?" Jeana suggested.

Billy Joe looked at her incredulously. "Do you have a tapeworm or something? A hollow leg maybe?"

"I'm hungry too," Allison said. "Come on, Billy Joe. Me and you can go get it."

Jeana eyed Mickey warily as soon as they were alone.

"Don't worry," he said. "I'm not even gonna ask. I know we wouldn't have enough time."

He set up her stereo for her and found a rock station on the radio. The honeyed tones of "Sukiyaki" floated out of the speakers, and he opened his arms to Jeana.

"This is a sad song," he said as they danced. "Promise you'll never take your love away from me."

She sighed. "Why do you say things like that, Mickey?"

"I'm just afraid you're gonna wake up one day and discover that you could have any guy you want, then you'll kick me to the curb."

"Don't be silly. You know you're the only guy I want."

161

His arms tightened around her. "I think my team has a weekend off in three weeks—that's the weekend of May thirtieth. Plan on spending it alone with me, because I can't go any longer without you."

An icy finger of fear poked her in the heart, but she said, "Okay, Mickey."

Billy Joe and Allison returned a few minutes later with two large pizzas. "I got one for Jeana by herself," Billy Joe said. "Maybe the rest of us will get at least one slice that way."

"That does it," Jeana said. "Mickey, beat him up."

"Why, baby?" he asked innocently. "Did you want two pizzas?"

She picked up one of the throw pillows and pummeled both boys with it. When all the pizza was gone, she put on her *Commodores Live* album, then she and Allison sat on the couch and laughed until tears ran down their cheeks while Billy Joe serenaded them with his lip-synced version of "Just to Be Close to You." Mickey accompanied him on air-guitar and contributed an occasional *Aw, baby* whenever Billy Joe gave him the cue. The girls agreed that Billy Joe made a believable Lionel Ritchie, but Mickey was a sad substitute for the rest of the group.

The boys left at seven with Jeana promising to call Mickey as soon as their phone was installed on Monday. She and Allison stood outside and waved until the El Camino was out of sight.

"I don't know why I ever thought this would work," Jeana said when they went back inside. "Mickey's coming back to Troy in three weeks. He'll know the truth as soon as he sees me."

Allison sat beside her on the couch. "Billy Joe's suspicious too. When we went to get the pizza, he asked me if I thought you really were gaining weight."

"Oh, great." Jeana leaned back her head and put her arm across her eyes. "I tried not to pig out in front of them,

162

but I stay hungry all the time. If I hadn't cut out soft drinks, I'd be as big as a house right now." She pulled up her shirt and displayed her little round belly.

Allison laughed. "Jeana, it's so *cute*."

"Oh, guess what. I felt the baby move Thursday night!"

"Can I feel it?"

"It's not big enough for anybody else to feel it yet." Jeana rubbed her stomach with a smile. "It's like someone's tickling me with a feather from the inside."

Allison sighed. "You should be sharing these things with Mickey."

Jeana's smile vanished, and her eyes filled with tears. "You don't know how hard it was not to tell him when I felt it Thursday."

"What are you gonna do when he comes back?"

"I don't know. I guess I'll worry about it when the time comes."

Allison put an arm around her shoulders. "Okay, Scarlett. We'll think about it tomorrow."

Chapter Twenty-one

The following Wednesday, the girls met with their advisors at Troy State to get their schedules. Allison had English on Monday mornings at nine, then she had basketball clinics in the afternoons every day except Friday. All Jeana's classes met on Tuesdays and Wednesdays: English, Child Psychology, and Issues Within Education Culture.

When Jeana left the campus, she found the public library and checked out two books on fetal development. After thoroughly scaring herself by reading the chapters on the complications of pregnancy, she called the Board of Health and got directions to the free clinic so a doctor could monitor her blood pressure, blood sugar, and the baby's growth.

Mickey called every night after eleven when the long-distance rates went down. His team was playing in Atlanta this weekend, so he didn't have to leave until Friday morning.

"I'm not sure I like you running around with Ty," Jeana said when Mickey called her on Thursday night. "Especially in strange cities with all those baseball groupies waiting to pounce on you."

"I won't let them catch me, baby," he said. "I sure do miss you at my games. It's no fun hitting homeruns without my Number One Fan there to kiss me for them."

"I'll pay up on the kisses later. You just keep hitting them for me, okay?"

"Yes, ma'am. Oh, and we do have the thirtieth open like I thought, so I'm definitely coming to see you." He lowered his voice and added, "All night long, Jeana.

Remember?"

"I remember, Mickey." She put a hand on her stomach. "I couldn't forget if I tried."

As the thirtieth approached, Jeana racked her brain for some excuse she could use to put Mickey off. If they made love like he planned, she didn't think he would believe she was just gaining weight because of stress or anything like that. The only possibility she came up with was faking an illness, and she wasn't even sure that would work. He was so determined to make love to her that he'd probably risk exposure to bubonic plague. She could just hear him— *What's a little Black Death gonna hurt? Kiss me, baby.*

At least he was playing well. He'd hit three homeruns and pitched a two-hitter when they played in Atlanta. Their next tournament was in Ft. Lauderdale, so the team had to leave on Thursday morning. Billy Joe called Allison Thursday afternoon and told her he was coming to Troy on Saturday.

Jeana wasn't worried about Billy Joe's visit. She should be able to easily hide her girth from him since he wouldn't be seeing her undressed and wasn't inclined to hug her all the time like Mickey. She had several oversized shirts that could be belted and bloused over to hide her belly, and she had a bulky robe to wear over her pajamas. She hadn't realized how homesick she was until she saw Billy Joe's beloved mop of hair framed in their doorway on Saturday afternoon when Allison answered the door.

"Somebody order stud services for the weekend?" he said when Allison opened the door.

"Yeah, but we'll cancel them since you're here." Allison laughed as Billy Joe swung her around and kissed her.

"Hey, Billy Joe!" Jeana said from the couch. She wanted to hug him herself, but she settled for pulling his face down to kiss his cheek.

"Hey, kiddo," he said. "Your folks sent a care package,

but I ate most of the cookies on the way."

"What a surprise." Jeana rolled her eyes.

The girls told him all about school—how much Allison liked her basketball coach and about Jeana's weird English professor whose right eye always seemed to be looking at the top of your head. Billy Joe confessed that he'd finally given in to his parents and put in an application at International Paper Company. He had an interview the following Tuesday and wasn't happy about it at all.

He and Allison were going out to eat and see a movie, but Jeana said she had a paper to write and declined to go with them. They still weren't home at eleven, so Jeana left a blanket and pillow on the couch for Billy Joe and went to her room. She was reading in bed when she felt a definite kick that startled her enough to make her jump.

"Oh my gosh! Do that again!" She pulled up her nightshirt to watch her belly and had almost given up when she felt another kick or punch—she wasn't quite sure which. She giggled and rubbed the spot where it had moved. "I see you, baby. I know you're in there."

She remembered an article in one of her pregnancy books that said experts believed reading to babies *in utero* aided in their developing intelligence. Her current reading selection was *The Dead Zone* by Stephen King, but she shrugged and began reading aloud. The baby might turn out to be possessed or something, but he'd know a good story when he heard one.

Jeana got so caught up in her reading that she didn't realize Allison and Billy Joe had returned until there was a knock on her door.

"I thought I heard you talking to someone," Allison said when she looked in.

"I was just reading aloud to the—" Jeana clamped a hand over her mouth.

Billy Joe's face appeared over Allison's shoulder. "Talking to your imaginary friend, Jeana? What was his name again?"

"Koo-Koo. I named him after you." She pulled the bedspread up to her chest. "Do you mind, Billy Joe? I'm in my pajamas here."

"Woo, *sexy*," he said with a whistle. "Is that Lamb Chop on your shirt?"

"Sorry, Jeana." Allison pushed him out of the doorway. "I'll try to keep him occupied so he won't bother you."

Jeana put her book away and turned off the light, hoping she hadn't made him more suspicious. She woke at three for her nightly trip to the bathroom and decided to tiptoe into the kitchen for a snack. When she came back to the living room with a glass of milk and her mother's chocolate chip cookies, Billy Joe was standing in front of her.

"Your belly keeping you awake, Jeana?"

She lowered her arms in a belated effort to hide her stomach, mentally kicking herself for not putting on her robe. "I figured I'd better eat these before you polish off the rest of them."

"You lied to me."

"What are you—"

"You told me you used protection."

Jeana sighed and didn't even bother to deny it. "We did, except for the first time. Rotten luck, huh?"

He walked away and sat on the couch in the dark. She put her milk and cookies on the table and followed him.

"You can't tell Mickey. You have to promise me, Billy Joe. I'll make you a million batches of cookies if you want, but you have to promise to keep this secret for me."

"Like hell I will! You can't keep this from him. Are you crazy?"

She told him about Mickey's promise to his dad that he'd make it to the majors if his dad quit drinking, but Billy Joe was unmoved.

"Do you want him to end up hating me?" she said.

167

"Because that's what'll happen if he quits school and never gets the chance to play baseball."

"I'm not buying that crap, Jeana. You can't keep this a secret from him. He has the right to know."

She covered her face and started to cry, but he pulled her hands away.

"That's not gonna work on me this time. You've been lying to everyone who loves you, and it's gotta stop!"

"You'd help me if you really cared about me!"

"Help you lie to my best friend?"

"You're supposed to be *my* best friend."

"Too damn bad! Mickey would never forgive me for lying to him about this. I'm telling him as soon as he gets back from Florida."

She stood up and pushed his shoulders. "And I'm supposed to believe you love me? Don't ever speak to me again!" She fled to her room and cried into her pillow until she fell asleep.

He was gone when she got up in the morning. Allison said he'd told her about the argument and had gone home to wait for Mickey.

"I tried to talk him out of it, Jeana, but he wouldn't listen to me either."

"Thanks for trying. At least I have one loyal friend."

She moped around the apartment all day, watching the clock speed toward the hour when Mickey would call and tell her he knew the truth. The phone rang at nine-forty, and Allison handed it to Jeana with a sympathetic look.

"Hey, baby," Mickey said when she answered. "I miss you so much."

He doesn't know! "Did you... just get home, Mickey?"

"About an hour ago," he said. "I've been talking to Billy Joe. It was funny, he was waiting in the parking lot when the bus pulled up. He said he was out that way and decided to wait for me."

"Did he... tell you he was here yesterday?"

"Yeah, he did. Listen, baby, I've got some big news. The weekend after next we play in Tampa at Legends Field where the Tampa Yankees play. They're one of the minor-league teams for the New York Yankees."

"That's great, Mickey," Jeana murmured, still wondering what in the world could've changed Billy Joe's mind.

"It's a big charity tournament the Yankees sponsor every year, and Brett said their scouts come to the games. He knows a guy who got a contract offer last year."

The implication of what Mickey was saying finally registered with her. "A contract to play for the Yankees?"

"Yeah, that's what I was talking to Billy Joe about."

"Oh."

"You sound kinda funny, Jeana. Are you mad because I didn't call you right away?"

"No, I'm not mad." Her mind was still processing what this tournament could mean for Mickey. "Did you play well in Ft. Lauderdale?"

"Yeah, I hit .450 for the tournament with two homeruns, and I pitched a shutout." When she didn't respond, he said, "Are you still there, baby?"

"I'm here. That's good, Mickey."

"Well, you don't sound too impressed, but I guess you can save all your enthusiasm for next weekend when I come to see you."

Oh, God. She couldn't let him find out about the baby now that he was so close to keeping his promise to his dad. Her mind searched frantically for some way to stop him from coming.

"About next weekend, Mickey. We have a problem."

"What do you mean? What kind of problem?"

Her gaze fell on one of her textbooks by the phone and she got an idea. "I have to go to a seminar in Montgomery with my Child Psychology professor."

"When did that come up?" His voice had an edge to it.

"You didn't say anything about it when I called you Wednesday night."

"My professor just told me about it on Friday. He gets to bring two students with him and picked me as one of them."

After a few seconds of tense silence, Mickey said, "I don't want you to go, Jeana."

"I have to, Mickey. This will help me a lot in my education classes. I was lucky to be picked and don't want to disappoint him."

"But you don't care if I'm disappointed?"

"Of course I do. When is the next weekend you have open?"

"Not until the Fourth of July. I can't believe you'd do this to me, Jeana."

"Don't be so selfish, Mickey." She winced as she said it. "Did I complain when you left after graduation to go play baseball?"

"No. In fact, it didn't seem to bother you much at all."

"I guess that's because I can keep things in perspective better than you."

"Perspective?" His voice had an edge to it.

"Yes, Mickey. We can't ignore our responsibilities just because we want to have fun, you know."

"Well, I guess the reason I don't have any trouble with *perspective* is because you always come first no matter what." Anger was clearly audible in his voice now. "I don't know where I rank with you anymore. Somewhere after college obviously."

"I don't think I want to talk to you anymore, Mickey. Call me back when you can be reasonable." She hung up with tears coursing down her cheeks.

"What were you talking about, Jeana?" Allison asked. "You're not going to any seminar."

"I had to say something to keep him from coming next weekend," Jeana said. "He's playing in Tampa in two weeks and *Yankee* scouts will be there. He can't miss a chance like that! And he wouldn't go if he found out about the baby. I just know it."

"Billy Joe didn't tell him?"

Jeana shook her head and looked baffled. "I guess not, but I don't know why. That's another reason I had to lie to Mickey. It's a miracle Billy Joe didn't tell him, so I can't waste it by letting him come and find out for himself."

"But how are you gonna keep Mickey from coming another weekend?" Allison asked. "Or what if he decides to come during the week?"

Jeana sat on the couch and covered her face with her hands. The thing she'd been telling herself would never be necessary had finally reared its ugly head, and she couldn't avoid it any longer.

"I have to break up with him, Allison."

"*Jeana!* You can't hurt Mickey like that."

"I don't have a choice. He'll be hurt a lot more in the long run if I don't."

Chapter Twenty-two

When Mickey called back an hour later, Allison told him that Jeana had left without saying where she was going, and they left the phone off the hook the rest of the night. In the morning after Allison left for her English class, Jeana got dressed to go to the library and hung up the phone just before she went out the door. It rang almost immediately. She stared at it a few seconds before she sighed and picked it up.

"Where were you last night!" Mickey demanded.

She gripped the receiver so tightly that it hurt her hand. "I had to go make travel arrangements with the other student who's going to the seminar, so we met for coffee."

"What other student? And you don't drink coffee!"

"His name is... Anthony. And I like coffee now."

There was barely controlled fury in Mickey's voice when he spoke again. "Why was the phone busy all night?"

"We didn't know it was off the hook until this morning. I don't have time to stand here and be grilled like this, Mickey. I have to go."

"Where are you going?"

"I don't have to clear my schedule with you." She was amazed that she could sound so hard-bitten with him. "I'm a big girl and I make my own decisions. I'll talk to you later."

She hurried out the door but still heard the phone when it rang again right away. She cried all the way to the library and spent the morning trying to escape into the world of *Little Women,* something she'd been doing to comfort herself ever since she was ten years old.

On her way home, she stopped at Piggly Wiggly and

bought ice cream and chocolate syrup, chocolate chip cookie dough, a giant bag of potato chips, and a two-liter bottle of Pepsi—the first one she'd had in months, and she couldn't wait to drink it. Allison wouldn't be home until after four, so Jeana planned to take the phone off the hook, eat until she was stuffed, then curl up in her bed to sleep. But when she pulled into the apartment complex, the unmistakable flames on Billy Joe's El Camino greeted her.

She parked and sat staring straight ahead. While she was trying to muster the courage to face him, her passenger door opened and he got in, but she still couldn't look at him.

"So if I help you," he said, taking her hand, "will you let me name the little rugrat?"

She burst into tears, and he pulled her over into his arms.

"Dry it up, kiddo. I'm on to you. I know that stuff you said at graduation about always being able to count on me was just an evil plot to make me feel guilty."

She nodded against his chest. "I knew it would get to you."

He put his cheek on the top of her head and closed his eyes. "Don't *ever* doubt that I love you. Do you hear me, Jeana?"

"I won't, Billy Joe." She looked up at him tearfully. "I'm sorry for what I said."

He kissed her on the forehead then let her go. "C'mon, let's get your groceries in the house. If my guess is right, you've got ice cream and a bunch of junk food in there. Besides, you need to get started on those million cookies you promised me."

She flashed a big grin. "I've got chocolate chip for the first batch."

They put the food away then sat on the couch together so Billy Joe could explain why he'd changed his mind about telling Mickey.

"I listened to Mick talking about the possibility of getting to play for any part of the Yankees' organization and how he'd give anything if his dad could be here to see it, and I knew you were right, Jeana. He'll always regret it if he gives it up now."

She hugged him again. "You're such a good friend to both of us, Billy Joe. I don't mind sharing you with Mickey."

"Listen, Jeana. I saw him this morning before I left and he said he's coming to Troy as soon as he gets through with practice today. What are you gonna do?"

"I'll just have to stay away from the apartment until he leaves." She started to pop her knuckles and he smacked her hand.

"Quit that. And you know Mick won't leave until he sees you. How did you think you could keep him away all summer anyway?"

She looked at the floor and swallowed before answering. "I have to break up with him, Billy Joe. I don't have any other choice."

He didn't sound nearly as shocked as Allison had been. "What the hell are you gonna give him for a reason?"

"Did he tell you what I told him this morning?"

"You mean about the seminar thing and the guy he's gonna flatten when he gets here?"

She had to laugh. "Yes, the imaginary guy going with me to the nonexistent seminar. He's going to be the reason."

"Get real, Jeana. You think you can look into those blue eyes of his and tell him you love somebody else?"

She put her head on his shoulder. "I know it's crazy, but it's all I can think of."

He put his arm around her and they sat that way without talking for several minutes. Then he met her gaze in the mirror on the wall across the room.

"You know, I did a sketch of us sitting this way a long

time ago," he said. "I never showed it to you because I felt guilty for trying to steal you from Wade while he was gone to that football camp the summer before the sixth grade. Some friend I was to him, huh?"

She sat up and turned to look at him. "Why are you telling me this now?"

"Because it gives me an idea," he said with a long sigh. "I sure as hell don't wanna do it, but I can't think of anything else Mickey would believe."

"What, Billy Joe?"

"Tell him..." He sighed again. "Tell him you finally realized that you love *me*."

She knew he was right. Billy Joe was the only person in the world that Mickey would possibly believe she could love instead of him. But she couldn't believe Billy Joe was willing to do it for her.

"Thank you for offering," she said, "but we can't ask Allison to go along with that."

"I'll talk to her first, but I think she'll do it. She's the greatest." He put his arm around Jeana again. "And it'll give me the chance to at least be a better friend to Mickey than I was to Wade."

She kissed his cheek. "Mickey just might believe that I love you, because it's not a lie." She jumped when she felt a sharp kick and got a quizzical look from Billy Joe in response, so she put his hand on her stomach and he felt it a few seconds later.

"Oh, man, that's *amazing*." He covered her stomach with both hands and had to wait over a minute, but the next one was harder than the first and made him let out a whoop. "He's a kicker like his Uncle Billy Joe!"

Jeana put the cookies in the oven, then she made ice cream floats for them to eat while they figured out exactly what to tell Mickey. They decided not to bring Billy Joe into the picture until after Mickey came back from Tampa, since they wouldn't be able to find out if any of the scouts had talked to him at the tournament if he wasn't speaking to either of them when he got back. When Mickey got to Troy that night, Jeana would tell him that he was being too possessive and they needed a break from each other. It wouldn't keep him away for long, but if it kept him from coming back to Troy until after he played in Tampa, then she would tell him that she loved Billy Joe.

"You'd better change clothes before he gets here." Billy Joe eyed the too-snug denim jumper she had on. "I was already suspicious, but I couldn't really tell how fat you are until I saw you in your pajamas."

She scraped the last bit of ice cream from her glass before she punched him. "This isn't fat, Billy Joe. It's *baby*."

"Yeah, whatever you say, fatso. Anyway, if you wear one of those big ugly shirts like you had on when I got here Saturday, Mickey shouldn't be able to tell."

"Okay." She set her glass on the table and put her arms around his neck. "I'd never make it through this without you, Billy Joe. I don't know how I'll ever thank you."

"I already told you. Let me name him. Oh, and the million cookies of course."

"What makes you so sure it's a boy?"

"Girls don't dropkick like what I felt. C'mon, Jeana. Can I pick his name?"

She sighed. "How can I tell you no when I owe you so much?"

"Promise?"

"I promise." She arched her eyebrow. "What did you have in mind?"

"Hmm…" He fingered his chin. "Either Jethro or Zeppelin, although I'm also partial to Boris."

She rolled her eyes. "Keep thinking."

Allison was surprised but happy to see Billy Joe when she got home. They sat on the couch together and he held her hands while he told her the plan he and Jeana had devised.

"For real, Al," he said. "If it bothers you too much, we'll think of something else."

She shook her head. "Like what? This is the only thing Mickey would possibly believe. And I'm sure he wouldn't want anybody at home to know about it, so I can handle it if you and Jeana can."

He tilted up her face to kiss her. "I told Jeana you were the greatest."

The girls made hamburgers for supper while Billy Joe watched *Wheel of Fortune* and made fun of the contestants.

"Don't buy another vowel, you moron!" he shouted at the TV. "There's only two letters missing! It's *potato salad.* POTATO SALAD!"

Allison and Billy Joe left after supper so Mickey wouldn't wonder why Billy Joe was there. Jeana tried to read *Little Women* while she waited, but when she heard the Mustang pull up at eight forty-five, she felt a giant hand squeezing her heart. She checked her shirt to make sure it was bloused over enough, then she took a deep breath and said a quick prayer before she opened the door: *Lord, give me the strength to get through this and I promise I'll never tell another lie for the rest of my life.*

She opened the door and remembered seeing him framed in her doorway the first time he came over to see her when they were sixteen. Neither of them was smiling this time.

"What are you doing here, Mickey?"

"You can't hang up on me in person." He came in and walked past her. But when she turned around after closing the door, he tried to pull her into his arms.

"Don't, Mickey." She forced herself to push him away. "We can talk if you want to, but that's all."

She sat on one end of the couch and turned away from him when he sat beside her.

"What's going on, Jeana?" he said, his voice full of fear

and confusion. "Why don't you want me to touch you?"

"Why are you here, Mickey?"

"Why do you *think?*" he asked incredulously. "You desert me next weekend to run off somewhere with another guy and you go out late at night to meet him, then you tell me it's none of my business what you do? How do you expect me to feel?"

"I haven't done anything wrong, Mickey." She was careful not to look at him. "I'm sorry you're disappointed, but my career is important to me."

"I thought I was important to you!"

"And I guess we both know why this weekend was so important to *you*, don't we?"

"What is that supposed to mean?"

"You know exactly what I mean, Mickey. That's all I've heard from you ever since I told you I was taking my scholarship—how you can't go any longer without making love again and how much you need it." She turned away from him even more. "I don't think you wanted to see me this weekend nearly as much as you wanted to sleep with me!"

"How can you say that, Jeana? Look at me!" He tried to turn her around, but she got up and moved to the chair.

"Here I am struggling to focus on the goals I've had for a long time, and you want me to feel guilty for trying to do the right thing."

"No, baby—"

"Don't call me that, Mickey. I'm not a baby."

He stared at her in disbelief. "What in God's name has happened to you, Jeana?"

"Funny you should say that, Mickey. God is the one who gave me the gifts I have, so the least I can do is make the most of them. If you can't support me in that..." She hesitated, because her next words were the ones that would hurt him the most. "...then I don't think we should see each other the rest of the summer."

She had sense enough not to look at him, but he sounded exactly the way she knew he looked—like he'd just taken a bullet to the heart.

"You don't love me anymore, Jeana?"

"I didn't say that, Mickey." She fought to steady her own voice. "I said I don't want to see you if you're going to pressure me. I think a break would do us good and would keep us from making mistakes we can't fix later on."

He knelt in front of her and grabbed her hand. "Please don't do this, Jeana! I love you... you *know* how much I love you." Tears spilled over onto his cheeks. "You told me I'd always have you. You *promised* me I wouldn't lose you!"

She pulled her hand from his and kept her face averted. "I'm sorry, Mickey."

He hung his head with his fingers clutching his hair, his sobs making her want to die for hurting him so much. She looked at him and felt like someone had hit her in the chest with a sledgehammer. Her hand moved instinctively to comfort him, but just before she touched his head, the baby kicked and made her stop.

This was for Mickey's own good. Did she want to see him breaking his back at some horrible job for the rest of his life because of her? With a Herculean effort she would never have believed she had in her, she left him there crying and ran to her bedroom.

Mickey rose to follow her, and as he wiped the tears from his eyes, he saw a pair of aviator sunglasses on the table and recognized them as the ones Billy Joe had been wearing that morning when he'd talked to him.

Billy Joe was in Troy.

Mickey stared at the glasses a few seconds, then he went to Jeana's bedroom door and found it locked. "Jeana, please let me in."

"I'm not going to change my mind, Mickey."

He pounded on the door. "I'm not leaving until you

come out and talk to me!"

She knew he meant it, so she wiped her eyes and opened the door. "You need to go, Mickey. There's nothing else to say."

He grabbed her by the shoulders. "What happened to make you act like this, Jeana? There's something you're not telling me."

"I told you everything you need to know. We need to concentrate on something besides each other for a while."

"I don't care about anything but you!"

She pulled away and walked to the living room. "That's exactly what I'm talking about. We're not sixteen anymore, Mickey. We have to be realistic about things."

"I don't believe all this is just because I asked you not to go to that seminar." His hands were white-knuckled fists. "Call this Anthony guy and tell him to get over here! I wanna have a little talk with him!"

"Don't be ridiculous, Mickey. He doesn't have anything to do with this."

"Then tell me what changed!"

She flinched but continued to stare out the window. Mickey came over to stand beside her and took her hand.

"I'm sorry I yelled at you, Jeana. I promise I won't interfere with your classes anymore, just please don't tell me I can't see you."

"That's how it has to be for now. Please respect me enough to listen." She withdrew her hand and went to open the door. "Go home, Mickey. And don't come back until I ask you to."

He stood in front of her and held her face in his hands. She couldn't stop her tears, but she kept her eyes closed in defense.

"Why can't you look at me, Jeana? You know this is wrong, don't you?"

She took his hands from her face and turned to look out the door.

"Goodbye, Mickey. Be careful going home."

He pulled her into his arms and kissed her, but she wouldn't return the kiss, her arms hanging at her sides as lifelessly as a doll's.

"Okay, I'll leave," he said when he let her go. "But I won't give up no matter what you tell me. We're meant for each other, and *nothing* can change that. I'll never stop loving you."

She didn't respond, so he walked out the door and she closed it behind him.

Ten minutes later, still sobbing against the door with her heart in fragments, Jeana heard the Mustang roar to life and listened as the person she loved most in the world drove away.

Chapter Twenty-three

Mickey drove around Troy in a daze for the next half hour, trying desperately to understand how his world could have fallen apart in a matter of minutes. How was he supposed to live without Jeana when she was everything he lived for?

He eventually had to stop for gas, and when he got back in the car, he looked at the passenger seat and remembered the countless times Jeana had sat there beside him. Tears blurred his vision again, and he threw the Mustang into gear then tore down the road back to her apartment to make her talk to him. But when he pulled into the parking lot and his headlights reflected off the metallic yellow flames on the side of the El Camino, he hit the brakes. Why was Billy Joe there?

After what Ty had told him about seeing Jeana kissing Billy Joe, Mickey couldn't help wondering if it had something to do with the way she was acting. And now that he thought about it, Billy Joe had been acting strange the night before, as if there was something he wanted to say but didn't know how. Mickey's determination to make Jeana change her mind dissolved into a terrible feeling of suspicion and dread. To tell the truth, he was afraid of what she might say if he went back.

It was after two o'clock when he finally got home. Marsha called out to him when he came in, but he went in his room without answering and sat on his bed—the same bed where he'd made love to Jeana and she'd told him he was her whole world. Mickey hung his head and cried.

Marsha knocked and when he didn't say anything, she opened the door and looked in. "Mickey, what's wrong?

Why are you sitting in the dark?"

"Don't turn on the light, Mom." Mickey's voice was choked with tears.

She went in the room and sat beside him on the bed. "What's the matter, baby?"

"Jeana made me leave."

"Why? Did you have a fight?"

"She doesn't want to see me anymore."

Marsha put her arm around his shoulders. "If she's mad about something, I'm sure she'll get over it."

He shook his head. "She told me not to come back. She wouldn't even look at me."

"Oh, Mickey." Marsha pulled his head to her chest and comforted him the way she had when he was little. "I don't know what's wrong, but I know Jeana loves you. Try to have faith, okay?"

"What if she loves somebody else?"

"That will never happen, Mickey. I don't believe it, and you shouldn't either."

She stayed with him until his tears stopped, then she kissed him and left him curled up on his bed.

~ * ~

Allison and Billy Joe came home to find Jeana also curled up in bed, crying and holding her baby. They tried to talk to her, but she only shook her head. When she still wouldn't talk to them an hour later, Billy Joe told Allison he was calling Mickey if she didn't come out soon. Allison agreed, but ten minutes later Jeana came out of her room and sat in the chair, looking at them with eyes so swollen from crying that her vision was impaired.

"Please tell me I'm doing the right thing," she said. "Tell me that Mickey will believe I only did this because I love him so much and that he won't hate me for hurting him."

"I know Mickey will forgive you," Allison said.

"That was the hardest thing I've ever had to do," Jeana

said. "To say things I knew would hurt him and watch as his heart crumbled. I don't know how I did it." She started to cry again, and Billy Joe went to pull her up from the chair and hug her.

"You did it because you love him." He rubbed the back of her head, then he held her away from him and grinned. "Hey, I thought of another name. Wanna hear it?"

She shook her head. "No, it will probably just depress me more."

"Don't say that, Jeana." He sat her down on the couch beside Allison. "What do you think of *Butkus?* Mickey will love having a kid named after the greatest middle linebacker ever."

"I hate it," she said with a weak laugh. "And besides, Mickey is the greatest middle linebacker ever."

Before long Billy Joe had them all laughing at his stories about working at Delchamps—the old folks who got hostile if the cream of chicken soup got mixed in with the cream of mushroom, and the little old lady who came in every Saturday morning at ten o'clock sharp and asked him which aisle the bouillon cubes were on, claiming she'd never shopped there before.

Around midnight, Jeana noticed the time and punched Billy Joe in the arm. "Did you forget about your interview at IP tomorrow?"

He looked at Allison and grinned. "Screw IP! I decided to give in to the *artiste* in my soul and make my living that way."

Jeana looked confused. "You're going to become a street artist for tips?"

Allison laughed. "I took him to the Fine Arts building at Troy tonight and got him to look at some of the catalogs." She held Billy Joe's hand with a proud smile. "He's gonna stay with us and take art classes."

Jeana's face lit up. "That's wonderful, Billy Joe! But how are you going to pay for them?"

"The Fine Arts bulletin board had ads for jobs and stuff," he replied. "There was one for a graphic artist apprentice that I'm gonna call about tomorrow. And I can get a student loan too, I guess."

Jeana threw her arms around him. "I'm so proud of you for having the guts to do this."

"Yeah, now I just gotta find the guts to tell my folks."

At the mention of his parents, Jeana realized she needed to call hers and tell them about Mickey. She definitely didn't want them to run into him and find out that way. The three of them went to bed at one-thirty, and Jeana woke up promptly at three for a bathroom run. She stopped at the couch on her way back to bed and looked fondly at Billy Joe's sleeping figure, and she said a silent prayer of thanks to God for giving her the most wonderful guys in the world to love her.

She couldn't get back to sleep, so she read *Little Women* awhile and the part about Jo's journal made her decide to start one for Mickey. She'd write in it daily and tell him all the things she wished he was sharing with her about their baby, and she'd tell him on every page how much she loved him. Tears blurred the date at the top of the first entry.

Dear Mickey ~

I broke both our hearts today. Please forgive me, and please believe that I love you even more than I knew was possible.

Let me tell you about our baby...

~ * ~

She called home after breakfast the next morning. Her

185

mother was shocked to hear the news of the breakup and wanted an explanation, but all Jeana would say was that things had gotten too intense and that she and Mickey just needed a break from each other.

Billy Joe got the apprentice job and was supposed to start the following Monday, so he went home on Tuesday afternoon to pack and tell his parents. The DuBoses took it fairly well, until Billy Joe told them he would be staying with Jeana and Allison.

"It's only temporary," he told his mother to calm her down. "I'll look for a place to share with another guy as soon as I get some money saved."

"But what will Allison's parents say?" Mrs. DuBose asked. "Especially that *mother* of hers."

"We're not gonna tell 'em, Ma," Billy Joe said. "If they knew I was staying there, they'd probably have Allison shot with a tranquilizer gun and ship her off to a convent." He paused and looked pensive a moment. "What's the Southern Baptist equivalent of a convent? The Ladies' Auxiliary?"

Wednesday morning he was all packed and ready to go, so he knew he couldn't put off talking to Mickey any longer.

"Hey, you gonna be home for a little while, Mick?" he said when he called.

"Why?" Mickey's voice sounded hoarse and tired, as though he hadn't been sleeping.

"I need to talk to you about something."

"I don't feel like any company."

"I'm real sorry about you and Jeana, buddy."

There was a pause, then Mickey said, "How'd you hear about it?"

"I called Allison Monday night and she told me."

When Mickey spoke again, every word was tinged with anger. "Does she know about you and Jeana, or have you been lying to her too?"

"What are you talking about, Mick?"

"I know you were in Troy Monday night! I saw your car when I went back to Jeana's."

It was what he and Jeana had planned to tell him, but not yet. And Billy Joe hadn't prepared himself for it yet either. After a guilty silence, he said, "I did go to Troy, but there's nothing going on between me and Jeana. Where'd you get a crazy idea like that?"

"Kissed anybody at McDonald's lately?"

That caught him completely off guard.

"I don't know who told you about that, Mickey, but it was nothing. Really."

"Sure," he said. "How about you keep your lips and everything else off of Jeana! She's still mine, even if she won't let me see her right now."

"Mickey—"

"And don't come anywhere around me! I don't wanna see you or talk to you!"

Billy Joe stared at the dead receiver in his hand, his breath catching in his throat.

"At least Jeana won't have any trouble getting him to believe what she tells him." He hung up the phone and his shoulders sagged. "And then he'll really hate me."

Chapter Twenty-four

Marsha was worried about Mickey.

Ever since the night he came back from Troy, he'd been staying in his room most of the time and barely spoke when he did come out. He wasn't eating and looked as if he wasn't sleeping either. The only time he left the house was for baseball practice, and for the past three nights he hadn't come home when practice was over. Marsha found his bed empty when she got up in the middle of the night, but he'd been asleep in it the next morning. When she asked him where he'd been, all he'd say was, "Fighting ghosts."

He began staying out every night until two or three o'clock, and all Marsha's attempts to question him were fruitless. It was the same scenario she'd faced when Stephen began drinking after the knee injury that ended his baseball career. Marsha was terrified that Mickey had strayed down the same path as his father. After it had been going on every night for a week, she decided to wait up for him and find out the truth.

"Sit down, Mickey," she said when he came in the door at three-thirty. "I want to talk to you."

He dropped his bag and sat on the couch beside her, staring at the floor. "About what, Mom?"

"Let me see your eyes."

He raised his head, and the intense blue of his eyes looked dull to her, as if some kind of gossamer fabric covered them. The whites were streaked and bloodshot. She didn't smell alcohol on him, but she knew from experience that you couldn't always go by that.

"Have you been drinking, Mickey?"

He laughed humorlessly. "You know I don't drink,

188

Mom."

He had never lied to her before, but Stephen had never lied either until he started drinking. Marsha faced her son with folded arms, determined to get the truth.

"Then tell me where you've been, and don't give me any more cryptic answers about ghosts."

He stared at the floor again. "I was playing baseball."

"In the middle of the night? You expect me to believe that?"

"You can believe it or not. I don't care. I don't care about anything anymore."

"Don't talk to me like that, Mickey Ray. I want the truth."

"I told you the truth!" He snatched up his bag and went to his room, slamming the door behind him.

Marsha tossed and turned in her bed for hours, frustrated because she wanted to help her son but didn't know how. She'd thought her battle with Valium had ended two years earlier, but this was a huge test of her self control. The memory of the blissful sleep the pills had always brought was dangerously tempting, and she was glad there were no drugs in the house.

With a bitter sigh, she thought about how it was no wonder if Mickey had succumbed to drinking. The poor boy had inherited a legacy of addiction from both of his parents.

~ * ~

Billy Joe enrolled in two art classes at Troy State that met on Tuesday and Thursday nights. He liked his new boss and would've been happy if he hadn't felt certain that Mickey hated him. When he told Jeana that Mickey thought they'd betrayed him and why, she took it as a possibility that she wouldn't have to lie to him about it herself, but she was wrong. Mickey called her the day he left for Tampa.

"I know you don't want to talk to me," he said, "but I have to know if it's true about you and Billy Joe. I have to hear it from you."

With her heart in her throat, she said, "It's true."

She had never heard such utter despair as she did in Mickey's next words.

"Why, Jeana?"

"I love him, Mickey."

His ragged breathing was audible, and she could tell he was crying. "This is why you wouldn't let me make love to you for the last month, isn't it? You wanted him instead of me."

"No, Mickey." She pressed her hand to her heart, hoping it might lessen the pain. "I didn't know how I felt about him until now."

"What about Allison?"

"We didn't plan any of this. She understands."

"I guess you think I should understand too, huh? Well, you can forget it because I *don't!* I'll never understand how you could tell me so many times that you loved me and you'd always belong to me, and then just change your mind!"

"I'm sorry…"

"Did you ever love me, Jeana? Or were you lying to me all along?"

"I meant everything I've ever told you when I said it."

"Then tell me what I did to make you stop!"

"Please don't do this, Mickey. It doesn't change anything and just hurts both of us."

He didn't say anything for a few seconds, and she knew he was fighting for control.

"Okay," he said finally. "I'll leave you alone if you can tell me you're sure you don't love me anymore."

That was one thing Jeana would *never* say.

"I already told you, Mickey. I love Billy Joe."

"That's not the same thing, Jeana. Tell me you don't love me."

"I love Billy Joe. That's all I need to say!"

"You can't do it, can you?" His voice was suddenly infused with hope. "You can't say you don't love me."

"I have to go—"

"Oh, God… you *do* still love me. Maybe you think you love Billy Joe right now, but you loved me first, Jeana. And a love like ours only comes *once* in a lifetime."

"I'm hanging up now, Mickey."

"You're *mine*, Jeana! You told me that the first time I kissed you because you felt it in your heart, the same as me. Billy Joe can't love you like I do—*nobody* can love you like me, because it's why I was put on the Earth. I don't know why you're confused right now, but when you wake up and see what a mistake this is, I'll be right here waiting for you to come back to me where you belong!"

She hung up the phone and fell to her knees, sobbing into her hands. When it rang again a moment later, she picked it up and shouted, "Don't do this to me!"

"Jeana Lee Russell, what in the world is going on?"

"Mama?" Jeana struggled to speak normally.

"Of course it's me. What were you talking about when you answered the phone?"

Jeana tried to lighten her voice. "Oh... I thought you were Billy Joe. He keeps calling and asking for people like I.P. Freely and Ivana Kissya."

Betty sighed. "Well, that's no way to answer the telephone. What if it had been someone you needed to make a good impression on?"

"Sorry, Mama."

"I called because I want you to come home this weekend, Jeana. We're having a special dinner for your daddy's birthday Saturday night, and I want you to be here. Billy Joe and Allison are welcome to come too."

"I can't, Mama. I have too much homework."

"I don't want to hear that, Jeana Lee. This is your daddy's fiftieth birthday, so he's already feeling down. He'll be heartbroken if you're not here and I won't have it.

Be here by four o'clock on Saturday and that's final."

Jeana knew better than to argue when her mother sounded like that. When she hung up the phone, she surveyed her protruding stomach in dismay. She looked like she was concealing a large cantaloupe under her shirt. The image of herself being detained in a grocery store for shoplifting melons flashed into her mind, and she found herself laughing in spite of the ache in her heart from Mickey's words.

She told Allison and Billy Joe about both phone calls while the three of them made tacos for supper. "How am I going to hide the little honeydew from them?" When they only stared at her in confusion, she said, "The baby. How am I going to hide it from my family?"

Billy Joe stopped shredding cheese and looked thoughtful. "They haven't seen you in almost a month, right?"

Jeana nodded. "Yes, so they're even more likely to notice the change."

"And they know you split up with Mickey and you're probably depressed about it?"

"Is there a point somewhere in all this, Billy Joe?"

He pinched some cheese between his fingers and popped it into her mouth. "Let 'em think you've been drowning your sorrows in junk food and it made you gain weight. Wear four or five shirts on top of each other so you'll look thick all over and not just in your stomach."

"It might work, Jeana," Allison said. "Especially when they see how much you eat." That cracked up Billy Joe so she added, "Sorry, but it's the truth."

Jeana went to her room after supper to see if Billy Joe's idea would look believable. She put on five T-shirts, tucking all but the last one into a pair of Billy Joe's sweat pants.

"It's hot and uncomfortable," she said when she went back to the living room. "But I do look chunky all over this way."

Billy Joe snickered. "If Mick saw you like that, he might've saved you the trouble of breaking up with him."

~ * ~

Betty was heartbroken when Jeana told her about breaking up with Mickey. She and Robert both loved him like a son and had been praying for a reunion. Betty was a firm believer in the power of prayer, but she decided that the Lord wouldn't mind getting a little help this time from a couple of concerned mothers. She called Marsha Friday morning to tell her that Jeana was coming home and to see if she'd send Mickey over to talk to Jeana. When Marsha told her that Mickey was gone to Tampa and wouldn't be home until Sunday night, the two women decided they would just have to take matters into their own maternal hands.

Chapter Twenty-five

Jeana didn't put on her "fat suit" until they stopped for gas in Bay Minette on their way home. When she came out of the restroom, Billy Joe greeted her with a wolf whistle.

"Very funny," she said. "I feel like the Michelin Man."

He put his arm around her as they walked back to the car. "I just wanted you to know you're still cute. For a fat girl."

She tried to elbow him but it was hard to move her arms, so she ended up giggling. They pulled into her driveway thirty minutes later, and Allison bid them goodbye until after lunch on Sunday. When Jeana and Billy Joe went inside her house, she had to fight the urge to laugh at her family's shocked faces when they saw her.

After all the hugging was done, Betty said, "We were just sitting down to lunch."

"Hear that, Jeana?" Billy Joe said. "One of your three favorite times of the day."

Jeana stuck her tongue out at him then went to the kitchen and fixed herself two sloppy joes. At least she didn't have to worry about eating too much in front of them. Betty invited Billy Joe to stay and eat with them, but he said his mother probably had something special waiting for him. He promised to come back later and give them all the details about his job and his classes.

After lunch, Jeana went to her room to unpack. As soon as she opened the door, memories rushed at her like a tsunami. Mickey was *everywhere*. Their prom picture stood on her dresser beside a plastic souvenir cup from last year's Senior Bowl, and spirit ribbons for Vigor's football games adorned her dresser mirror, all of them notated on the back with the number of tackles, assists, and interceptions Mickey had made in the game.

She picked up Mickey's first homerun ball at Vigor from the lap of a stuffed bear he'd won for her at last year's Greater Gulf State Fair, running her finger over the words written on the ball in Mickey's flawless printing: *For Jeana, my inspiration. Love, Mickey.* (*It was a homerun, not a touchdown.*) She laughed despite the longing she felt for that time when they'd simply taken it for granted that they would always be together.

She wiped her eyes and started to unpack. When she took the prenatal vitamins out of her suitcase to hide them in her chest-of-drawers, a dark blue item in the back corner of the top drawer caught her eye. It was one of Mickey's shirts that he'd taken off and forgotten one day when he was playing basketball in Billy Joe's driveway. She held it to her face and breathed in deeply, sobbing because it smelled like him. She put the shirt in her suitcase so she could sleep in it when she got back to Troy, then she got her journal and took it with her to go sit on the porch.

Betty came out a few minutes later and sat beside her in the swing. "Honey, I think we need to talk."

Jeana closed her journal. "About what, Mama?"

Betty put her hand on Jeana's stomach. "About my grandchild."

For a second Jeana couldn't do anything but look at her mother with frightened eyes, then she hung her head and whispered, "How'd you know?"

Betty tugged on one of the T-shirt sleeves. "This disguise of yours might've worked if I hadn't already noticed how much you were eating and going to the bathroom before you left for Troy."

"I'm sorry, Mama." Jeana stared into her lap. "You must be so ashamed of me."

"*Never*, Jeana." Betty pulled her daughter into her arms.

"I'll always be proud of you. I just don't understand why you've been hiding this from us and why Mickey obviously doesn't know."

Jeana told her about Mickey's promise to his dad and how she feared he would quit school if he found out.

"It's so like you to put Mickey's dreams above everything else," Betty said. "But this isn't something you can decide by yourself, honey. It's his baby too."

"Mama, I know we should've waited until we were married, and I guess I even feel like the misery we're going through right now is a little bit deserved, as a penance or something. But I don't believe God would want us to be unhappy for the rest of our lives because we made one mistake in judgment, and that's what will happen if Mickey has to break his promise to his dad."

"Still, Jeana—"

"Mama, I *know* Mickey." Jeana's tearful eyes pleaded with her mother. "If he knew I was pregnant, he'd insist that we get married right now and take any job he could get to support us, no matter how much he hated it. He'd never complain, but I'd know he was miserable. And if there was ever anyone who deserves to be happy, it's Mickey. He doesn't know how to be anything but fine and honorable and dedicated. If I can help him keep his promise to his dad, I'll feel like I've at least come close to being as good of a person as Mickey. Please don't tell him, Mama. *Please.*"

The depth of Jeana's love was impossible to ignore, and it touched Betty's heart.

She put her hand on her daughter's cheek. "What mother wouldn't be proud of a daughter who possesses the kind of selfless love that most people spend their entire lives searching for?" She leaned over and kissed Jeana's forehead. "Okay, honey. I won't tell Mickey. I still don't believe this is right, but I do believe in *you.*"

"Thank you, Mama. I love you so much." Jeana hugged

her then asked, "Does Daddy know too?"

"No, I wanted to talk to you first."

"Do we *have* to tell him?"

"Of course we do," Betty said. "But I think we'll wait until after his birthday dinner tonight. I don't want to spoil his appetite."

They went inside, and Jeana promised to help with dinner as soon as she put her journal away. Robert was gone to the grocery store and Shelly was at Sissy's house, so Jeana took off all but one of the T-shirts so she'd be more comfortable. The doorbell rang on her way back to the kitchen, and Betty arrived just in time to witness Marsha's shocked expression when Jeana opened the door. Since Jeana had no idea why Marsha was there, she misunderstood her reaction and grabbed her hand.

"What's wrong, Mrs. Royal? Did something happen to Mickey? Is he okay?"

"Mickey's fine," Marsha said. "But I think I need to sit down."

The three of them went to the living room and Betty told Jeana how she and Marsha had planned to ambush her about breaking up with Mickey, but they had other things to discuss now. For the second time that day, Jeana explained her reasons for not telling Mickey about the baby, but she didn't have to convince Marsha of what he'd do if he found out.

"You're right, Jeana," she said. "Mickey's proud and stubborn like his father, and that's why I'm so worried about him. I'm afraid he's too much like Stephen and will make the same mistakes."

"What do you mean?" Jeana asked.

Marsha told them why she thought Mickey was drinking. "He gave me some crazy story about playing baseball in the middle of the night, but I don't believe it. This is exactly what happened to Stephen and me, and I'm afraid Mickey will end up like his dad if he loses his chance

197

to play baseball too."

Jeana put her arm around Marsha. "We won't let that happen to Mickey, Mrs. Royal. I'm hoping he'll get an offer from one of the scouts in Tampa this weekend. That's why I had to break up with him—so he wouldn't miss that tournament."

Marsha looked surprised. "Mickey didn't tell me anything about Yankee scouts being there this weekend. Oh, that would be the answer to our prayers, Jeana! Stephen would've been happy to just play in the minors, but Mickey's an even better player than his father."

"So you won't tell him I'm pregnant?"

Marsha was silent a moment, then she sighed. "I certainly understand your reasons, Jeana. I would've done the same thing for Stephen in a heartbeat if I'd had the chance. Mickey might end up hating all of us for deceiving him, but I'll keep your secret." She kissed Jeana's cheek. "I knew you still loved him. I told him you'd never fall for somebody else."

"Why on Earth would he think a crazy thing like that?" Betty asked.

Billy Joe walked in the door, took one look at Marsha and spun around to leave.

"Come back here, Billy Joe!" Jeana called, laughing.

He peeked around the corner. "Did Mick send his mom over to kill me?"

"What in Heaven's name is going on?" Betty demanded.

Jeana explained to her what Mickey believed about Billy Joe, and Betty shook her head in disapproval. "Good gracious, poor Mickey. He thinks he's lost his girl *and* his best friend. I hate to think how bad he must feel."

Billy Joe took a handful of peanuts from the dish on the coffee table and tossed them into his mouth. "I hate to think how bad I'll feel if he rearranges my pretty face."

Marsha promised to call if Mickey came home from

Tampa with any offers, and Jeana promised to keep her informed about the baby.

"We both look much too young to be grandmothers," Marsha said to Betty as she was leaving, "but it's exciting, isn't it?" She kissed Jeana and hugged Billy Joe. "Take care of them for Mickey, and don't worry about him hating you. He'll know what a true friend you are when all this is over."

Betty and Jeana broke the news to Robert and Shelly after supper. Robert was understandably upset, but he also told Jeana that his pride in her was unchanged. However, it took quite some doing to convince him not to tell Mickey. Only after he heard that Marsha had agreed to keep the secret did he grudgingly acquiesce.

Shelly was actually relieved. Not only was she happy to find out that Jeana still loved Mickey, she was also glad to know that her sister wasn't destined to look like Gerta, the German shot-putter Mickey had tutored in math a few years earlier.

Betty and Robert wanted to pay for Jeana to see a private obstetrician, but she assured them that the doctors at the clinic were more than competent and were carefully monitoring her B vitamin levels because of her history with pernicious anemia. She did have confidence in the clinic doctors, but the real reason was that she knew Mickey wouldn't want her to let anyone else pay their bills.

She slept in Mickey's shirt that night and fell asleep with it pulled up to her face so she could smell him and pretend he was really there. She dreamed he climbed in her window and slept with his arms around her.

~ * ~

When Mickey got home from Tampa on Sunday night, Marsha called Jeana in Troy.

"He said he hit well in the whole tournament, but his pitching was really off in the last game. He hit two batters."

"Oh, no," Jeana said. "So none of the scouts talked to

him?"

"He didn't say anything and I couldn't ask him because I wasn't supposed to know anything about it."

"Where is he now?"

"I don't know." Marsha sounded anxious. "He left a little while ago and wouldn't say where he was going. It's hard to get him to talk to me at all anymore."

"Try not to worry, Mrs. Royal. I really can't believe Mickey would be drinking."

"I hope you're right, Jeana. And I think I'd like you to start calling me Mom."

"Okay, and I guess you should also be thinking about what you want the baby to call you. Grandma or Nana or—"

"Oh, Lord," Marsha said. "I'm not ready for that yet."

Jeana laughed. "My mama said the same thing. Bye, Mom."

~ * ~

The first time Mickey went to the batting cages after practice, he discovered that if he hit the balls hard enough, he was able to release some of the frustration and rage that was always inside him now. The pain he felt over losing Jeana was like a cancer eating away at what was left of his heart, but when he was in the cage, it wasn't quite as bad. It was almost as if he could kill some of the pain by killing the ball, so he stayed in the cage until the park manager made him leave, and he did the same thing the next night and the next.

After watching Mickey crush the ball repeatedly one night, the park manager asked him if he played anywhere locally. When he found out that Mickey would be playing at South in the fall, the manager offered him access to the cages late at night, along with a passkey so he wouldn't have to use any money. In return, Mickey promised to get the man tickets to the Jags' home games.

Mickey stayed in the cage every night until he was so

200

exhausted that he thought he might be able to sleep in the bed where he'd made love to Jeana without the memories torturing him with the ghostly touch of her hands on his skin, teasing him with the scent of her hair on his pillow, and mocking him in the dark with the whispered promises she hadn't meant.

It wasn't something he could talk about with his mom or anyone else. The only person who would have understood why he went there was the reason he had to go.

Chapter Twenty-six

Betty went to Troy the next week and took Jeana shopping for maternity clothes. The timing was fortunate, because the baby had a growth spurt at the end of June that made Jeana's regular clothes obsolete. She no longer looked like a melon thief. Now she looked like a basketball smuggler.

Around the same time that the baby and Jeana got bigger, Billy Joe suddenly developed a new passion for fat jokes. Whenever he and Jeana would pass each other in the apartment, he'd flatten himself against the wall and slide past her. Then there was the morning he and Jeana left the apartment together and saw two little girls playing in the doorway of the apartment next door. One little girl was upset about something and Billy Joe told her not to cry—it wasn't a school bus coming to take them to school, it was just Jeana wearing a yellow shirt.

Also around the end of June, Jeana began receiving a card in the mail every week, signed only with *I Love You* in incredibly neat printing. She started a scrapbook and put the cards inside, along with her journal pages for the week and the handouts she got from the clinic about the baby's development.

Mickey played in New Orleans, Little Rock, and Tallahassee in the month of June. All the time in the batting cages showed in his hitting, and he led his team in homeruns. They didn't have a tournament the weekend of July 4th, so Ty persuaded Mickey to go to Atlanta with him for a Braves-Dodgers game. Since Mickey would be out of town, Marsha called to tell Jeana it was safe for them to come home and spend the holiday with their families.

Thursday afternoon, Jeana and Billy Joe loaded the car while they waited for Allison to get home from her basketball clinic.

"I don't think we forgot anything." Billy Joe closed the trunk and scratched his head. "I got the suspension checked and made sure all the tires were aired up to handle the extra weight. I guess we'll be okay."

"Ha-ha," Jeana said. "I hope you get shot in the butt by a Roman Candle."

She went inside and nudged the thermostat down a little more. The daily high temperatures averaged ninety-seven degrees, and she wondered if she'd ever feel cool again.

"I've got to get this hair cut before it kills me." She piled her thicker-than-usual curls on top of her head and secured them with a clip.

"Don't you *dare*," Billy Joe said. When he got a surprised look from Jeana, he added, "I mean, I don't think Mick would want you to cut it. He loves your hair." He bent to put a large sketch pad inside his portfolio.

"He wouldn't love it if he had to lug it around all the time." Jeana sat on the couch and fanned her neck with a Piggly Wiggly sales flyer. "It feels like I'm wearing a thermal ski cap."

They left as soon as Allison got home and were in Chickasaw by seven-thirty. Billy Joe carried Jeana's suitcase inside for her when they arrived.

"She's kinda sensitive about her size," he told the Russells. "So try not to make any fat jokes. And don't let on that she's wearing two different shoes. She hasn't seen her feet in weeks, you know."

Jeana pushed him out the door. "I think I hear your mama calling you, Billy Joe."

~ * ~

Ty and Mickey's plans were to leave for Atlanta after practice on Friday, so they went to Mickey's house to get cleaned up and eat before they left. While Mickey was in the shower, Ty decided to call Sissy to see if he could stop by her house when he brought Mickey home on Sunday.

"I'd love to see you again, Ty," she said, "but I can't talk right now. I was just leaving to take Shelly home."

"You mean Jeana's sister?"

"Uh-huh. Jeana's home from college this weekend."

Ty said he'd give her a call when he got back from Atlanta, then he went to the kitchen and fixed a plate of the chicken and dumplings Marsha had ready for them.

"Guess what Sissy just told me on the phone," he said when Mickey came in the kitchen.

"She found out about your other fifty girlfriends?" Mickey got a plate from the cabinet and filled it with food.

Ty grinned. "It's fifty-five, but that's not what I'm talking about."

"I give up," Mickey said as he sat down. "What did she say?"

"Your beautiful but unfaithful girlfriend is home for the weekend."

Mickey's fork froze halfway to his mouth. "How does she know that?"

"Jeana's sister told her."

The fork clattered to the plate as Mickey jumped up from the table. "I can't go to Atlanta with you. I have to see her."

"You gotta be kidding me, Mickey." Ty followed him to his room. "I never would've told you if I'd known you were gonna torture yourself some more."

Mickey took a shirt from his closet and tossed it on the bed. "I don't expect you to understand. You don't know what it's like to love somebody the way I love Jeana."

"You're right," Ty said. "I don't understand, and I hope I never do if this is what love does to you."

"I'm sorry for leaving you in the lurch like this, but I have to get her back."

"Mickey," Marsha said from the doorway, "why did

you fix a plate of food and just leave it?"

"Jeana's home, Mom. I'm going over to see her." He looked up from tying his shoes, and his face showed some animation for the first time in weeks.

"Well, you can at least eat your supper before you go," Marsha said.

"I'm not hungry. I can't think about anything until I see her."

Marsha put her hand on his shoulder. "Don't get your hopes up too much, baby."

"He won't listen, Aunt Marsha," Ty said. "He finally stopped acting like a zombie all the time, and now he's gonna do it to himself all over again."

"Why don't either one of you believe that she'll come back to me?" Mickey jerked his shirt over his head. "You told me to have faith—remember, Mom?" He snatched up his keys and walked out.

Marsha ran to the phone to call Jeana as soon as Mickey was gone.

"He's on his way over there right now, Jeana. Is there somewhere you can go?"

"He'll only come back later, unless he just stays here and waits for me," Jeana said. "I'm not sure my daddy won't tell him the truth if he does that. I'll have to tell him I don't want to see him when he gets here."

She was on the verge of tears at the idea of another scene like the one in Troy, but she got an idea while she waited for Mickey to get there. The evening's forecast called for thunderstorms, and she could already feel the rain in the unseasonably cool breeze when she went outside. She put on one of her father's windbreakers and zipped it up all the way before going to sit in the porch swing.

Her heart went to double-time as soon as she heard the Mustang approaching from a block away. She hadn't seen Mickey in two months, so the sight of him when he got out of the car was almost too much for her. She literally had to grip the arm of the swing to keep from running to him. She closed her eyes and prayed: *Lord, help me be strong one more time.*

When he came up the steps and saw her in the swing, he stopped and stared at her a moment.

"I had to see you."

"How did you know I was here?" she asked despite the gigantic lump in her throat.

"Sissy told Ty." He took a cautious step toward her, as if he were afraid she'd run away. "Will you talk to me, Jeana?"

"There isn't anything to talk about, Mickey. Nothing's changed."

He walked over to her slowly. "You still think you love Billy Joe?"

"I do love him."

Tears magnified the blue of Mickey's eyes. "You know I'll never stop loving you, Jeana."

"I'm sorry I hurt you, Mickey."

He sat beside her in the swing and leaned over to stare at his hands clasped between his knees. "Do you tell him all the things you used to tell me?"

"Please don't do this." She thought her heart would stop if the pain got any worse.

"Maybe he's loved you longer than me, but he doesn't love you more."

She got up to go inside but he grabbed her hand and stopped her.

"I can't live without you, Jeana. If you give me another chance, I promise I'll love you so much you won't be able to think about Billy Joe or anybody else!"

"Let me go, Mickey." She tried to free her hand but he held it tighter and pulled it to his lips.

"Please come back to me, Jeana—I'm *nothing* without you! Just let me hold you one more time and I'll make you remember how much we love each other."

She looked at him and regretted it immediately. His beautiful face covered with tears was a testament to the agony she was putting him through, and it was more than she could bear. She touched his cheek and was about to give up and tell him how much she loved him, but just as she opened her mouth to say it, their baby moved again and reminded her of what she had to do.

She pulled her hand free and ran inside, praying he wouldn't follow her. She knew that if he got his arms around her, she'd tell him to never let her go.

~ * ~

Billy Joe heard the Mustang too and went to check on Jeana as soon as Mickey left. Betty told him she was in her room crying and he was welcome to go cheer her up if he could. He closed Jeana's bedroom door and sat beside her on the bed.

"Well, kiddo," he said as he rubbed her shoulder. "We had to go through a helluva lot to get here, but we're alone in your room and your mother told me not to come out until you were smiling."

She sat up and put her arms around his neck. "I can't do that again, Billy Joe. The next time I see him, it will all be over."

"You think he'll come back?"

"You know Mickey. What do you think?"

"We can leave in the morning," he said. "I'll call Al when I get home and tell her."

Fresh tears ran down Jeana's cheeks as she put her head on his shoulder. "Y'all shouldn't have to leave because of me."

"It's no big deal. You know there'll be fireworks wherever I am anyway." He gave her a squeeze and stood up.

"What are you doing?" she asked, wiping her eyes.

He pulled off his shirt. "Time to put that smile on your face."

She laughed and threw her pillow at him.

~ * ~

Mickey stayed in the batting cage until after four the next morning. At one point, during a downpour sometime around midnight, he started across the park toward Jeana's house but changed his mind before he got there because he was afraid he'd find her with Billy Joe. He was even more exhausted than usual when he got home, but sleep still eluded him.

In addition to the raw pain he felt from this latest heartbreak, something else was bothering him about when he'd seen Jeana. He couldn't put his finger on it, but there was some niggling detail that hadn't made any sense, lurking on the outskirts of his consciousness. He finally fell asleep around dawn and went to see Jeana as soon as he woke up, but she'd already gone back to Troy.

~ * ~

The next few weeks were relatively uneventful. The baby continued to grow, and Jeana's increased size gave her difficulties she hadn't experienced before. Tying her shoes became a challenge, and since her feet stayed swollen all the time anyway, she bought some rubber flip flops and wore them whenever possible. She also found it hard to get up from a seated position—a sight that never failed to entertain Billy Joe.

The oppressive heat finally got to her one day when the temperature peaked at ninety-nine degrees with one-hundred-percent humidity. She drove to the nearest hair salon and had them cut her long curls into a short layered style that she and Allison thought looked quite chic and that Billy Joe said made her look like a poodle.

Allison and Billy Joe made plans to celebrate the end of the summer college semester at the beach and convinced Jeana to go with them. Panama City was only two hours from Troy, and unlike Gulf Shores, it was doubtful they would run into anyone from Chickasaw there. Bright and early on the first day of August, they packed a day's worth of drinks and snacks and headed south on Highway 231 to Florida.

"I'm glad you came, but I don't think you should swim, Jeana," Billy Joe said when they'd been driving about thirty minutes.

"And why is that?" she asked with narrowed eyes.

"People could drown from the rise in the water level when you get in the Gulf."

Jeana sighed. "Why do I even talk to you?"

"You know you love me, Fifi." He reached back and mussed her hair.

They were on the beach by nine. Jeana slathered herself with sunscreen and tried to find a comfortable way to sit and read on the sugar white sand. Billy Joe and Allison joined a volleyball game and made an intimidating pair, setting each other up for the spike while Jeana cheered them on. She was able to stay cool by taking frequent dips in the emerald water, so they stayed until the sun had almost surrendered to the horizon.

They stopped to eat in Dothan on the way home and found a Wendy's because Jeana wanted a baked potato with the works. While they were standing in line to order, Jeana wondered aloud why the restaurant was so crowded, and a man in front of them told her they were in town for the American Legion Baseball Association's Regional Tournament.

"Mickey's team plays in that association," Jeana told Allison and Billy Joe. "They must be here."

They got their food and were lucky enough to snag a table by the window so Jeana could keep a wary eye on the parking lot while they ate.

"Don't get your panties in a wad, kiddo." Billy Joe slurped the last of his drink. "Mickey probably won't leave the park between games. You know he likes to scout the other teams when he's not playing."

209

Jeana poked at her baked potato. "I know. I just wish I could see him play. I love watching him hit home runs, and he looks *so* good in his baseball pants." She glanced at Allison and they both laughed.

Billy Joe went to get a drink refill and was grinning when he came back. "You can stop worrying about Mickey showing up here. They're playing a team from Baton Rouge right now at the Westgate Complex."

"How'd you find that out?" Jeana asked.

"That man who told us about the tournament had a copy of the bracket with him. You wanna ride over and see if we can watch the game from the parking lot?"

Jeana's face lit up, and she threw her arms around his neck. "Billy Joe, you're the best!"

"You can cut out the flattery," he said. "You're not getting my Frosty."

When they got to the complex, they discovered that there were two fields next to the parking lot, and Mickey's team was playing on one of them. From their vantage point in the car, they could see all the outfield and the infield up to the pitcher's mound. Mickey's team was ahead 4-1, and he was playing center field. Jeana's eyes filled with tears as soon as she saw him, but she was glad she had a new image to replace the one of him in utter despair that had haunted her since the last time she'd seen him.

The next batter hit a fly ball to center field that Mickey caught at the fence. The runner on second tagged up, but Mickey threw him out at third to end the inning. Jeana couldn't see the plate because of the bleachers, but she could hear the scorekeeper in the press box announce the batters as they came up and got goose bumps when he said, *Now batting... number 7, the center fielder, Mickey Royal.*

With a runner on first and two outs, Mickey ripped one to deep left field. The outfielder sprinted to the fence and jumped, but the ball sailed over his glove by a good three feet for a home run.

Jeana pulled her earlobe and whispered, "Happy Birthday, Mickey."

Chapter Twenty-seven

Marsha called the next day with the news that Mickey's team had won the regional tournament and would be going to the World Series in Shelby, North Carolina the following weekend. She didn't have the heart to tell Jeana that Mickey had been crushed when he came home and found out that Jeana hadn't even sent a card for his birthday. He told Marsha he'd felt something on Saturday while he was playing and had hoped it meant Jeana was thinking about him.

Jeana saw the doctor at the clinic on Monday, and he estimated her due date as September 17—six more weeks. When she stepped on the scales and discovered she had gained thirty pounds, she swore off all junk food for the rest of the pregnancy.

Mickey's team took third in the World Series, but he didn't come home with any contract offers. When he ran into Shelly at Delchamps and she let it slip that Billy Joe was living with Jeana and Allison in Troy, the fragile thread of hope he'd been clinging to all but disappeared.

~ * ~

The last week in August, Allison wanted to go home before their fall classes started since they'd cut their visit short in July, but Jeana didn't want to go. She was terrified of seeing Mickey again and was too uncomfortable to ride in a car for four hours anyway. She told Allison to take Billy Joe and have a good time without a pregnant woman to worry about for a change.

While Allison was gone to the store the night before they were supposed to leave, Billy Joe came into the living room and sat beside Jeana on the couch.

"I don't think we should leave you here alone," he said. "I think I'm gonna stay here."

Jeana put down her book. "Don't be silly. The baby's not due for another two weeks. Allison wants to go home, and you can't expect her to make the trip by herself."

"I'll talk to her. She'll understand."

"Absolutely not, Billy Joe. You can't ask her to give up anything else because of me. You're going with her and that's final."

"Don't tell me what I'm gonna do!" He got up and walked to the window. "I said I'll talk to her and I will."

"Why are you being so insensitive and stubborn?"

He whirled around to face her. "How the hell will I ever get Mick to forgive me for lying to him if I let anything happen to you or the baby?"

Before she could respond, he jerked open the front door and went outside. She stared at the door after it slammed shut and realized she wasn't the only one who missed Mickey. Billy Joe had lost his best friend and was obviously afraid he'd never get him back. She felt incredibly selfish, and when she finally managed to get up from the couch, she followed him outside and found him sitting on the hood of the El Camino, staring across the street.

"It's too hot for you out here," he said when she walked up.

She slipped her hand into his. "Then come back inside with me. I don't think I should be left alone."

He looked at her a second, then he slid off the car with a sigh. "What's the matter? Don't trust yourself alone with the doughnuts I bought this morning?"

"For your information, I haven't even thought about eating one. Every time I look in the mirror I lose my appetite." She eyed her prodigious belly with scorn. "If Mickey saw me like this, he'd probably say you're welcome to me."

Billy Joe stopped and turned her around to face him. "You're wrong, Jeana. Nobody with a brain in their head would give you up voluntarily, and Mickey's no fool. He'd think you'd never looked more beautiful."

She tiptoed up to hug his neck. "I hope I never have to find out what I'd do without you."

When Allison got home, Billy Joe took her in the bedroom to talk. Jeana heard their voices rise and fall for the next half hour and hoped she wasn't causing major problems between them. Allison stayed in the room with the door closed when Billy Joe came out.

"Is she mad?" Jeana asked.

"A little, but I'll make it up to her when she gets back. Don't worry about it." He sounded reassuring but didn't look it.

Jeana woke up at eight the next morning—the first day of September. Allison had already left, and Billy Joe was making pancakes.

"When did you learn how to cook?" she asked in amazement.

"It was either fix my own breakfast or do without when my mother worked at the hospital." He expertly flipped two pancakes. "But I only cook breakfast, so don't get your hopes up."

"Don't make much for me." She eased herself gingerly to the couch. "My back ached all night and I barely slept."

She didn't mention the pains she'd been having in her lower abdomen since early that morning. They were probably only Braxton-Hicks contractions, and Billy Joe would just stress out over them.

When the pancakes were ready, he found her asleep on the couch with her feet stretched out in front of her and her head against the back, so he let her sleep and saved her three pancakes. He sat on the end of the couch after he ate, and she stirred in her sleep.

"Mickey..." She opened her eyes and smiled at Billy

Joe. "I was dreaming."

"So I guessed." He picked up one of her swollen feet and massaged it.

"Oh my God," she said ecstatically. "What did I do to deserve this?"

"I feel sorry for these little tootsies. They got a mighty tough job, you know."

"Make all the jokes you want as long as you don't stop."

He switched to the other foot. "You know I only tease you to make your eyes flash, don't you?"

"It doesn't bother me," she said. "I know you're pathologically irritating."

He laughed. "You're actually kinda cute. In a chubby, poodle sort of way."

She stuck her tongue out at him then pressed her hands to her stomach. "Oh! That was a good one."

His fingers froze on her foot. "A good *what?*"

"Just false labor pains." She motioned for him to keep rubbing. "They're called Braxton-Hicks contractions and they're normal, so don't get excited."

He narrowed his eyes. "How do you know for sure that's all it was?"

"Because I've been reading about this stuff for the past six months. You know I'm an honor student. I know my material."

"You'd better tell me if you get any other symptoms."

"I don't have a disease, Billy Joe. They're called 'signs of labor.' I'll tell you if I have any, but it's too soon for that. First babies don't come early and this one's not due for another sixteen days."

He still looked doubtful. "Yeah, but look who his mother is. If Leonardo is anything like you, he thinks he knows it all and does everything his own way."

She arched her eyebrow. "Leonardo? As in Da Vinci?"

"Whatsamatta?" He made a Mama-mia gesture. "You

don't-a like-a that name?"

"I like it better than Heisman, but not much. Have you given any serious thought to a name yet?"

"I gotta see the little guy first. Then I'll know." He grinned at her suddenly. "Hey, lemme paint your toenails for you. It'll drive everybody crazy trying to figure out how you ever reached 'em."

The contractions continued throughout the day, increasing in frequency as well as intensity. Jeana believed what she'd said about first babies, so she tried to hide her growing discomfort from Billy Joe to keep him from panicking. But by late afternoon, she was unable to sit still and he commented on her restlessness.

"My back is still bothering me," she said. "It helps when I walk."

He opened the front door and peered out. "Looks like we're gonna get another afternoon shower, but it's fairly cool out here right now. Wanna go for a walk?"

They were two blocks from the apartment when the downpour started. Since running was not an option, they were both drenched when they got back inside. The phone was ringing as they came in and Billy Joe answered it.

"Bill's Bar and Grill." He shook the water out of his hair like a dog, spraying Jeana and making her laugh. "Bill speaking."

Silence on the other end of the phone. Then: "Let me talk to Jeana."

Billy Joe handed her the phone with an apologetic look. "It's Mickey."

Her laughter died as she took the receiver and said hello.

"I called to tell you I start school next Monday," Mickey said, "and to see if anything was different. But since it sounds like you and Billy Joe are having such a good time, I wouldn't want to interrupt you!" He hung up before she could say anything.

She cried with the receiver still held up to her ear. Billy Joe hung up the phone and put his arms around her.

"Whatever he said, he didn't mean it, Jeana."

She let him hug her a minute, then she pulled away wearily and went to her room to put on dry clothes. She tried to lie down on her bed for a nap, but the contractions and the backache were worse than ever.

~ * ~

Marsha had never seen Mickey as angry as he was when he hung up with Jeana. He almost tore his bedroom door off the hinges, only to come charging out again a minute later and storm through the house. He had a boxer's heavy bag hanging from a crossbeam on the back porch, and when Marsha looked outside, he was brutalizing it with his bare fists. When he'd worn himself out and was clinging to the bag in exhaustion, she went and pulled him into her arms.

"Don't do this to yourself, baby."

He leaned against her with his eyes closed. "I lost her, Mom. She's the only girl I'll ever love, and she loves somebody else. And I can't even hate him because it's Billy Joe."

"I know it hurts, Mickey, but don't give up."

He shook his head. "I know she's not coming back to me. I just don't know how I'm supposed to get over her." He pulled away and went back to his room.

The doorbell rang a moment later and Marsha went to answer it. When she let Ty in, she warned him that Mickey was upset over the phone call to Jeana. Ty found him lying on his bed, staring at the ceiling.

"Let's go, Cuz," Ty said. "We gotta get your mind off that girl."

"I'll never get her out of my mind."

"Maybe not the first time or the second, but you'll find somebody who'll make a difference."

Mickey put his arm across his eyes. "Forget it. It'll never happen."

"Then come with me because you owe me," Ty said. "You dumped me the weekend we were going to Atlanta and need to make up for it, so get dressed and come on."

Mickey sighed. "Where are you going?"

"Just trust me. You'll have a good time if you give it a chance."

Mickey didn't want to go anywhere, but he also didn't want to spend more endless hours in the room where he'd held Jeana, knowing that she was probably in Billy Joe's arms now. He got dressed, and an hour later he was sitting at a reserved dinner table at Mobile Greyhound Park with a girl he'd never seen before hanging on his arm.

Ty's date, a platinum blonde named Heather, had insisted that he bring someone for her visiting friend from Savannah. Within ten minutes of meeting Mickey, Candy had asked him what kind of car he drove, what business his dad was in, and what career plans he had for himself. She didn't seem to care much for any of his answers, but that didn't keep her from draping herself across his broad shoulders.

The dog races didn't appeal to Mickey, and Ty's conversation with Heather wasn't any more interesting than Candy's endless prattle about her social life in Savannah. While she was describing the dress she was wearing to her cousin's wedding in excruciating detail, the announcer's voice drew Mickey's attention when a dog named Yessir That's My Baby was declared the winner of the seven o'clock race. He got an odd feeling when he heard the greyhound's name, and the hair on the back of his neck stood on end.

Mickey supposed the food was good, but there was little pleasure in anything for him anymore. He thought the evening would never end, and when it was finally time to leave and the girls were in the restroom, he told Ty his debt was paid and he just wanted to go home.

"Not so fast, man." Ty slung an arm around Mickey's

shoulders. "The best part of the night is still to come. The girls want to see the house, and the rest of the family's gone to the Gulf."

"No way." Mickey shrugged off Ty's arm. "If you don't wanna take me home you can drop me anywhere, but I'm not going to your house with that girl."

"What's the problem, Cuz? She likes you, and you know what they say in the song—love the one you're with."

"I hate that song," Mickey said.

Ty looked baffled. "I don't get you, Mickey. Everybody knows the best way to get over a redhead is with a blonde or a brunette."

"I feel sorry for you, Ty. These girls you date can't compare to Jeana. They don't even come close."

Ty held up his hands in surrender. "Fine, you win. I'll take you back to Chickasaw."

Sitting in the back seat of Ty's Firebird with Candy babbling in his ear about her "coming out" in Savannah, Mickey willed the car to go faster. He knew he'd have to go to the batting cages to get through the night, and he was eager to get there.

Heather turned around and leaned over the front seat. "Candy, guess what Ty has up here in his glove compartment! Your very *favorite* thing to drink—teeny-weenie bottles of Jack Daniels." She handed one of the miniatures to Candy along with an open can of Coca-Cola.

Candy squealed and opened the bottle. "Do you like whiskey and Coke, Mickey?"

"I don't drink," he replied.

Her blue-frosted eyelids blinked in surprise. "You don't drink whiskey?"

"I don't drink any kind of alcohol."

She was pouring the whiskey into the Coke and was apparently so amazed at Mickey's answer that she overflowed the can and spilled it on his lap, soaking his pants. With only a perfunctory apology, she moved away from him on the seat.

"Thanks a lot, Heather," she said. "You got me a date with a real party animal."

Mickey didn't even bother to respond. He'd be free in a minute and didn't care what she thought about him anyway. When Ty pulled into his driveway, Mickey got out but Candy was right behind him. She put her hand on his chest and looked at him from beneath lashes thick with mascara.

"I really shouldn't offer since you're passing up your chance to be with me tonight," she said. "But I guess you can kiss me before you go. Maybe it'll change your mind."

He looked from the drink in her hand to her artificial face. "I'll tell you what. If you can answer one question for me, I'll kiss you *and* go to Ty's house with you."

"Okay," she said. "Ask me anything."

"Have you ever heard of The Mick?"

"Of course. Mick Jagger, right?"

Mickey smiled. "Just like I figured. I'm gonna have to pass on that kiss, but I'm sure Ty will make it up to you. See ya later."

Candy's mouth fell open as she watched him walk away. She got back in the car with Ty and Heather and said, "Let's go. We don't need him anyway."

Ty looked at the tag on the front of the Mustang before he backed out of the driveway.

"Saints deliver me from true love."

Chapter Twenty-eight

Billy Joe checked on Jeana a little later and found her tossing restlessly on her bed.

"Turn over on your side and I'll rub your back for you," he said.

"You're too good to me, Billy Joe. At least I didn't lie to Mickey when I told him I loved you." She started to cry again and said, "You'd think I'd run out of tears eventually, wouldn't you?"

He stretched out beside her on the bed and kneaded his thumb into the small of her back. "Just listen to the rain and try to sleep. You'll feel better when you wake up."

They both fell asleep and were awakened an hour later by a window-rattling clap of thunder. Billy Joe opened his eyes and realized he'd been holding Jeana in his sleep, and she had his hand clutched to her heart. He pressed his face into what remained of her curls and kissed the back of her head. When thunder rumbled again she squeezed his hand.

"What did you say, Jeana? It sounded like *knock-knock*."

"Never mind." She turned over and wiped her eyes. "Why is it so dark?"

"The power must be out. Is there a flashlight in here?"

"There should be one on the top shelf of my closet."

On his way to get the flashlight, he banged his thigh on the corner of the bed and uttered a few choice words. Jeana stifled a giggle.

"I heard that," he said, shining the light in her eyes.

She blocked the beam with her hand. "There's another flashlight in the kitchen. Help me up so I can go get it."

He pulled her to her feet and she felt a gush of water

221

run down her legs and puddle on the floor between them.

"Oh, God…"

"What's wrong?" Billy Joe asked.

She pointed the flashlight in his hand at the floor, and the puddle looked black in the darkness.

"What the hell is that?" he demanded.

"My water just broke. We have to go to the hospital, Billy Joe!"

"Oh, *shit!*"

She whacked him on the arm. "Stop cussing. And don't just stand there. Go get me the other flashlight so I can get changed and pack my suitcase. I don't even have it ready yet."

He left the room muttering about how she *obviously* didn't know her material as well as she *thought* she did, and he came back in a minute with the other flashlight and a towel.

"You want me to call your folks?"

"I guess so," she said. "And tell Mama to call Mickey's mom."

He closed the door so she could change but knocked on it a minute later. "Jeana, the phone's dead. The storm must've knocked down the lines."

"Oh, great. Well, I guess you can call from a payphone at the hospital."

She pulled on a dry pair of shorts, and just as she got them up, a contraction doubled her over and made her moan. Billy Joe rushed into the room.

"What's wrong now?"

"It was a contraction," she said when the pain ended. "A strong one."

He helped her sit on the bed. "Aren't we supposed to be timing 'em?"

She nodded. "Do you have on your watch?"

He shined the flashlight on his arm. "Damn! It got wet and I can't read it."

"It's okay, Billy Joe. Mine is over there on the chest-of-drawers."

He got her watch and said, "Tell me when you feel another one."

"Don't worry. You'll know when I do." She started to get up, but he pushed her back down on the bed.

"No, just stay there," he said. "I'll get your stuff for you. Tell me what you want."

"Mickey." She closed her eyes, but the tears still leaked out.

He sat beside her on the bed and sighed. "Sorry. I wish you had him instead of me too."

"I don't want him *instead* of you." She wiped her eyes and leaned her head on his shoulder. "I want you both."

By the time they had her suitcase packed and were ready to leave, her contractions were coming at two-minute intervals and Billy Joe's pulse rate was 150. They tried the phone again before they left but it was still dead. When they got to the entrance of the apartment complex, they found out why. A huge pine tree had fallen across the power and phone lines, blocking anyone from entering or leaving.

Billy Joe got out of the El Camino and grabbed the first person he encountered. "We gotta get out! My friend's having a baby!"

A man in the crowd from the apartment management overheard and said, "No one's going anywhere until the power company gets here and secures these lines. Someone could be electrocuted."

"You don't understand!" Billy Joe shook the man by the shoulders. "She's having the baby NOW!"

A middle-aged woman came over and tried to pry Billy Joe's fingers from the poor man's shoulders. "Take it easy, son. I'll help you."

"Are you a nurse?" he asked hopefully as they walked to the car.

"No, but I have seven children so I know how it's done." She opened the El Camino's passenger door and leaned in. "How you doing, sweetie?"

Jeana was in the middle of a contraction and could only grimace at the woman with her hands pressed to her belly until it was over.

"I'm fine," she said. "But they're getting closer."

Billy Joe grabbed two handfuls of his hair. "Why the hell didn't I pay attention in biology instead of flirting with Allison?"

Jeana laughed up at him and said, "Shut up and drive me back to the apartment, Billy Joe. I don't want my baby born in your ugly car."

"She's right," the woman said. "Your car *is* ugly and we need to get her back inside. Then I'm gonna need your help, son."

"But I—"

"Oh, God!" Jeana grabbed his arm, giggling hysterically. "This is where you say 'But I don't know nuthin' 'bout birthin' no babies!'"

Billy Joe gaped at her a moment, then he broke into a laugh too. The woman eyed them as if she suspected they were both on drugs.

Billy Joe ran around to get in the car. "Our apartment is number 3A, right over there."

The woman looked where he'd pointed. "Okay, I'm gonna grab one of these rubberneckers and see if they can flag down someone to call for an ambulance. I'll be there shortly."

He got Jeana inside and helped her into bed. When he came back to her room with more towels, he said, "I can't boil any water because the power's off."

"Don't worry about it. That's just something they tell men to get them out of the *waaaahhhhh...*" She lapsed into a yell as she felt the next contraction, and Billy Joe ran to the front door.

He found the woman poised to knock when he flung it open, so he grabbed her arm and pulled her inside. "Hurry!"

"I'm sorry it took me so long," she said as he dragged her to the bedroom. "I went home to get this hurricane lamp so we'd have some light." She put the lamp on the chest-of-drawers, then she went to the bed and held Jeana's hand. "My name's Sarah Wade, honey. Don't worry, I'm here to help you."

Jeana exchanged a bittersweet look with Billy Joe when she heard the woman's name. "Thank you, Mrs. Wade. I'm Jeana and this is Billy Joe."

"How long have you been having contractions?" she asked.

"Since early this morning, but they got a lot stronger after my water broke about an hour ago."

Mrs. Wade told Billy Joe to leave the room while she helped Jeana out of her shorts. When he came back, Jeana was wearing Mickey's Yankee shirt and had the sheet pulled up over her lap.

He pushed the damp hair from her forehead and gave her a lopsided smile. "I suppose you think I'll name the kid something like DiMaggio or Gehrig if you wear that shirt."

"I hope not." She pulled his face down and kissed his cheek.

Mrs. Wade told Billy Joe to take off his shoes and sit behind Jeana on the bed so he could support her while she had the contractions, and the next one started as soon as he was in place.

"You're crowning, honey," Mrs. Wade said when the contraction ended.

"What does *that* mean?" Billy Joe's eyes were wide.

"It means I can see the baby's head. Jeana needs to push when she has the next contraction, and you need to remind her to breathe."

"Who's gonna remind me?" he muttered.

225

Less than a minute later, Jeana had another contraction. "Okay, sweetie," Mrs. Wade said. "Time to push."

"Breathe, Jeana." Billy Joe winced because she had his hands in a vise grip.

Jeana strained until the contraction ended, then she collapsed against him.

"You did great, honey," Mrs. Wade said. "This baby's like you—no bigger than a popcorn fart. One or two more good pushes like that ought to do it."

When she felt the next contraction coming, Jeana said, "Billy Joe, this is it!"

She pushed as hard as she could, but Mrs. Wade still prompted her for more. Billy Joe leaned forward with Jeana and pressed his cheek against hers.

"Here's your chance to prove you're not a weenie, kiddo! Just a little more and I'll tell Mick you played like an all star. Come on, Jeana—PUSH!"

She reached behind her head and grabbed Billy Joe's hair with both hands. With an impassioned cry from both of them, she pushed with everything she had.

"We have a boy!" Mrs. Wade exclaimed.

"You did it, Jeana!" Billy Joe held her in a bear hug as they both laughed and cried at the same time.

Mrs. Wade wrapped the baby in one of the towels and held him face down while she cleared his airway. When he started to wail, she turned him over and put him in Jeana's arms and looked at her watch.

"Seven o'clock straight up," she said. "Lucky seven!"

Jeana struggled to see him through her joyful tears, gazing into the little face that was all screwed up and red from crying. "Have you ever seen anything so beautiful, Billy Joe?"

"Yeah," he said in a voice thick with love. "His mama. Both of you are amazing."

~ * ~

Alabama Power got the lines cleared from the road and the

ambulance arrived shortly after the baby was delivered. Billy Joe followed them to the hospital in the El Camino and used the payphone in the emergency room to call Jeana's parents. They said they were leaving right away for Troy. He asked them to call Mickey's mom, then he called Allison and his own parents.

It was after nine when Jeana was finally taken to a room and Billy Joe was allowed to see her. Visiting hours were over, but the nurses must've thought he was the baby's father because they told him he could stay a little while longer. Jeana didn't correct them.

"When will they bring me my baby?" she asked the nurse who was trying to take her temperature. The staff had rushed the baby off to the neonatal nursery as soon as they'd arrived.

The nurse replaced the thermometer under Jeana's tongue. "They're checking him out and doing all the newborn procedures. They should be bringing him to you around ten."

"Can I stay to see him?" Billy Joe asked.

Before the nurse could answer, Jeana took the thermometer out of her mouth again. "He's not leaving until he sees the baby. I don't care what anyone says."

The nurse folded her arms. "If you don't leave that thermometer in your mouth, young lady, it'll be even longer before you see him."

When the nurse was gone, Billy Joe sat on the bed and kissed Jeana on the forehead.

"You did so good, kiddo. You had him without any drugs and didn't scream or cuss or anything."

"I couldn't have done it without you." She hugged him, and the clock on the wall behind him caught her eye. "It's nine *fifty*. Why haven't they brought him yet?"

Billy Joe grabbed her hand before she could push the call button. "If you don't stop harassing them, they're gonna kick both of us outta here."

"But I haven't even had a good look at him yet," Jeana said. "It was too dark to see what color his hair or his eyes are. Could you tell?"

"Nope. Everything looked gray to me."

"He's probably scared to death. He needs his mama, and they'd better bring him to me in the next five minutes or—"

The door opened and a nurse pushed a rolling bassinet into the room. "I hear somebody's mighty anxious to see this little fella."

The baby wasn't crying, but he was making little whimpering sounds. Jeana craned her neck to see into the bassinet.

"It's okay, baby. Mama will have you in just a second." She held out her arms to the nurse. "Give him to me now."

"Bossy little thing, ain't she?" The nurse, a rotund black woman with a face creased by deep laugh lines, winked at Billy Joe as she picked up the swaddled bundle.

"You don't know the half of it," he said.

She put the baby in Jeana's arms, and Billy Joe sat beside them on the bed. Jeana pulled the blanket away from his face so they could see him. He had cherubic little features and a layer of fine red fuzz covering his head.

"He's got your hair," Billy Joe said. "And almost as much."

The baby began to cry halfheartedly so Jeana murmured, "Shh... Mama's got you now, baby." He turned his head toward the sound of her voice and blinked rapidly. "Why can't he open his eyes very well?"

"He got drops in them just a little while ago," the nurse replied. "They'll be swollen for a bit, but he can't really see right now anyway. His vision won't clear up for a few weeks."

"But he's trying to see me," Jeana insisted.

The baby continued to blink and managed to keep his eyes open long enough for Jeana to get a quick glimpse of them, and it made her gasp.

"Did you see that, Billy Joe? He's got Mickey's blue eyes!" She looked up tearfully. "Oh, *thank* you, God."

The nurse patted Jeana's shoulder. "All babies have blue eyes when they're born, honey. They might change later on."

Jeana frowned at her. "They don't all have eyes *this* blue."

The nurse peered over Billy Joe's shoulder and caught a flash of brilliant blue. "Hmm, you may be right. I think that *is* a true blue."

Billy Joe's head jerked up, and he snapped his fingers. "That's it!"

"That's what, Billy Joe?" Jeana said.

"That's his name. *True*."

A smile spread slowly across Jeana's face. "True Royal—it even means true blue. You're a *genius*, Billy Joe!"

"Oh, I like that name," the nurse said. She took a card from the slot on the end of the bassinet, and underneath I'M A BOY she wrote MY NAME IS TRUE.

The baby was now crying in earnest. The nurse told Jeana he hadn't been fed yet because they didn't know her feeding preference.

"I'm definitely going to breastfeed," she said. "I read all about how much better it is for babies." She smiled sweetly at the nurse and added, "Will you show me how to do it, please?"

"You decided to be polite now that you need my help, huh?" The nurse looked amused and went around to the opposite side of the bed where she eyed Mickey's shirt dubiously. "You're not exactly dressed for it, sugar. Are you at least wearing a nursing bra?"

Jeana shook her head. "But I have one in my suitcase, and a gown too. Get them for me, Billy Joe."

He got the items from the suitcase and handed them to

Jeana. Miraculously, he didn't make any jokes about the size of the bra. "Can I hold him while you change?"

The nurse gave him a gown to wear over his clothes, and he sat in the chair beside the bed. Jeana put the baby in his arms and reminded him to support his head, then she went into the bathroom to change. She kissed Mickey's shirt and held it to her heart before folding it tenderly.

Billy Joe was whispering to True when she got back into bed. "I'm your Uncle Billy Joe and I named you. Don't believe anything your mama tells you about me."

Jeana laughed. "He's hungry, Uncle Billy Joe. Give him back and you can go get me a Pepsi while I get situated and covered up."

"Oh, great," he said as he handed the baby back to her. "You make me work all day and then send me out of the room when it's time for the good stuff."

The nurse laughed as she shooed him out. She showed Jeana how to get True started, and Jeana was amazed at how naturally he took to nursing. She thought her heart would overflow with love as she watched him.

Jeana's family was with Billy Joe when he came back. Jeana showed them the baby the best she could, because there was no getting him to stop nursing.

"He's got Jeana's hair *and* her appetite," Billy Joe said.

When True was fed and properly burped, Jeana and Betty unwrapped him and inspected all his parts while they changed his diaper.

Shelly peered over her mother's shoulder and exclaimed, "His eyes are just like Mickey's! Wait until he sees..." She stopped and looked at Jeana apologetically.

"It's time he knew the truth anyway," Robert said. "I saw him the other day and he looked absolutely terrible."

"We can't tell him yet, Daddy," Jeana said. "He starts school on Monday. I want him to be committed to the baseball team before he finds out."

"It's not right to do the boy this way," Robert said,

shaking his head.

"Don't worry, honey." Betty put her arm around Jeana and gave Robert a stern look. "Your father isn't going to tell Mickey anything because it's not his place to do it."

The nurse came back and told everyone they would have to leave, but they could come back in the morning at eight.

Before Jeana surrendered True to the nurse, she kissed him and whispered, "Mama loves you and so does your daddy. He just doesn't know it yet."

She kissed her parents and Shelly goodbye, but she grabbed Billy Joe's hand before he could leave.

"Thank you, Billy Joe," she said, giving him one last kiss. "When Mickey finds out how much you've done for us, you'll have your best friend back. I promise."

She wrote down every single detail of the day in her journal for Mickey, and she ended with this:

> *I held him in my arms and looked at your eyes, and I knew just how special he is. God gave us both more than our fair share of gifts, Mickey. We have so many things we can do better than most people, but when I looked at our son, I knew without a doubt that he's the best thing either of us will ever do.*
>
> *I remember watching you once while you were sleeping, and I couldn't imagine ever seeing anything as beautiful as your face. You have some competition now, because True is just as beautiful as his father.*
>
> *I've loved you since the first time*

231

you kissed me and I'll love you throughout eternity. Just a little while longer and we'll be together again. Always and forever.

Chapter Twenty-nine

Mickey was still out with Ty when his mother found out that she had a grandson.

"I'd give anything to go see him," Marsha said when Betty called and asked her to come with them to Troy. "But I don't know what I'd tell Mickey. I couldn't leave without saying where I was going, and I don't want to lie to him. God knows I'm deceiving him enough already."

"We'll bring back plenty of pictures for you," Betty promised.

But the more Marsha thought about it after she hung up, the more she believed she should tell Mickey the truth when he came home. He'd been so desolate after he talked to Jeana earlier, and Marsha could tell he'd lost all hope. She convinced herself that the fears she'd had about him drinking were unfounded and decided to tell him about the baby as soon as he got home.

She was reading in her bedroom when she heard him come in. She called out to him, and as soon as he walked into her room, a sickly familiar smell assaulted her nostrils.

"*Mickey.* Why do you smell like whiskey?"

"I don't want to talk about it," he said, staying in the doorway. "It was just something stupid I let Ty talk me into."

"Come over here so I can see you," Marsha said. "I want to talk to you."

"Not now, Mom. I don't feel like talking to anybody. I just came in to change clothes, then I'm going out again."

Marsha's fears returned in full force and she changed her mind about telling him. She'd wait for Jeana the way they'd agreed. When Mickey's playing future was secure, they'd tell him he had a son and all this drinking nonsense would come to an end. There'd be no reason for him to drink anymore, and he'd be safe from the demons that had taken his father away from them. The same ones Marsha had so narrowly escaped herself.

~ * ~

Before Jeana left the hospital on Friday morning, someone from Records came to get the information for the birth certificate.

"Father's name?" the woman asked.

"Mickey Ray Royal," Jeana replied. "And you'd be smart to remember that name, because he's going to be a famous baseball player one day."

The woman gave her a patronizing smile. "Do you want the baby to have your last name or the father's?"

"His father's of course," Jeana said. "We'll be married soon and it will be my name too."

From the look on the woman's face, Jeana could tell she didn't think it was such an obvious conclusion.

She was able to leave as soon as her family arrived and the nursery brought the baby. On the ride to the apartment, she and Shelly sat on either side of the car seat and laughed at the faces True made in the bright daylight. Allison had returned to Troy that morning, and she ran out of the apartment to greet them when they drove up.

"Oh, Jeana, he's precious!" she exclaimed when she saw True. "He's a little mixture of you and Mickey."

A bassinet filled with baby items greeted Jeana in her bedroom. Betty told her the bed was from Marsha and the other things were from them and Billy Joe's parents. The Russells had to leave after lunch because Shelly was cheering at Vigor's first football game that night. When Jeana's family was gone, Allison told her they needed to talk.

"I'm so sorry for the way I acted about Billy Joe staying with you," Allison said. "I'm ashamed of myself for being so selfish. Can you ever forgive me?"

"Allison, you're the most *un*selfish person in the world," Jeana said.

She shook her head. "You would've been all alone in a storm when True was born if Billy Joe hadn't stayed here. Thank God he didn't listen to me."

"No danger of that," Jeana said. "When does he listen to anyone?"

"Can it, Poodle," Billy Joe said, his hands on Allison's shoulders. "We've got something to tell you."

Allison held up her left hand for Jeana to see. "When I came home this morning, Billy Joe asked me to marry him!"

Jeana squealed over the small diamond glittering on Allison's tanned finger.

"Oh, I'm so happy for you!" She hugged her then frowned at Billy Joe. "Why didn't you tell me you were going to ask her?"

He shrugged. "I told you I'd make it up to her when she got back, didn't I? It was the only thing I could come up with."

~ * ~

September passed for Jeana in a sleep-deprived parade of diapers, spit-up, and endless feedings, until she and True established a routine they both could live with. Jeana excelled at motherhood as much as she did everything else, and True was a complacent baby who began sleeping through the night at three weeks, a cause for celebration to everyone in the apartment.

On the first Friday in October, Jeana woke at seven and threw her arm over the side of the bassinet, sighing when she realized it was empty. She went to the living room and found Billy Joe reading a Spider-Man comic book on the couch with True sleeping contentedly on his chest. She grabbed a handful of curls and shook Billy Joe's head.

"Quit stealing my baby, Billy Joe. You're going to give

me a heart attack."

"It was his idea," he said. "I told him you'd be mad but he said he's not afraid of you."

Jeana picked up the baby and he immediately turned to her breast. "Sometimes I think you only love me as a food source."

True looked up at her and studied her forehead as if it were the most interesting thing he'd ever seen. Then he smiled, and his mama's heart swelled with love.

"There's my morning smile. I'm pretty sure I see dimples hiding in these chubby little cheeks, Uncle Billy Joe. Maybe we'll get to see them one day soon."

They were leaving after breakfast to go home for the first time since True's birth. Jeana had talked to Marsha the night before, and they'd decided that the only way to find out what was going on with Mickey and the school baseball team was for Jeana to talk to him. Since the last time he talked to Jeana on the phone, he'd basically turned into a hermit when he wasn't at school or baseball practice, and Marsha couldn't get him to tell her anything.

Allison and Billy Joe were also going home with a purpose—they were going to tell their parents they were engaged. Allison was almost nineteen, so her parents couldn't keep them from getting married, but she hoped they would come around and see how wonderful Billy Joe was.

They were all full of nervous anticipation when they left for Chickasaw. True proved to be an excellent traveler as long as he was fed on time, so it was a good trip for everyone. Betty came out to meet them as soon as they pulled into the driveway.

"Hand him over, Jeana," she said. "I can't wait another second to see him."

Jeana unbuckled the car seat, and Betty laughed when she saw the sentiment printed on True's little T-shirt: IF YOU THINK I'M CUTE, YOU SHOULD SEE MY

UNCLE BILLY JOE.

"I guess I don't have to tell you who got him the shirt," Jeana said.

"I can't believe how much he's grown," Betty said as she carried him inside. "And I didn't think he could get any cuter, but he did."

"He was an absolute angel on the trip, Mama." Jeana smiled proudly as she smoothed his red curls.

Billy Joe carried in the last of their bags. "I think that's everything, Jeana. We'll see you later."

"Is your dad home?" she asked.

"Yeah. We're gonna drop the bomb on 'em, so watch for fallout."

Jeana explained to her mother what he meant, and Betty said, "I've always loved that boy, but after everything he's done for you and True, I'd give anything to see him happy."

Marsha arrived a few minutes later and hugged Jeana when she answered the door. "You look wonderful, Jeana! Your hair is adorable."

"What do you think Mickey will say about it?"

Marsha gave her a wry look. "He'll probably hate it, but don't let that bother you. Stephen never liked me to cut mine either. It's a man thing."

Jeana linked her arm with Marsha's. "Come on, Mom. There's someone I want you to meet."

"Hey there, Grandma," Betty said when they walked into the living room. "Look who's here." She put the baby in Marsha's arms.

"He's so beautiful…" Marsha started to cry, then she read his shirt and laughed. "Hello, True. You look just like your daddy when he was a baby, except for this gorgeous hair you got from your mama." True was looking studious again, then his face crinkled into a big smile. "Oh, Jeana, this baby has God's fingerprints all over him."

Jeana sat on the couch beside her. "Is Mickey home

right now? I can't wait to see him even though I'm scared of how I'll react."

"He has classes until two and then baseball practice." Marsha gave the baby back to Betty and turned to take Jeana's hands. "Now that I've seen True, I don't see how we can keep him from Mickey any longer."

"Do you think he'll stay in school if he finds out now?"

"I don't know, Jeana, but I do know he's miserable without you, and that baby is much too precious a gift to keep from him."

"You know I don't want to hurt Mickey anymore," Jeana said, "but if we tell him too soon and he quits school, all this will have been for nothing."

"I got an idea last night that might help," Marsha said. "Maybe we can convince him that the three of you can live with me. I think I can get the doctor I work for to let me do my transcription at home so I can keep True for you. That way you and Mickey can both keep going to school."

"That would be wonderful," Jeana said. "I'm just afraid Mickey won't agree to do it. He told me once that he didn't want to ever have to borrow money from anyone."

"I know he's proud like his dad," Marsha said, "but I think he'd be willing to accept help if we can make him see that it would also be helping me to have all of you there instead of being alone." She put her hand on Jeana's cheek. "Just give it some thought, okay? I won't tell him about the baby, but I really think it's time you did."

~ * ~

Billy Joe's parents surprised him by being excited about the engagement. They even offered to invite the Whites over for supper so Billy Joe and Allison could break the news to them, but Billy Joe said he didn't want any knives close by when Allison's mother found out he was gonna be her son-in-law.

After Allison left, Billy Joe said he was going over to see Jeana and asked his mother if she wanted to come with him to see True.

"I have an appointment at the beauty shop in ten minutes," she said. "But I want you to bring them over as soon as I get back."

He waited until he saw Marsha's car pull away from Jeana's house, then he walked across the street with his sketchbook. Betty told him Jeana was in her bedroom trying to get the baby to sleep.

"She's wasting her time," he said, taking a cookie from a platter on the table. "He won't go to sleep until we've had our lunchtime chat."

Betty smiled and kissed him on the cheek. "Go on in there, Billy Joe. I can see you're almost as attached to him as you've always been to his mama."

When he got to Jeana's room, she was on her bed with True squirming beside her. "He's so sleepy, but he's fighting it. It must be the new surroundings."

"Nah, that's not it." Billy Joe stretched out on the other side of True. "He was waiting for me to come talk to him. We do this every day."

"Oh, really?" Jeana arched her eyebrow. "And what do you talk about?"

"Guy stuff. Chicks, cars, where to get the best milk."

She laughed. "How did your parents take the big news?"

"They were happy—can you believe it? I guess they're relieved to know somebody else is willing to put up with me. We're gonna tell Allison's folks tonight." He turned onto his back and patted his chest. "Put him up here for me."

She put True on Billy Joe's chest and kissed him on the cheek. "Well, just remember that I'll always put up with you."

"What did Mick's mom have to say?"

Jeana sighed. "She wants me to tell Mickey about True, but I'm afraid it's too soon."

"I think she's right, Jeana. True's only a month old, and look how much he's changed already. It's not fair for Mick to miss any more time with the little guy."

"I know, but—"

"No buts, Jeana. Time is something that can never be retrieved after it's lost. Somebody real smart said that once."

Her eyes filled with tears. "Maybe you're right. I don't think I'll be able to keep from running into his arms when I see him anyway."

"Cheer up, kiddo." He brushed her chin with his knuckles. "If Mick gives you any lip about staying in school, just take off your shirt. He'll be at your mercy."

"You're awful." She elbowed him and they both laughed at the way True was bobbing his head around like a pecking chicken. "Hey, why did you bring your sketchbook with you?"

"Since you wouldn't let us take any pictures of you while you were pregnified, I did some sketches so Mick could see how beautiful you looked. I thought you might want to put 'em in his scrapbook."

She squeezed his cheeks together and kissed him. "How can you be so obnoxious one minute and so utterly sweet the next?"

"I told you a long time ago," he said. "I'm a complicated personality."

Chapter Thirty

Mickey stopped on the way to his car after baseball practice when he heard someone calling his name. He turned to see Coach Laird and another man walking toward him.

"Mickey, this is John Ashworth," Coach said. "He's a scout for the Tampa Yankees and wants to talk to you."

"I saw you play in Tampa last June," the man said as he shook Mickey's hand. "I intended to talk to you then, but I had to leave unexpectedly because of a family emergency."

Mickey looked surprised. "I didn't play very well in that tournament. Hard to believe you wanted to talk to me."

"You're quite a power hitter from what I saw," Mr. Ashworth said, "and an excellent outfielder. I understand you also pitch."

"Yes, sir. That's what I did so bad in Tampa, but I guess you missed it if you left early."

The man took a leather case from his pocket and handed Mickey a card. "Coach Laird tells me you've been looking good on the mound at practice here. I'd like to see you in action when you start playing your fall games. You can leave a message at either of these numbers to let me know when you'll be pitching. I'll make the arrangements to get to the game."

Driving home, Mickey wondered why he wasn't excited about what had just happened. This man was with the *Yankees*, and they were interested in him. It was what he'd always wanted, and it didn't mean anything to him without Jeana. His dad had told him a long time ago not to forget that baseball wasn't the most important thing in the world. He sure knew it was true now.

He exited the interstate at Highway 45 and pulled in at the Exxon station for gas. While he was getting a Gatorade from the refrigerated case in the back of the store, he heard a familiar voice coming from the front and realized it was Billy Joe's mother talking to another woman at the register. Mickey ducked behind the magazine rack before she saw him.

"It's so good to see you again, Carol," the woman was saying to Mrs. DuBose. "And how is that adorable son of yours?"

"Jack and I are so proud of him for taking art classes at Troy State," Mrs. DuBose replied. "He came home today with his girlfriend and just gave us the most wonderful news. They're engaged, and we couldn't be happier about it."

Mickey felt the store start to spin and had to grip the magazine rack to steady himself. He couldn't have heard right—Jeana and Billy Joe were *engaged?* He closed his eyes against the vertigo, and when he opened them again, he realized he must've been standing there longer than he thought, because both of the women were gone.

He paid for his gas and left the store still in a daze. He didn't know where he was going, but he couldn't go home. He didn't want to see or talk to anyone. After driving around aimlessly for half an hour, he ended up in Saraland at a place he didn't recognize and had no idea why he was there.

He sat in the Mustang and stared out at Chickasabogue Creek, wondering how his life had gotten so messed up. This same month three years ago, he'd kissed Jeana for the first time and she told him she would always be his. *Always.* Now she was going to marry the best friend he'd ever had. How was he supposed to live without her when he wasn't sure he wanted to live at all?

The misery he'd endured all summer had been bad, but it was nothing compared to the torment he felt from knowing that Jeana wanted to spend her life with somebody else. He'd tried to hold on to the small hope that she was just confused about her feelings for Billy Joe, but if she'd agreed to marry him, she must really love him after all.

His grip on the steering wheel tightened as he honestly wondered if he could go on living without Jeana. The black depths of the creek seemed to summon him, promising to end the crippling pain in his heart.

"Now I know how you felt, Strickland."

Agony and frustration welled up inside him. He beat his hands against the wheel and turned his eyes heavenward.

"Why, God?" he cried. "What did I do that was so bad you have to take everybody I love away from me!" He buried his face in his arms and cried himself into an exhausted sleep.

The next thing he knew, he was standing on a barren landscape that stretched out before him in all directions. Off in the distance, he saw two figures and immediately knew they were Jeana and Billy Joe, their heads bent together over something in their hands. Mickey had no idea what it was, but he knew Jeana needed him and that he had to get to her.

But with every step he took, gaping black holes appeared in the ground and Mickey found himself teetering on the edge, fighting for his balance. Behind him the ground was solid again, but he knew he couldn't quit. He took another step just as an enormous hole appeared in front of him and he tumbled into it, barely managing to cling to the side and pull himself back up.

When he was standing on the ground again, Jeana looked even further away than before, and Mickey felt his hope start to die. He was so incredibly tired. Maybe he should just give up. Billy Joe was over there with Jeana and would help her. Mickey knew he would take care of her, because Billy Joe had always loved her too.

He looked at the hole he'd just pulled himself from and

thought how easy it would be to just fall in and not have to hurt anymore. He took a step toward it but stopped when the sound of an approaching car made him look up. A yellow Corvette skidded to a stop in front of him, and the driver leaned out the open window with a familiar sneer.

"What the hell is your problem, Yankee-boy?" Wade shouted. "You mean to tell me I couldn't take her away from you, but you're just gonna give up and let DuBose have her? What was the last thing I said to you? *Take care of Jeana!* Now move your Yankee ass and go get her!"

He gunned the Corvette, spraying rocks and dirt on Mickey as he sped away in Jeana's direction. Mickey started to run after the car and had already covered fifty yards before he realized the holes were gone. Just as he got within twenty yards of Jeana, the Corvette disappeared.

Mickey tried to call out to her that he was coming, but no sound would come out of his mouth. A few more steps and he was able to see what Jeana and Billy Joe were looking at, and it stopped him abruptly in his tracks. Billy Joe was trying to put an engagement ring on Jeana's left hand, but he couldn't because there was a ring already on her finger. Mickey started to run again and reached out to pull her away from Billy Joe, but she disappeared just before he touched her. He woke with his heart hammering in his chest and Jeana's name on his lips.

As he struggled to catch his breath, he finally knew what had been wrong the last time he saw Jeana. *She was still wearing her engagement ring!* Now he remembered seeing it on her hand when he'd kissed it just before she ran inside. If she was so sure she loved Billy Joe, why had she still been wearing her ring?

He started the car and pulled out onto Highway 158 with renewed belief that it wasn't over with Jeana yet. Somehow he'd make her see that they were meant for each other. Hope lived in his heart again, and all thought of ending his life disappeared.

As he drove back to Chickasaw, Mickey wondered who would've ever believed that Wade Strickland would be the one to help him find his way back to the girl they both loved more than anything.

Chapter Thirty-one

Billy Joe went to see Jeana as soon as he got back from Allison's house.

"Well, they know," he said, taking True as he sat beside her on the couch.

"What did they say?"

"They said we were too young. They said Allison had to finish school. They said I'd never be able to make a decent living as an artist, and they said I needed a haircut." He fluffed up True's curls and sighed. "They said just what I expected."

"I'm sorry, Billy Joe." Jeana put her hand on his arm. "What did Allison tell them?"

He looked at her and grinned. "She told 'em they could either learn to like me or they'd never see their grandchildren. You should've seen their faces when she stood up to them. It was *sweet*."

"Good for her!" Jeana said.

"Hey, my mother wants you to bring True over later so she can see him."

"Okay, but let's go now because I'm going to see Mickey as soon as he gets home."

"You gonna tell him about True?"

She took the baby again and smoothed his hair back down. "I thought about it all afternoon, and I decided you're right. It's not fair for Mickey to miss any more time with his son. I did all I could to keep him in school. We'll just have to hope he won't quit."

She got a blanket for True and told her mother where they were going. Five minutes after they went inside Billy Joe's house, Mickey pulled into Jeana's driveway.

"I'm sorry to bother you, Mrs. Russell," he said when Betty answered the door. "But I have to see Jeana."

"She's not here, Mickey," Betty said. "She's at Billy Joe's."

His newly restored hope faltered at the prospect of seeing Jeana and Billy Joe together, and he hung his head.

"Why don't you go over there and talk to them?" Betty said. "It's time they told you the truth."

"I can't do that. I have to see Jeana alone." He stared across the street, and there were tears in his eyes when he looked at Betty again. "Can you do me a favor, Mrs. Russell?"

"Of course, Mickey. What is it?"

"Tell Jeana I really need to talk to her and I'll come back tomorrow if she'll let me. If she doesn't want to see me…" He struggled to continue. "I'll know she doesn't love me anymore, and I won't bother her again."

"I'll tell her, Mickey." Betty patted his arm. "I know she'll talk to you. She has something very important to tell you."

He thanked her and walked to his car, not sure if he would come back or not. The last thing he wanted was to hear Jeana tell him she was going to marry Billy Joe.

~ * ~

Jeana and Billy Joe came outside a few minutes after Mickey drove away. As they started to cross the street, she stopped and grabbed his arm. "Shoot! I need to get diapers. Will you take me up to Delchamps?"

"Sure," he said, "but me and True will just wait in the car. I don't wanna listen to them begging me to come back and organize the soup aisle."

When they got back from the store, Betty met them at the door and told Jeana that Mickey had been there.

"You have to tell him the truth *now*, Jeana," Betty said. "It broke my heart to see him like that. I almost told him myself."

247

Jeana called Mickey's house, but Marsha told her he wasn't there and she hadn't heard from him. She promised to call Jeana as soon as he got home.

"Where could he be?" Jeana said when she hung up.

"We can go look for him if you want to," Billy Joe offered.

"I might take you up on that if he's not home soon," she said. "I'll wait awhile longer to see if his mom calls."

After Billy Joe left, Jeana gave True his bath and fed him, then she lay with him on her bed until he fell asleep. Using two rolled-up quilts, she made a barrier around him on the bed and turned on her old "Kukla, Fran and Ollie" nightlight before she left the room.

She tried to watch TV with her parents, but mostly she just stared at the telephone and willed it to ring. When Robert and Betty went to bed, Jeana checked on True then turned off the television and went out to sit in the porch swing. Running her hands over the worn boards, she remembered all the times she'd been there with Mickey. Where could he be? And how ironic was it that she'd spent the past nine months doing everything she could to keep him from finding out that she was pregnant, and now that she was ready to tell him about their baby, she couldn't find him.

She looked over at Billy Joe's house and considered taking him up on his offer to go look for Mickey, but his house was as dark as all the others on the street. She wasn't sure of the time but knew it was late because the whole neighborhood was cloaked in the kind of gloomy quiet that only comes in the wee hours, when even the crickets are asleep. In fact, the only noise she heard at all was a distant, intermittent *whack* that sounded like…

A bat hitting a baseball!

She jumped out of the swing and bounded down the steps, praying that she wouldn't break her neck before she could get to him. Once she was inside the park, she forced herself to walk for safety's sake, and as soon as she came around the dugout on Field B, she saw him in the same batting cage he'd been in on the day she met him.

Despite her heart trying to jump out of her chest toward Mickey, she watched him as she'd done three years earlier, but he didn't swing the bat the same way anymore. With every pitch, he swung with such vicious force that he'd almost lose his balance, and she knew immediately that this was how he'd been coping with their separation. When he hit the last ball and the machine whirred to a stop, he stood with the bat on his shoulder and his head hanging in such desolation that it hurt Jeana just to look at him.

How could she have ever thought that hurting him this much was for his own good? She was suddenly terrified that he'd never forgive her and almost turned to run away. But then the very thing that had gotten her into trouble became her salvation when her body took over for her head, and just like that other day three years earlier, she felt her feet move as if of their own accord.

"Hey, Mickey! Don't you know it's football season?"

He froze at the sound of her voice, and when he turned to look at her, it was almost in slow motion.

"Jeana..."

The look on his face was that of a dying castaway who'd finally spotted a ship. He dropped the bat and flung open the gate to get to her. When Jeana started to run, he opened his arms to catch her in an embrace so consuming that it took their breath away.

"I love you, Mickey! I never stopped loving you!"

He enveloped her head in his hands and turned her face up to his. "Oh, God... Jeana. You came back to me!" He ran his fingers over her features. "Are you really here? Please tell me I'm not dreaming."

"I'm here, Mickey. Please say you'll take me back."

"How could you ever doubt it, baby? I haven't lived since I lost you." He wrapped her in his arms again and kissed her. "My Jeana... I love you more than you'll ever know! I'm never letting you go and I'll never let you leave me again, never, ever, ever, ever—"

She put her fingers on his lips to stop the avalanche of words. "I'm so sorry I hurt you, Mickey. Can you ever forgive me?"

He pressed her hand to his cheek and closed his eyes. "Nothing matters except that you love me! Tell me again, Jeana. Tell me over and over."

"I love you, Mickey. You're the only one I've ever loved, and I'll always belong to you."

He picked her up by the waist and swung her around with a shout of pure joy.

"I tried to believe you still loved me," he said. "I held on to that when I thought I couldn't make it another day. But when I heard you were gonna marry Billy Joe, I wanted to die."

She brushed the tears from his cheeks. "What are you talking about, Mickey? I'm not marrying Billy Joe."

"I heard his mother tell somebody he's engaged."

"He's engaged to Allison." She held up her left hand. "Whose ring is this?"

Confusion clouded Mickey's eyes. "I don't understand..."

"I know you don't," she said. "But you will after we go to my house. I have to show you something."

"Show me later, baby." He pulled her against him tighter. "I don't want to let you out of my arms yet. I need to hold you until this fear that's been torturing me goes away forever."

"Mickey, my one and *only* love"—she put her hands on his cheeks—"I have to show you now. But I promise you won't be sorry, and after I show you, I'll stay in your arms all night long."

Chapter Thirty-two

When they got to Jeana's house and went inside, Mickey said, "Show me whatever it is so we can go, baby. I don't want to share you with anybody tonight."

She smiled and took his hand to lead him to her bedroom. Before she opened the door, she stopped and said, "Everything I did was because I love you so much, Mickey. I always have and I always will. Promise me you'll remember that."

"I promise, Jeana."

She led him across the dimly lit room and stopped beside the bed, then she took his face in her hands and looked into the blue tunnels that connected his soul to hers.

"Mickey Ray Royal, this is your son."

She turned his face toward the bed and he stopped breathing. His astonished gaze returned to her face just before his legs lost the ability to support his weight, and he fell to the edge of the bed beside the waking baby.

"My... son?"

Jeana picked up True and whispered to him. "Wake up, baby boy. It's time to meet your daddy."

Mickey was overcome when she placed his son in his arms, his breath coming in gulps that made his chest jerk and hitch. Tears streamed from his eyes, but he kept them on the baby in his arms who was yawning and stretching inside a sleeper that was a miniature version of the Yankees pinstripes.

Jeana knelt on the floor at his feet so she could watch Mickey's face as his son saw him for the first time. When True looked up at Mickey with eyes identical to his own and smiled as if he recognized his father, Mickey's breath

251

was stolen along with his heart.

"Oh my God, he's unbelievable."

"His name is True," Jeana said, "and he was created by the truest love ever shared by two people."

"I have a son… and his name is True." Mickey seemed to be trying to convince himself it was real. "When we thought you were pregnant…?"

"Yes, and I promise I'll explain everything to you," she said. "But right now I just want to share our baby."

Mickey lifted his tearful gaze heavenward. "Thank you, God. For giving my Jeana back to me, and for giving me a son." He looked at True again and touched Jeana's face. "He's so beautiful, baby. Just like you."

"Like *you*, Mickey." She rose to kiss him and laughed when True whimpered. "It's okay, baby. I'm allowed to kiss him. He's your daddy."

Lying on Jeana's bed with True nursing between them, Mickey watched in wonder. "This is such a miracle. A few hours ago I was trying to figure out how to go on living, and now I can't imagine ever being happier." He touched True's hand and laughed when his thumb was squeezed in the tiny fist.

Jeana traced the side of Mickey's face with her finger. "I'm so sorry I hurt you. I hope I can make you understand why I did everything."

Mickey kept his gaze on the baby. "I know why, Jeana. You thought you loved Billy Joe."

She almost laughed because he still believed it. "No, Mickey. You've always been the one and *only* love of my life."

He looked up at her in confusion. "But you told me…"

"I had to tell you that to keep you away from Troy. So you wouldn't find out I was pregnant."

"But if you didn't love Billy Joe, why didn't you tell me you were pregnant?"

"Because you made a promise to your dad." She started

to cry. "And I wasn't going to be the reason you had to break it."

She told him the whole story, how and why she'd done everything. He listened without interrupting, and there was a shocked look of utter amazement on his face when she finished.

"I can't believe you did this, Jeana." He rolled onto his back and closed his eyes. "All that time I thought I'd lost you... we could've been together if you'd just trusted me and told me the truth!"

"I couldn't let you break your promise, Mickey."

He turned toward her again and squeezed her cheeks together to make her look at him. "You promised me a long time ago that you'd never keep anything from me again. Remember *that* promise, Jeana?"

"Yes and I'm sorry, Mickey. I don't blame you for being mad, but—"

He cut her off with an astounded laugh.

"I'm not *mad* at you, Jeana. I'm just having a hard time wrapping my brain around the idea of how a girl who swears she doesn't like sports would sacrifice everything to make sure I played baseball, and how you could break all your promises to me so I wouldn't have to break the one I made to my dad. The logic is so totally *Jeana*-fied, it's mind boggling! You make me crazy, do you know that?" He shook his head and sighed. "And that's part of why I love you so much."

"I couldn't let you give up your future, Mickey. I know how much you love baseball."

"Jeana, I want you to listen to me very carefully," he said. "I do love baseball. I love the game for itself and for the way it challenges me to get my brain in sync with my body. I love how it feels to face the pitcher when I'm at the plate, knowing he's gonna do everything he can to outwit and outplay me and finding out if I've got what it takes to beat him. And most of all, I love baseball because I hear my dad's voice when I'm playing—all the times he coached me and the things he taught me. Baseball keeps my dad alive for me."

He paused and leaned forward to hold her face again.

"But as much as I love baseball, I love you a trillion times more, and I'd give it all up for you in a heartbeat. There *is* no future for me without you, Jeana. I died when I lost you. Don't *ever* leave me again."

She looked at him through her tears and marveled again at how blessed she was to have him.

"I won't, Mickey. I promise. And I promise I won't break any more promises too." She hadn't meant it to be funny, but as soon as she said it they both laughed. "What will you do now, Mickey? Will you stay in school?"

His expression sobered and he touched his son's cheek. "I don't know. I have to take care of us, baby."

"Your mom wants us to live with her, Mickey. She said she'd keep True for us so we can both keep going to college."

She could tell he was surprised to hear that his mother knew about True. She explained why Marsha thought he'd been drinking, and he looked contrite.

"I should've known she'd worry about that because of my dad. I was going to the—"

"Batting cages," Jeana finished for him. "When I saw you there tonight, I knew that was where you'd been going all summer."

He leaned over and kissed her. "That's because you understand me better than anyone."

"Your mom really wants to help us, Mickey, and I think it'd be good for her too. It would make her feel like she's helping to make your dad's dream a reality. I can tell she loved him the same way I love you."

He told her about his conversation with the Yankee scout that afternoon, and she was elated to hear the news.

"But even if they want to sign me, Jeana, it'd be at least

a year or so before I'd make any money. Would you be okay with not having our own place that long?"

She smiled as if he were a slow-witted child. "I'd be happy with living in a cave as long as I was with you, Mickey."

"I guess we can give it a try," he said. "Right now I can't see the future as anything but bright. Everything I need to be happy is right here beside me." He flicked her earlobe and touched True's tiny one.

When the baby was fed and changed and sleeping soundly again, Jeana made a pallet on the floor beside her bed and started to put him on it.

"Give him to me, Jeana," Mickey said. "I'll hold him."

She shook her head. "No, Mickey. You're going to hold *me*."

His dimples appeared and his eyes turned a sultrier shade of blue. "Okay, hurry up and c'mere."

She got True settled then went to Mickey's waiting arms. "Hold me tighter, Mickey. Hold me and don't ever let me go."

"Anything for you, Jeana." He ran his fingers through her short curls and turned her face up to him. "Even without your beautiful hair, you're like a vision. Tell me again that you won't ever leave me."

"I'll never leave you, Mickey. Now that we're together again, I don't think I could go a single day without you."

She ran her hands over the muscles in his arms and back, thrilled to find them even more defined than she remembered. When he pulled her against him, she felt the same searing heat he had always ignited in her.

"I've wanted your arms around me like this for so long, Mickey. I missed you so bad."

He kissed her shoulder, his lips moving slowly up to her neck. "I dreamed about making love to you every night we were apart."

"Show me what you dreamed, Mickey."

Lying on her bed with nothing between them but the love that had sustained them for the past five months, Mickey touched every inch of her body, as if he needed to reassure himself that she was really there. While his hands and his lips caressed her, she told him over and over that she loved him and would never leave him again.

Their bodies became reacquainted slowly, and they made love tenderly at first. But their time apart from each other and their shared passion soon drove them to the fury of a recurring tempest that barely allowed time to catch their breath before they needed each other again, like an addict needing a fix. Finally they lay wrapped in a blissfully spent tangle, adrift on the ocean of their love in the peace after the storm, still enmeshed in each other because neither of them was willing to let go.

Mickey lay with his head on Jeana's chest, her heartbeat a reassuring rhythm in his ear. "Let's get married on your birthday, baby."

Her fingers played in the damp curls at his neck. "Whatever you say, Mickey. I'll marry you tonight if you want me to."

They put the baby back in the bed with them and made spoons, Mickey's arm around Jeana and his hand on True's back so he could hold them both.

Just before she drifted off to sleep, Jeana heard Mickey whisper, "Thank you, God. I'll do my best to deserve them."

~ * ~

She woke to the sight of Mickey sitting beside her on the bed, staring enraptured at his son in his arms.

"Have you been holding him all night?" she asked.

"He's so perfect." Mickey traced the shape of True's eyebrow with his finger. "I can't believe we made him."

"He's better than perfect," Jeana said. "He's Mickey-*esque*. See, you're not the only one who can coin an adjective."

256

After breakfast with her overjoyed parents, Jeana and Mickey went to tell Marsha that they'd take her up on her offer. When they got back to Jeana's house, Mickey sat beside her on the couch and watched in fascination while she nursed True.

"He's got a big appetite, doesn't he?"

"Billy Joe says he gets it from me." Jeana looked cautiously for his reaction to Billy Joe's name.

Mickey kept his gaze on his son. "Ty saw you kissing Billy Joe when I was in Memphis. That's why I believed you when you said you loved him."

"That was only a goodbye kiss, but I do love him, Mickey. He's the best friend either of us will ever have. He hated lying to you and thinks you'll never forgive him."

"I tried to hate him," he said, "but I just couldn't. That was part of what drove me so crazy."

When True finished eating, Jeana went to her room and got the scrapbook. "This is how I survived while we were apart, Mickey. I wrote in it for you every night." She took the baby back so Mickey could look at the book.

He opened it and saw the sketches first. "God, look how beautiful you were, baby."

He read the whole thing, laughing at Billy Joe's fat jokes and the names he'd gone through. He was touched when he found out that Jeana had seen him play on his birthday, and the entry for the day True was born made him cry.

"Thank you for this, baby. It means the world to me."

"Billy Joe did the sketches for *you*, Mickey. He loves both of us."

Mickey ran his finger over the lines of one of the sketches, then he stood up. "I'll be back in a little while."

When Billy Joe answered the door, he and Mickey didn't say anything at first. They just stared at each other.

"You lied to me," Mickey said finally. "You moved in with the girl I love behind my back, and you didn't tell me about my son. I thought we were friends."

Billy Joe looked as though he'd been kicked in the stomach. "Mickey, I—"

"I just have one thing to say to you." Mickey paused, then his face slowly broke into a smile. "Thanks for taking care of them for me. I love you, buddy."

Billy Joe sputtered something and Mickey grabbed him by the shirt to pull him into a rough embrace.

"I knew you loved me," Billy Joe said, wiping his eyes. "Jeana thought you were pining for *her*, but I knew the truth."

They sat on the porch steps together, Billy Joe's hands clasped between his knees

"I guess you've known for a long time how I feel about Jeana. I lost her to Wade when we were kids and did everything I could to steal her back, even though he was my best friend. But I'd never do that to you, Mick. I hope you know that."

"I do now," Mickey said. "I missed your scrawny butt this summer. Not as much as I missed Jeana, but almost."

"That's quite a kid you got, huh?" Billy Joe grinned.

"Definitely." Mickey put his arm across Billy Joe's shoulders. "Jeana told me you named him. I think you did a fine job, buddy, but there's something I gotta ask you."

"What's that, Mick?"

Mickey shoved him off the steps. "How could you let Jeana talk you out of *Butkus?*"

Chapter Thirty-three

On Jeana's birthday a month later, she sat at an antique vanity in one of the guest rooms at Ty's house while Shelly and Allison pinned a crown of baby's breath and miniature carnations in her hair.

"Do you think Mickey will like it this way?" Jeana asked.

Marsha smiled and held True higher so he could see his mama. "Mickey is so happy he's barely touching the ground. He'll think you're beautiful."

"It feels like I haven't seen him in weeks," Jeana said, wiggling True's foot. "But it's really only been fifteen hours, twenty-two minutes and... thirty seconds."

Everyone laughed and Betty said, "I think Jeana's floating a little herself."

Robin knocked and told them everything was ready in the garden, and the guests were beginning to arrive. "You look gorgeous, Jeana," she said. "Mickey's liable to blind everyone with the glow from his eyes when he sees you."

Jeana hugged her. "Thank you again for letting us have the wedding here. It's like getting married at Tara."

"I was happy to do it." Robin smiled in Shelly's direction. "And look at the good it's done for Ty."

Shelly and Ty had been dating ever since they'd gotten to know each other three weeks earlier when the wedding was first being planned. Ty was so enamored that he hadn't even called another girl since their first date, and he told Mickey he was finally beginning to understand about "this love stuff."

As the ladies got ready to go downstairs and start the ceremony, Billy Joe showed up with a package wrapped in wedding paper. He spoke to Allison briefly then lingered behind until Jeana was alone in the room.

"The best man is supposed to be helping the groom," Jeana said as she straightened his tie.

Billy Joe scoffed. "He doesn't need me. He's been dressed since four o'clock this morning."

"You look exceedingly handsome. You should wear a tux more often."

"Not bloody likely." He affected a British accent. "In fact, if I can talk Al into eloping, we'll skip all the nonsense her mother's got planned for us next June." He touched the flowers in Jeana's hair. "What's with the horticulture?"

"You don't like it? Shelly and Allison did it for me."

"It's okay. Makes you look like an extremely busty Flower Child."

"Thanks a lot. Does that mean you'd be embarrassed to escort me downstairs?"

"In a minute." He led her over to sit on the bed. "I need to talk to you alone and didn't figure I'd get the chance after the wedding. I know Mick will be in a big hurry to start the honeymoon."

She laughed and pointed at the gift. "Is that for me?"

"Yeah, but that comes later." He set the gift aside then touched her chin. "I know this is supposed to be the happiest day of your life, and I sure as hell don't wanna do anything to spoil it for you, but there's something I gotta tell you."

"What is it, Billy Joe?"

He hesitated, and his face looked conflicted for a moment. "You know what happened last year on your birthday."

She nodded. "I took flowers to his grave this morning."

"He asked me something after the banquet that night, Jeana. I didn't think much about it at the time, but I remembered this morning." He took both her hands in his before continuing. "He said there was no telling where we'd all be in a year, so he wanted me to do him a favor."

Jeana was almost afraid to ask, but she had to know.

"What did he want, Billy Joe?"

"He asked me to tell you something for him if he wasn't around to tell you himself. I figured he meant because you'd both be off in college somewhere, but I promised him I'd do it." He leaned over and kissed her on the forehead. "Happy Birthday from me and Wade, the other two guys who'll always love you."

"Thank you, Billy Joe." She took the handkerchief he offered and wiped her eyes. "Did Mickey tell you the dream he had the night I told him about True?"

"Yeah, that was wild."

"I think Wade was trying to make up for some of the things he did. And I think he'd be happy for us if he was here."

Billy Joe looked skeptical. "I don't know about that, but I know he'd definitely want to kiss the bride. And then the groom would deck him and I'd have to come to the rescue since I'm the best man. It'd be a helluva mess."

"You're probably right," she said, laughing. "May I have the gift now?"

He nodded and picked it up. "Remember when you made me promise to paint a picture of you that everyone could see?"

"Yes, but I thought that was why you did the sketches."

"Those were for Mick," he said. "This is yours."

He handed her the package, and she tore off the paper to reveal a framed watercolor of herself holding True right after his birth. Her hair was sweaty and tousled and Mickey's shirt was wrinkled, but Billy Joe had captured perfectly the overwhelming love on her face as she looked at True for the first time, and the picture was breathtaking.

"I love every sketch you ever gave me, but this one I'll treasure forever, Billy Joe. Just like I treasure you." She hugged him then kissed him on the lips. "Don't ever forget how much I love you."

"Yeah, I know," he said. "Everybody loves Billy Joe—you, Mickey, Allison, True. I'm just everybody's fantasy." He stood up and held out his arm to her. "It's a tough job, but somebody's gotta do it."

They went downstairs together, and he left her on the verandah with her attendants and her father.

"Ready, Hot Shot?" Robert asked.

Jeana took his arm. "Daddy, I've been ready for this day since the first time Mickey smiled at me."

Shelly and Allison led the procession to the garden, followed by Susannah as the flower girl, then Robert escorted Jeana down the petal-strewn path to the floral arch where Mickey and Billy Joe waited. Robin had been right about the glow in Mickey's eyes, because they shone with an even brighter blue than usual, stoked by the profound love for Jeana that he was eager to profess before God and everyone.

Jeana didn't take her eyes off Mickey's face as she walked to him—the face she loved more than any other, the one she'd seen in her dreams every night for the past three years. She walked to him confidently, without the slightest doubt or nervousness, because she loved and trusted him completely and knew their love would last forever.

Now the rest of the world would know it too, and Mickey would never again have to ask if she still loved him. From this day on, he'd know without a doubt their love was True.

Epilogue

Jeana sat in the stands at Legends Field and tried to keep her son in his seat by playing his favorite word game with him.

"Okay, True, here's an easy one: hot and house. What's the middle word?"

His three-year-old face looked thoughtful momentarily, then he grinned. "Dog!"

"Right!" Jeana smiled and kissed him on the nose. "Hot *dog* and *dog* house. You are *so* smart."

"Wike you, Mama?"

"Yes, smart like Mama and handsome like Daddy." She realized her slip too late and winced.

"Where *is* my daddy?" True started bouncing in his seat again. "I wanna see him play baseball!"

"He'll be out in a little while." Jeana could see the impatient protest forthcoming from her son, so she added quickly, "Help me watch for Uncle Billy Joe and Aunt Allison."

His blue eyes lit up. "And Uncle Bildy Joe will let me ride in his car with the fire on it?"

Jeana smiled and nodded. A few seconds later, the music playing over the public address system stopped abruptly and the booming voice of the announcer filled the stadium.

"Ladies and gentlemen, here are your Tampa Yankees!"

The players waved to the cheering crowd as they took the field to warm up. Jeana put True on her lap so they could both wave at Mickey when he came through the gate. She barely managed to keep True from jumping out of her arms in his excitement.

"*Daddy!* That's my daddy!"

Mickey spotted them and waved back. Jeana wondered if he had weights on his cleats to keep him anchored, because she knew he was almost as excited as True about playing in his first minor league game.

"True Blue, my *main* man!" Billy Joe scooped up the little boy and walked over to the guardrail with him. "Who's that guy down there in those pinstriped pajamas?"

"That's my daddy, Uncle Bildy Joe. He's a Yankee!"

Jeana hugged a very pregnant Allison and helped her sit down. "It's so great to see you. I'm glad you convinced your doctor to let you come."

Allison eased herself into the seat. "Billy Joe told him he had experience and knew what to do if the baby decides to come early. You know we wouldn't have missed this for anything."

Billy Joe came back and Jeana hugged him too. "Are you sure your heart can withstand another delivery? You almost had a stroke when True was born."

He scowled at her. "You were the one doing all the complaining. I was calm and collected." He ruffled True's auburn curls. "Me and my little buddy are gonna go down and say hey to Mick."

"Uncle Bildy Joe's gonna buy me a hot dog and you can't eat it, Mama." True leaned his head against Billy Joe's, and they both snickered.

Jeana rolled her eyes and put True's Yankee hat on his head. "Give Daddy a kiss for me, okay?"

True looked at Billy Joe and sighed. "Mama and Daddy kiss *aww* the time."

"I know, I know." Billy Joe shook his head. "Want me to bring you anything, Al?"

She fanned herself with her program. "Lemonade and an air conditioner."

Jeana sat beside her again and held her hand. "The last

month is the hardest, but it's worth it."

"I know." Allison rubbed her stomach affectionately. "I'm just impatient to see the little guy."

"No, it's going to be a girl," Jeana said. "You are much too wonderful for God to make you put up with a miniature Billy Joe."

~ * ~

Mickey started in center field and batted third in the lineup. He got a single his first at-bat, and when he came up in the bottom of the third inning, he got the high fast ball he'd been waiting for and sent it flying over the left field fence to put the Yankees ahead 2-0. As he crossed the plate, he looked up into the stands and pulled his earlobe, smiling at the faces of his two biggest fans.

On his way to the dugout, Mickey lifted his blue eyes heavenward. "Tell God I said thanks again, Dad."

~ ~ ~

Thank you for reading the True Blue Trilogy. I know some of you may be unhappy about some of the things that happened, but don't despair. In the world of fiction, all things are possible!

Here's a preview of my next book coming in 2017.

After You
The Unfinished Series Book Two

From Chapter One

Wade's eyes widened as a thought occurred to him. He took his foot off the accelerator at the same instant the headlights reflected off the curve warning signs. What the hell was wrong with him? He stomped the brake, causing the rear end to fishtail just enough to put the driver's side to the fore when the Corvette took flight into the curve.

Just before impact with the tenacious scrub oak that had managed to escape Frederick's wrath, Wade had just long enough to whisper, "I'm sorry, Redhot. I didn't mean to spoil your birthday."

His eyes aren't working, and there's something stiff around his neck. He can't see who's doing all the yelling, but he can hear the whoop-whoop-whoop *of a helicopter and can feel hands rolling him onto some kind of board. That's all he feels, and he knows he should probably be thankful for that. He wishes he could tell them all to just leave him the hell alone, but his voice isn't working either.*

Everything goes away for a while.

Then he's awake again and doesn't hear the helicopter anymore, but there are even more people yelling now, all of them pulling and poking at him. He can hear hospital sounds too. Don't they know it's too late? He really screwed up bad this time.

He can't black out again no matter how hard he tries, so he does the next best thing and goes away to the only place he's ever been happy.

He's ten years old and can't stop smiling because Jeana is going swimming with him, and he'll have her all to himself. Billy Joe is on vacation with his parents, and Jeana's bratty sister has a cast on her arm and can't tag along like she usually does.

They're at the pool and he's showing off for her, doing half-gainers and handstands. He challenges her to a Dead Man's Float contest and lets her win so he can look at the way her red hair gets all billowy around her when she's in the water. She laughs and teases him about winning so he pretends to be upset, but the truth is the way she looks when she laughs is what he sees in his dreams.

A storm comes and they have to leave the pool. They take shelter at the school on the way home because she's afraid of the lightning, and he can't believe he has her in his arms, close enough to smell the heavenly scent of her hair that even the chlorine from the pool can't mask. He touches one of her curls and thinks it must be what it feels like to touch strands of silk. For once his stupid brain doesn't fail him, and he thinks of a way to keep her from being frightened. When she kisses him on the cheek before they leave and looks at him like he's a hero or something, he knows he will love her as long as he lives...

"Pressure's dropping—he's flat lining!"

"Give him an amp of epi!"

As long as he lives...

"Asystole. We lost him."

"Shit. Call it."

As long as he lives...

And longer.

~ * ~

When Wade opened his eyes again, he was sitting in some

kind of pristine waiting room across from a girl wearing a long white dress. He looked down and was surprised to see that he was also dressed in white pants, shirt and shoes. What the hell was going on?

"Where are we?" he asked the girl, but she only put a finger to her lips and pointed at the wall behind him. When he got up to look, he saw a sign in gold paint that read TAKE A SEAT AND WAIT TO BE CALLED. NO TALKING. And the door to the left of his chair bore a sign lettered in the same glowing paint.

AFTERLIFE ADMISSIONS

"You gotta be kidding me."

~ ~ ~

About the Author

JOYCE SCARBROUGH is a Southern woman weary of seeing herself and her peers portrayed in books and movies as either post-antebellum debutantes or barefoot hillbillies á la Daisy Duke, so all her heroines are smart, unpretentious women who refuse to be anyone but themselves. In addition to her novels, Joyce also has several short stories available as free downloads. She writes both adult and YA fiction and is active in her local writers' guild as well as the regional chapter of SCBWI. Joyce has lived all her life in beautiful LA (lower Alabama), she's the mother of three gifted children and a blind Pomeranian named Tilly, and she's been married for over 30 years to the love of her life—a superhero who disguises himself during the day as a high school math teacher and coach.

Web site – http://www.joycescarbrough.com
Blog – http://joycescarbrough.blogspot.com
Facebook – https://www.facebook.com/pages/Joyce-Scarbrough-Books-225355834210672
Twitter – @JoyceScarbrough

More books by Joyce Scarbrough

True Blue
True Blue Trilogy, Book One

Royal Blue
True Blue Trilogy, Book Two

Different Roads

Symmetry

After Me

Shades of Blue

Made in the USA
Charleston, SC
29 September 2016